THE
JADED
KIWI

The Jaded Kiwi, Nick Spill – 1st US Edition

The Jaded Kiwi

Library of Congress Cataloguing-in-Publication Data
Spill, Nick
Crime – Fiction Mystery- Fiction
Action and Adventure – Fiction
Thriller – Fiction
New Zealand–Fiction

ISBN: 978-0-9839080-9-8

Book Cover: Jeroen ten Berge

Format and Design: 52 Novels

Back cover photo: Leon Smith Photography

More information about The Jaded Kiwi can be found at http://nickspill.com and http://nickspill.blogspot.com

To Ken Friedman who coined the phrase the Jaded Kiwi, and to my wife Joy who has to put up with a Jaded Kiwi.

And to Wiremu, wherever you are...

THE
JADED
KIWI

Nick Spill

1975 in Northland, New Zealand

Thousands of seeds floated from a giant net, changing colors in the golden dawn. The helicopter flew low over the kauri forest until it came to a wide clearing and released its harvest into a massive bonfire.

The flames illuminated the faces of the policemen and officials. Police Commissioner Ian Thompson and Inspector Bernie Grimble looked over at the TV news crew and journalists from Radio New Zealand, the *Herald*, the *Auckland Star* and the local Whangerei paper. The five photographers looked more concerned than the others at the destruction.

Commissioner Thompson approached the makeshift podium. He took out a piece of paper and began to read his speech. The journalists did not look interested. They had already received their copies.

"Let's hope the wind changes, then we'll all get high!" one of the photographers grumbled.

Three Maoris sat on a couch and listened to every word the police commissioner said. Wiremu Wilson was bolt upright in the middle, with his hands on his knees. In his thirties, with masses of curly hair, he wore a black singlet, green army pants and spit-shined black boots. Hone Wilson, his younger and larger brother, sat on his left in an ironed plaid shirt with glasses and short hair. His face was blank. Hei Hei, usually the clown, was at a loss for words and cupped his face in his hands. He made up for his lack of size with a beer belly and longer hair. Hei Hei stared at the bonfire.

"Operation Weedout has wiped out all illegal marijuana growing in Northland. We have seized all plots of the foul narcotic and are now arresting the criminals who have grown this vicious weed that threatens our children and our community."

"It's 'whom,' not 'who.' He can't even speak English." Hone muttered and he lowered his eyes, unable to look at the remains of their year's work.

"With help from our friends in the United States, we have eradicated the illegal narcotic from our land. This is a tribute to the hard work and dedication of our police force."

They watched a Huey helicopter release another net full of plants into the fire. There was a huge upheaval of flames and sparks. The down draft from the helicopter created dense white whirlwinds around the assembled police and press. Men coughed and covered their mouths as they leaned over and choked on the thick fumes.

"Do you think they got stoned?" Hei Hei asked.

The screen changed to a windswept commissioner who smiled at the camera despite the fact that strings of his white hair now stood straight up behind his ears. The talking head in the studio continued.

"This morning, Police Commissioner Thompson called Operation Weedout a huge success as an estimated five thousand marijuana plants have been seized from public and Maori lands and destroyed."

Wiremu leaped up from the couch and kicked the TV over. It sputtered and died.

"Shit! I was going to watch the *Avengers*," Hei Hei yelled.

"I'll give you vengeance!" Wiremu growled back. "All that work. For nothing."

"There's next year," Hone offered.

"Fuck me! What about our plans?" Hei Hei held his head again.

"Look at those seeds. They flew all those plants bursting with seeds over half of Northland. They've done our work for next year," Hone explained.

"Yeah! They reseeded the whole of the fucking forest. We won't know what to do with all the plants that will shoot up next season." Hei Hei threw up his hands. "Fucking pahekas! God bless the fucking idiots!"

The previous week Wiremu had been in that forest. He had stepped into a wedge of light and turned to cast his shadow over a male cannabis sativa plant that was six feet tall. He knelt on his right knee to examine the plant. His face touched the serrated edges of the leaves as he inhaled the damp smell of the forest. He lifted his head to see a piwakawaka singing above him. The bird kept flicking its grey and white tail in the air while it sang its small song. Tane, god of the forest, must have approved of his project, he had mused.

The piwakawaka hovered over Wiremu as he stood up and walked to the next plant. Under his breath he muttered, aware of the irony now invested in the ancient proverb, Noku te whenua, o oku tupuna. (Mine is the land, the land of my ancestors.)

Chapter One

Friday

Police Commissioner Thompson teed off. Inspector Grimble followed the ball as it floated in the early soft light to land near the pole. He placed his ball on the tee and looked up at the surrounding pine trees. The dew on the grass and the distinct smell of pine needles made Grimble feel very much alive. He loved the clarity of the early morning and what such a meeting with the commissioner would bring.

The two policemen had the Point Chevalier course to themselves.

"There's a Maori I want you to investigate for me," the commissioner said at the ninth hole.

"You're finally allowing me to take on these Maori gangs?"

"Oh no. Not those. Much too perilous. Leave them alone. Our target is more dangerous in the long run, because he can attract more moderate Maori and liberal Pakehas to his cause."

Grimble was aware of Thompson staring at him, as he took his shot. The ball rose high and veered towards the trees. Grimble would let his boss win, but he was playing a poor game naturally. Golf was not his sport.

"Wiremu Wilson. You know him, don't you?" The commissioner dropped the name casually.

"Oh yes. I know him." Grimble let out a quick smile.

"My sources say he's got too much money and is buying land in Northland. Putting it in other peoples' names. Hiding his ownership. They worship him up there. You swing too far to the right, your left elbow moves up when you swing, you have to learn to relax more, Grimble."

As they walked, wheeling their bags, Grimble could hear the sound of a tui, a black bird with a white parsons collar, on a nearby pine tree. He thought the bird's honking mocked his golf game.

"You mean he's growing marijuana?" the inspector asked. "I thought we eradicated all those public plots last season."

"Don't believe what you read in the papers, Grimble."

They came to Grimble's ball off to the right by the pines. Grimble could hear the tui honking again.

"Is this going to be like the others?"

"Yes. Report directly to me. Pick a trusted partner. Bring in others if there's anything public, but don't talk to Drug Squad. They're a bunch of cowboys."

At the next hole, the commissioner cleared his throat.

"We need to get to the bottom of the Maori gang problem, Grimble. I think Wilson is the key. We haven't been able to penetrate his organization, and as for those burnings, well, I don't want him to be my Hone Heke."

"But Hone Heke was the first to sign the Treaty of Waitangi," Grimble stated.

"Yes. But you know what I mean. He disrupted everything. Just like Wilson is going to. We've put him away before and we're going to put him away again. For ever."

Grimble selected an iron and looked to his boss for confirmation. The commissioner nodded.

"I understand." He lined up the shot, taking care to keep the distant green in his sights.

"I'm retiring soon. If all goes well, I won't forget you."

Grimble's ball went too high and landed in a sand trap. The commissioner shook his head.

"When are you going to learn to play golf?"

Henry Lotus stood opposite the Jolly Rodger, a two-story Victorian building. He held Mel Johnson's hand and gazed up at the huge skull and crossbones flag that hung over the entrance.

Every few steps they had stopped to kiss. He inhaled the thick fragrance of gardenia flowers in the humid air. A Bob Dylan song came from somewhere beyond overgrown oleander bushes.

"You know our lives have been defined by going through doors. I first saw you when I walked into your dojo and watched you fight, then you burst into my hotel room in New York, where you saved me from those crazy Albanians."

"Bulgarians," Mel corrected as she turned around to see a tall man and on his arm a young Chinese woman whom Mel thought she recognized. The man opened the double stained glass doors to the pub and let the woman in.

"Now we are about to go through these doors on our first Friday down under. Do you think we should?"

"Bad things happen in threes, you know."

"You wanted to come here. Relive your student days. And I thought it was good things happen in threes. For a physicist, you're pretty superstitious."

Henry looked at the limp flag, then at Mel.

"So we're at the third door. Do you want to go in?" Henry offered.

"If you weren't so recalcitrant, I'd call you the jaded kiwi."

Mel and Henry crossed the road and swung open the high double doors. They were engulfed in a wall of noise. The entire pub was packed. John Mayall and the Bluesbreakers were playing "Have You Heard" on the jukebox, loud. Henry was thrilled. New York radio had been playing "Welcome Back" by John Sebastian, but here in the summer of 1976, they were listening to Eric Clapton from the sixties. The pub had that old-fashioned stink of cigarettes and stale beer. A smaller skull and crossbones flag hung above the long polished wooden bar that was, one hour before closing time, choked with overflowing ashtrays, empty beer mugs and foam caked beer pitchers. Mel squeezed to the front of the bar and managed to catch the eye of one of the overworked bartenders. Henry paid for the beer and carried the two mugs and pitcher behind Mel, who parted the crowds as they moved towards the back. No glass only plastic, New Zealand had definitely become more civilized, Henry thought.

There was nowhere to stand or sit. The bar was packed elbow to elbow, men with long hair and earrings and women with crew cuts. You could not tell the poet truck drivers from the philosophy professors. Groups of young people were engulfed in clouds of cigarette smoke made denser by the stifling humidity. Packs of men in sweat stained T-shirts ordered two or three pitchers at a time. A group of young Maori men were clustered at the opposite end of the bar making a lot of noise. There was not a sober person in the house. Everyone seemed to be swaying to their own inner beat, not the jukebox's, intoxicated but secure in their communal drinking.

"Nostalgic enough for you?" Mel yelled in Henry's ear.

"Don't know, hardly ever came here," he screamed back.

Henry spotted two chairs at a crowded table, and they worked their way around so they could sit down. Henry poured the beers without spilling any. They raised their plastic mugs to toast each other.

"But you've been talking about nothing else all week, Friday night at the Jolly Rodger, as if it's the center of your universe!" Mel screamed at him. "You're not jaded, you're …"

"From New York to Auckland!" Henry roared in celebration, getting into the Friday night spirit. He ignored Mel's look.

She pushed back her hair as she surveyed the room. A big bear of a man turned around to look at Mel. Mel had seen him enter the pub. He had a thick red beard, long red hair swept back over his shoulders and a ruddy complexion that bore a smile from ear to ear.

"You've come from New York? We just got back too!"

He had his arm around a woman who looked fourteen years old. She was a little plump, with a pageboy fringe and black hair to her shoulders. With high cheekbones, big almond brown eyes and a nose that was too small for her wide face, she looked deceptively innocent. She was a third generation Chinese New Zealander.

"Yes. Got back Monday. Been away years. Cheers, mate!" Henry raised his mug and the four of them sipped their cold beer as if it was the finest they had ever consumed.

"I'm Henry Lotus," he began with a mock Yankee accent. "Retired physicist. At your service." Henry would never have been so outgoing without the aid of the beer.

"Clovis Tibet. Violinist and liberator of young damsels in distress!" Clovis let out. His companion tried to whisper in his ear.

"That's Dr. Johnson, the gynecologist!"

"That's wild because we've just come from there too," Mel added somewhere in the conversation, though they were all confused as to who had been introduced to whom, and what the other person had just said.

"Yeah, it's nice to be back down under!" Clovis shouted. "My girlfriend, Plum Blossom."

They had moved their chairs and managed to shake hands. Mel shook Plum's hand as if she had just met her, a situation she would have to get used to, bumping into patients in social situations. She felt uncomfortable. What could she say? "Hey, never seen anal scarring like that before!"

The jukebox blared out a very distorted "Purple Haze."

Henry looked around and noticed the group of Maoris by the far corner of the bar.

"Drink up. I'll get a refill!" Henry topped off everyone's beer mug and stood up with his empty pitcher. "I think I recognize that Maori."

Henry edged in between two large Maoris. He was so hot he had undone another button to his shirt, something he never did. He didn't feel any cooler as he tried to catch the attention of the barman.

The Maori to his right turned and looked into Henry's eyes. They were the same height, although the Maori seemed taller.

"Hey! Henry, right?" His eyes shifted to the pendant. He embraced Henry. The piece of jade was shaped like a large tear, with a color so dark green, it was almost black.

"Wiremu! It's you! My God!" Henry grinned as he looked over Wiremu then across to Mel who had been watching.

"I always wear it."

Wiremu smiled.

"Hey, I want you to meet my little brothers Hone and Hei Hei."

Suddenly a wave of cold air swept through the bar and the noise level dropped for a second. Two policemen, in their summer blue shirts, stood in the double doorway. They looked more like targets than law enforcement officers as they surveyed the crowd in their high, white metal helmets, although neither was tall enough to see across the heads of the drinkers. A plastic pitcher went flying through the air to greet them. The taller policeman's helmet was knocked off and both were covered in beer. The policeman picked up his wet helmet and retreated, followed by his partner. The doors shut behind them. Henry had not seen who had thrown the pitcher, for he was shaking Hei Hei's hand, a greeting that seemed to go on forever, with Hei Hei fixing him with his dark eyes.

"What a waste of beer!" Wiremu roared and the others followed in a manner that suggested to Henry that Wiremu was the leader and these men would laugh when he laughed, cry when he cried and would follow him anywhere.

"At least they're plastic now! Can't hurt anyone." Henry shrugged. There was more laughter, but not as defiant as Wiremu's.

The packed room erupted again into a louder chaos of shouting and drinking.

• • •

Mel thought it was the tall Maori next to Henry who had thrown the beer. Clovis looked at Plum then over to Henry, trying to figure out what had just happened. There was another group of Maoris standing shoulder to shoulder nearby. Perhaps they had done it.

It was too noisy to conduct any conversation, so Mel was about to go to the bar to escape Clovis's close scrutiny when Henry appeared at the table with Wiremu, carrying three large pitchers. Beer spilt onto the crowded table as they plunked them down.

"Wiremu." Henry waved to his long lost friend. "Meet Mel and these are our new friends." In the excitement of seeing Wiremu, he had forgotten the couple's names.

"Hi. I'm Clovis and my girl, Plum."

They shook hands and Henry noticed how big Clovis really was.

A few inebriated couples started to work their way through the packed bar to the front door. But no one else could be drawn away from their precious pitchers of beer.

"Me and Henry go way back. Quite a story. Must tell you some time. Excuse me. I have to look after my mates. Talk to you in a minute." Wiremu turned and waded through the crowd to the bar.

"Is that who I think it is?" Mel asked Henry. Plum noticed Henry's pounamu pendant. She could not take her eyes off it.

"Look at that pendant! It's greenstone! Will you buy me one like that, Clovis?"

Clovis got goose bumps up his forearms when Plum spoke in her distinctive pleading voice. It bought back the recorded sex call he had listened to, too many times, alone in his cockroach-infested sublet on St. Marks Place. It seemed like a lifetime ago, but it was only two weeks.

Clovis grinned. He was broke. He had spent his life savings to fly to New York to find Plum and bring her back. Now he needed work. He had an audition with the local orchestra next week. If he got that position he could pay next month's rent and contemplate buying Plum a modest present, but first things first. On returning to New Zealand with Plum, he had sent her to a Women's Clinic. He dared not think what Plum had done in New York. The tests had cost him $15 in Auckland, rather than the $250 they would have cost in Manhattan. Plum had gotten the results that afternoon, negative. If he thought she was infected with some sexually transmitted disease, what did that say about him? If he flew halfway round the world to rescue her, how could he not trust her? Tonight they were celebrating, in Clovis's favorite Ponsonby pub. Only Plum's doctor was sitting right next to him, and he could not take his eyes off her, she was so beautiful in a powerful, confident way.

"I think they're going to come back in force!" Clovis shouted. "Why don't we go up the road to the Three Lamps?" He stood up and swayed on his feet. No one responded to his suggestion. Perhaps they did not think the police would reappear, and one pitcher of beer would scare the police away, forever, and allow them to drink in peace. The heat and beer were going to Clovis's head, but he did not want to get beaten senseless by cops in a brawl, especially with his audition coming up. He had to protect his musician's fingers, as well as his Plum Blossom. Clovis had witnessed a saxophonist have his front teeth punched out when he refused to play "Ten Guitars", back when he was in a rock band misnamed the Cat's Pajamas. He knew Plum would love to see a New

Zealand bar brawl, where everything unbreakable got broken. He bent down and addressed the table again.

"Look. I live nearby, why don't you come over to my place. We can pick up some beer." Clovis had shouted, nervous about what could happen next. He had had enough of men in uniforms. At Auckland International Airport, Clovis had been separated from Plum Blossom, put into a windowless room and made to strip naked before three customs agents. He had flown from New York with Plum and paid for his tickets in cash, the day of departure. He had long hair, a beard and a scruffy rucksack and a violin case as his only luggage. He had to be a drug dealer, according to customs.

Clovis was ordered to bend over a desk, while one of the agents inserted a surgical gloved hand, one finger only, he hoped, although he had dared not inquire, up his anus. Right up, till he could feel his prostate being tickled. It was unpleasant and humiliating.

Plum had fared worse. She had endured the deep cavity search, at both ends. Lying flat on her back with her knees pressed up to her ears, two butch custom's agents with spiked hair had probed around inside her while a third had held her ankles. "What could they be looking for? It was like being raped by a gang of lesbians," she had told Clovis in the taxi from the airport. "And they didn't wear gloves, only lots of Vaseline. Ugh! I feel so unclean. I need a bath!"

"Let's do it. Buy some beer and get outta here!" Henry announced.

Henry Lotus led them past the group of Maoris. Wiremu dramatically clutched him by the shoulders again and let out a big yell. Mel, Clovis and Plum came to a halt behind Henry. The other Maoris were crowded around their leader. No one could move.

"Hey! My mate!"

"When was it? 1965?" Wiremu recalled.

"Yeah! That party!" Henry looked back at Mel who shrugged her shoulders. She could barely make out what they had said. While Henry had been partying his youth away with oversized Maoris, Mel had been at Dunedin Medical School, cramming for interminable exams under a desk lamp, worrying about intercellular leakages and macrophages, wondering if she would ever hold a normal human conversation again.

The scene came back to Henry fueled by the beer he had just consumed. Police cars had been lined up outside the party house. Their blue lights bounced against the stonewalls. Swarms of policemen wielding truncheons threw everyone out of the house. They punched and beat the bikies, Maoris and any young man with long hair they could lay their hands on. They struck them in the stomach, the chest, the legs, but not the face, where the cuts and bruises would show in court.

Wiremu had given Henry the greenstone pendant, the Tear of Tane, after Henry had saved him from being arrested in that police raid.

The head bartender, sweat dripping from his large red nose, rang the ship's bell that was suspended over the bar. He yelled at the top of his lungs, "Last call!"

The entire beer-crazed mob responded in unison, sending their delegates to the bar to refill their pitchers. The more pitchers of beer they had on their tables, the safer they would feel. The public drinking house had to close, by law, at exactly 11:00 PM. The drinkers had a few more minutes to empty their mugs. Then, at twenty minutes after closing time, the police routinely entered and flushed out the remaining drinkers.

Henry was jammed up against Wiremu, as other Maoris with their empty pitchers tried to put their stomachs to the bar and claim the attention of the bartenders.

"Hey, I like your pendant," Hei Hei shouted. "Wear that and you'll always be protected!"

"Doesn't mean you'll be safe," Hone added, laughing as if he were privy to a secret joke.

"Yeah! I proved it three times!"

Hone chuckled; his eyes shone, not from too many beers but from the joy of being surrounded by his mates, particularly his brother. Wiremu had been out of Paremoremo's D block for over two years. As a multiple offender, the next time he was arrested, he would be put away for a long time. Hone had not even received a parking ticket. He had lived in Auckland the last two years, the better to assist his brother in their tribal business and work on his political science thesis.

No one left. The patrons were too busy hoarding beer for the closing minutes, determined to last as long as possible in the communal madness of drinking. Suddenly the double doors swung open and three policemen with metal helmets stood shoulder to shoulder, reinforced by a wall of blue behind them. They were, at first, ignored.

Henry saw Mel wave a $10 note to a bartender, as she tried to get his attention. Then he noticed the policemen and thought how odd that they should arrive before 11:00. Why couldn't they wait until after closing time? Then Henry remembered the thrown pitcher. "Oh shit!" he said to himself.

A loud explosion went off next to him. His ears rang. He saw Wiremu fire both barrels of a sawed-off shotgun. The shots blew out the stained glass windows above the doors, covering the three policemen in a shower of glass splinters. They stood frozen, then, when they realized that they were still alive and unharmed, they retreated and the double doors closed. There was a huge hole above the doors, where the stained glass windows had been.

After the shock of silence that followed the shotgun blast, panic erupted inside the bar. As if on cue, the juke-box started up again even louder with "Wild Thing" by Jimi Hendrix. Most patrons were too drunk to move, and if they could, there was nowhere for them to go. The front doors were the only exit. But the doors were now closed, creating the illusion that the shotgun blast had blown away the police. But they had formed a circle outside, blocking anyone from leaving. Those patrons who were still aware of their surroundings had dived under their tables, knocking over full ashtrays and mugs of beer. Or they crouched behind their chairs, expecting another blast.

Henry looked across at Wiremu who bent down and stuffed the shotgun into his trousers. Mel had seen everything and shouted in Wiremu's ear as he righted himself.

"We better get out of here. They'll be coming back in force any second!"

She looked around. Patrons pushed and shoved each other to get to the entrance and escape. Such was the mass of bodies trying to get to the front doors that it appeared the crowd was dancing in slow motion, swaying back and forth, but getting nowhere.

"Nah! They'll wait for the Armed Offenders Squad! They're too chicken!" Wiremu replied to the woman he had been introduced to. He looked at her with interest, not only was she beautiful, for a white sheila, but she had said "we."

The screams and shouts grew louder. Henry struggled to keep his feet on the ground without being swept away. He yelled to Wiremu while holding onto him for balance.

"There must be an exit in the back!"

"Nah! It's sealed! You'se guys go out the front. I'm goin' to disappear. I'll call! Okay?" Wiremu addressed Hone, Hei Hei and his other young men with a sense of authority they did not question. They nodded and began to move in unison, like a bulldozer, to the doors. Wiremu started to elbow his way to the back of the bar. Henry followed him with Mel right behind.

Clovis looked at Henry then at Wiremu, undecided on what to do. He sensed he was on the verge of missing out on an adventure. If he were truthful with himself, he would have admitted that he would have followed Mel to the ends of the earth; he was so attracted to her. He got in step behind Mel as they pushed their way against the panicking crowd.

"Why are you following me?" Wiremu yelled over his shoulder. "You're safe to go out."

"Heh. I just met you again after all these years. We're with you," Henry yelled back.

"I have a bad feeling about this," Mel whispered to Henry. "Let's get going."

Wiremu worked his way to the door at the end of the bar that led to a narrow corridor and two toilets. The five went unnoticed by the drunken crowd evacuating the pub. The corridor stank of piss.

Opposite the toilets was a large casement window. Wiremu drove his right elbow into the lower pane, shattering the frosted glass. He kicked out the remaining pieces to reveal a set of iron bars. He took a step back and aimed the heel of his right boot at the iron. The bars vibrated, but remained in place. Clovis led Plum into the corridor, to join Henry and Mel. They watched Wiremu kick the bars for a second time. Nothing moved. The third time, one of the bars came loose at the bottom.

Using his full weight, Wiremu threw his right shoulder at the bars. They gave way and Wiremu fell out into the courtyard hitting his head on the concrete. He continued his interrupted forward roll, stood up and brushed off the shards of glass. He turned to the others who looked at him through the broken window.

"Why don't you lot go out the front? We'll meet up later."

Henry already had one leg over the windowsill. He was on tiptoe, careful not to catch himself on the jagged glass. Here he was following the man who had given him the greenstone pendant. He felt lucky, as he lifted his other leg over the glass. Mel was right behind him. She had traveled all the way to New York to rescue Henry, and she was not going to let him out of her sight now.

Clovis picked up Plum and propelled her through the gap, feet first. He sensed something unusual was about to happen. He had survived New York and felt he could handle anything in New Zealand, including the Armed Offenders Squad. He had invited his new friends to his home, and he wanted to play the gracious host. He looked down at his favorite khaki shirt. It was ripped at the left elbow. A trickle of blood ran down to his wrist. He started to panic. All his false courage left him. That was his fingering arm. Maybe he should have left through the front door? But it was too late to turn back. He caught Mel throwing him a quick smile, and his confidence returned. He could still hear "Wild Thing."

The small triangular yard was enclosed in empty beer crates stacked high against the walls. Wiremu quickly rearranged some of the crates to form a steep stairwell to the top of the wall farthest from the pub, next to the gasworks. He climbed up and disappeared with a quick curse. The others followed him. Clovis caught Plum as she jumped over last.

They crouched against the wall and adjusted their eyes to the dark. Wiremu could identify the back of one police van nearer the Jolly Rodger entrance. There were more police cars around the corner. They could see the blue flashing lights reflected off parked cars. The bar was still being emptied. The police were too busy sorting out the rowdy drinkers outside the entrance to pay attention to the back of the pub and the side street.

"Here. Follow me. Ponsonby is Clovis's land." Clovis stepped out of the shadows and casually walked across the street holding Plum's hand. Henry and Mel took Wiremu by the arm as they ambled after them. The small wooden houses had hedges and picket fences separating their tiny front gardens from the pavement. They walked up the hill until they came to a lamppost with a broken light. Here, Clovis ducked behind a tall hedge. The others followed him. Through the branches, they spied an ambulance scream down the street followed by two police cars. The cars stopped directly by the wall they had jumped over. Four policemen emerged with rifles. A light went on in the front room directly over their heads.

Clovis put his finger to his lips and pointed to a narrow path between the two houses that led down to a pitch-black garden. He slowly duckwalked down the path, feeling in front of him, for any obstacle. At the end of the property he came to a tall corrugated fence with ivy growing up it. The fence was over six feet high and was not solid enough to scale. He felt for the join between two sheets. He tore out one side of the corrugated iron sheet. The sheet groaned as it was wrenched from its flathead nails. Clovis! Your violinist fingers! Wiremu held the sheet back and Clovis crawled on both hands through the opening into the next yard. He slid into a freshly dug garden. Standing up, he took a step forward. He began to sink into a large hole.

A dog started to bark nearby. Clovis felt his knees disappear into the sludge. Then Wiremu slipped through the fence and stepped on Clovis's shoulders. He sunk deeper into the compost. The barking dog seemed very close.

Lights went on up the valley of back gardens, as the dog's barking grew louder.

"Watch out!" Clovis whispered. They could both hear the deep growl of a large dog.

Wiremu leapt off Clovis to dry land and pulled him out of the pit. Clovis held his breath. There was an atrocious smell coming from his trousers, and he found his boots made a squelching sound. In the darkness, Wiremu organized the others around the manure trap. Clovis tried to wipe some of the decaying vegetable matter off his trousers and shirt. Taking another step forward he became caught in netting for string beans. He lost his balance and fell over. The more he struggled, the more entangled he became. The dog was closer and louder. Henry and Wiremu, trying not to laugh, ripped the netting apart and pulled Clovis out of his bean cocoon.

A nearby neighbor yelled at his dog, "Shut the fuck up!" followed by a crash and a whimper. Clovis checked to see that Plum and the others were following him and continued his trek across the booby-trapped Ponsonby garden.

A chorus of dogs barked at their own echoes up the valley. There was another dog who sounded nearer. Clovis took another step forward in the darkness and came nose to nose with a huge Rottweiler at the end of a tight metal chain. The guard dog strained on his hind legs and snarled into Clovis's eyes. He could see into the dog's mouth. Its teeth were so white with froth dribbling down its wide-open jaw, that they looked fluorescent. Clovis took a step back and found the proper path away from the reach of the dog. He led the others to the front gate, where they crouched down behind a hedge, out of sight.

Wiremu turned to face the others after checking the street. It was deserted. He raised his hands. By now, Wiremu knew the police would have seen the broken back window and bars and realized a man, the size of a gorilla, had escaped. There would soon be roadblocks with police and dogs scouring the area.

'Here. Let's split up. There's no reason for you lot to get caught," he whispered.

"No," Clovis found himself saying. "Two doors up across the street, they're some friends of mine. I'll borrow their car and take us to our place. Stay here." He ran across the street before Wiremu could protest.

Clovis ran down the side path to the back of the house. The path was full of overgrown weeds. The back door steps were covered in slippery moss. Clovis fell against the wooden door and knocked three times. There was no reply. He turned and saw a light farther down the yard, seeping out of the partially opened door of a large shed. He heard the sound of an electric sander coming from inside.

He opened the door and was immersed in a bright light softened by the suspended dust. A kauri hull of a half-finished thirty-foot yacht emerged out of the dust cloud. Clovis felt he had walked onto a surreal stage set. The electric sander whined. Wedged under the hull was his friend, Rodney, on his back with a discolored mask and steamed up, sawdust caked eye goggles, sanding a kauri plank. Rodney was oblivious as Clovis shouted at him. After a fit of coughing, Clovis found the power cord and pulled the plug out of the transformer. In the abrupt silence, Rodney, after examining his sander, slowly pulled off his goggles and mask and gazed up through the dust to see an upside down figure in front of him. The figure was covered in brown smelly compost and had beans in his hair and beard.

"Rodders! It's me! Clovis!"

"Shit! I thought you were in New York?"

"No. I'm back and being chased by cops. I need to borrow your car, just for tonight."

"New York cops or the locals?" Rodney asked, still lying on his back.

"Locals. Can I? Please, Rodders."

"Here. Fill it up with gas when you return it by ten tomorrow. And I want details. You with Plum?"

"Yes, but…"

Rodney searched in his overalls and pulled out a set of keys that he threw up to Clovis.

"Figures. Now plug it in."

"I promise."

Clovis caught them and put the plug back into the transformer. He rushed out of the door as he heard the sander start up.

Clovis found the cream colored 1965 Vauxhall Victor parked two doors up the road. The engine started immediately and he made a three-part turn, slowly backing to where he had left the others behind the hedge. He leaned over and opened the side door. Four figures came out of hiding one house farther down the street and ran to the car.

The Vauxhall struggled up the Ponsonby hill on a cold engine with its cargo. Clovis turned left at the top onto Ponsonby Road and headed towards Summer Street, a narrow road with cars parked on either side. The small wooden houses seemed to lean against each other they were so close together. Very few had any front garden to speak of. Young professionals had restored some to their earlier splendor, whilst others exhibited the neglect of absent landlords and overcrowded occupants paying too steep a rent. Clovis stopped near the end of the street, at his newly rented cottage.

"Here. I've got a few beers in the fridge, and I baked a couple of loaves of bread." Clovis turned off the ignition and opened his front door. The light went on in the car. He turned to his mandatory guests, smiling. Mel, Henry and Wiremu burst out laughing. Plum, in the front seat, put her hand over her mouth. They knew he smelt bad, but he did not know he looked so ridiculous.

Plum brewed some tea while Clovis quickly bathed and put on fresh khakis. Wiremu went straight to the kitchen. His nose told him where the whole wheat bread was. When Clovis appeared, clean, from the bathroom, Wiremu was on his third piece of bread and manuka honey.

"Did you really make this, Clovis?" he asked, honey dripping down his fingers. Clovis nodded. "Then for a Pakeha, you're okay!" Wiremu grinned and chomped into his unevenly cut thick slice. "My mother baked rewena with white flour. This is so much better. You must give me the recipe."

Henry and Mel sat at the red Formica table and quietly sipped tea, black with no sugar.

"Tell me, why on earth were you carrying a shotgun up your pants and why fire it at those cops?" Henry asked what everyone had been thinking.

Wiremu finished his slice, savoring the last piece of crust as it disappeared into his mouth. He sat down on a red chair. Plum gave him a big mug of tea with lots of milk in it, as requested.

"After I gave you the pendant, about a week later, they raided my house. They found various weapons and charged me with anything they could think of. Illegal possession of drugs, although there were none in the house, illegal possession of weapons, consorting with known criminals, no TV license, no dog license and, of course, the classic resisting arrest.

"Well, all my friends, they've been arrested at least once over Maori land rights, you know, stuff like that. I must've been on probation at the time.

"'Now, Mr. Wilson,'" Wiremu put on his Pakeha bureaucrat voice and held his sweater as if it were a judge's cloak. "'This is your last chance to go straight and become a worthwhile member of the community.'"

Wiremu put his hand in his trousers and pulled out the shotgun. It was a Remington side-by-side double barrel, with as much of the stock and the barrel sawed off as possible. To Clovis's untrained eye, Wiremu broke it in half. Wiremu took out the spent cartridges and left them on the table before putting the gun up his leg again. This was done casually, as if he was retying his shoelaces. Clovis noted that Plum's eyes were the widest he had seen them since she first unzipped his pants.

"I was in Mount Eden for almost two years. There was no window in my cell. In the summer I had cockroaches and in the winter rats. It was so cold, I couldn't sleep at nights. We only got one blanket. I got out and went back to Opononi. Things were going okay for a while, and then one night I was back in Auckland in a pub with me mates. I got involved in a brawl. It was stupid. Not even my fault. In fact, I tried to break it up. But that officer walked in with two other cops. You remember the one, Henry? At the party."

"The cop with the close-set eyes?"

"Yeah. Grimble's his name. Did he have it in for me. Three cops who weren't even there testified that I started it!"

He paused to take a deep breath. There was no artifice in his delivery. He was, Clovis thought, giving them a full explanation.

"I got seven years. I was one of the first to go to Para. Paremoremo, their maximum security prison. D block. No grass, no earth, no land to see or touch. It was designed specifically to break Maori spirit. This was their secret plan. And that's who they put in there. Maori. After all, we're the most locked-up race in the world, after the Aussie Abo. Over half of all prisoners are of Maori blood, and one out of three Maori men will appear before a court by the time they're seventeen. That's what they say. And I've seen it.

"I refused to let the Pakeha beat us. I became the head of the debating team. A librarian. A big brother to all Maori boys they put in there. We grew strong and built solid friendships. No, the Pakeha wouldn't beat us."

"But why carry that?" Henry asked. He was angry at Wiremu. It was one thing to claim you were downtrodden. It was another to be so stupid.

"They'll put you away for life now. Attempted murder of a cop," Mel shot out.

"They'd put me away, regardless. Besides, I need to protect myself. I'm not going back in again. I have too much to do."

"But you can't rely on violence to achieve your goals." Mel made an effort to calm down. She had felt an immediate empathy for this giant Maori, but she was exasperated by his attitude.

"Yeah." Wiremu bowed his head. "I don't. We don't. It's only a last resort. They use fear and violence to maintain their safe little status quo. But we don't want that."

"What do you want?" Mel's tone was a little patronizing, although that was not what she intended. Her eyes were fixed on the spent cartridges.

"Where have you been? The so-called Treaty, the Springboks tour, the Land March? Uh?" Wiremu said this gently, not wishing to aggravate Mel anymore.

Clovis looked up at the thick patches of grease on the kitchen ceiling and the spider webs in the corner. It did look disgusting, but he had sworn to Plum that he was not going to paint another rented house. Besides he had his violin practice everyday. At least four hours of fiddling. Clovis began to move his right arm.

"Your arm!" Plum let out a scream.

He looked down saw a large bloodstain. He thought it had stopped bleeding in the shower.

Plum undid the buttons, whilst Mel quickly slid his shirt off his back. An experience he would have relished under different circumstances. She bent down and examined his wound.

"A superficial laceration, no stitches required. You're a little flabby, Clovis," Mel whispered as she dressed his arm, pinching his waist playfully. Clovis was more flattered by the attention than by the truth of her observation. He looked guiltily at Henry who was absorbed in buttering the last piece of bread.

"So what happens now?" Henry asked. He stuffed the bread into his mouth. What was he doing in a rundown Ponsonby shack with a Maori radical who had just tried to blow away the Auckland police force, an overweight redhead from the hippie era and a Chinese girl who looked so innocent she must have been a hooker? And Mel was tending to this redhead's injured elbow like he was the reincarnation of bleeding Jesus Christ himself. Just an ordinary Friday night in Ponsonby. How he loved being back in New Zealand. He was alive again. Back in the magical land. God's Zone. Here was his home, where something unexpected always happened. How amazing it was to be with Mel. Now he had three new weird friends. Expect the unexpected should be the motto for the country. Not like New York at all. There you were lucky if anything happened. It was far too provincial, far too insular. There was no spontaneity with the people. They all seemed so closed off. Here he felt positively unjaded. Here, everyone was alive. So alive they were bleeding in the kitchen!

"You've got your audition tomorrow, Clovis." Plum gave her lover one of her cross-eyed looks.

"Tomorrow?" Clovis looked confused.

"What do you play?" Henry asked, but Clovis was already addressing Wiremu.

"You can stay here as long as you like. Violin," Clovis answered Henry. "I audition for the Symphony Orchestra. Second fiddle."

Clovis wanted to get to know this huge Maori who had mana and a princely bearing. Clovis had spent hours describing Maoris to Americans in New York, not always accurately, and yet he had been close to only one, Rua the drummer. Clovis did not know their history or understand their language. Now was his chance.

"Yeah, Clovis. I won't be able to go home. They'll be watching for me."

Plum shot another cross-eyed glare at Clovis when she thought nobody was looking. She sensed they were getting involved in an affair that would have an unpleasant end, for everyone involved.

They retired to the small living room, which contained one sofa facing an empty wall with faded carpet covering the wooden floor. The bare walls had been painted an off-white over layers of aged wallpaper. The entire house was a dry cinder box.

Clovis got the last brown bottle of DB beer. He came back to see Wiremu sitting on the sofa next to Mel. Plum sat cross-legged on the carpet looking like she belonged there, whilst Henry, with a wry smile, stretched out on the floor with his back to the wall directly opposite Wiremu.

"I have no other way to do this in the Pakeha's world. What do you expect me to do? Sell life insurance? Or work in the freezing works with a bunch of embittered commies?"

Clovis held up the bottle. "Last one. Any offers? What do you expect freezing workers to be like? You don't expect them to run around in tutus or 'Desert Song' outfits? Singing 'I like bananas 'cause they've got no bones!' Do you?"

Mel laughed. Clovis threw the bottle to Wiremu who caught it and tore the cap off with his teeth, took one long swig and offered it to Mel. She declined, and Wiremu passed it to Henry. He checked the level of the liquid and took a polite drink before offering it to Plum and Clovis. They both shook their heads. He handed it back to Wiremu.

Plum Blossom rolled her eyes behind her eyelids, a favorite trick of hers that indicated, "here we go again!" When Clovis had teased her about this, she had replied, "Clovis, when you fiddle, the cows hide behind the moon." She was kidding, she loved his violin playing. It turned her on. That such a big man with long thick fingers could draw from that instrument such a delicate sweet tone never ceased to amaze her.

Henry turned to Clovis and asked him. "What kind of music do you play?

Wiremu was still trying to talk to Mel. "...you know there's a saying take away their language and you'll take away their culture. That's what Franco did to the Basques. It was illegal to speak Basque in Spain. He tried to destroy their culture. The same happened here. Up until 1952 it was illegal to speak Maori in our schools. My father used to be caned and sent home if he spoke

Maori. And my grandmother would always take him back to school and curse the teacher in Maori. A real heavy makutu."

"Anything," Clovis replied to Henry. "I love classical, baroque and jazz rock fusion, even learned some ragas, but that takes some doing and it blew off my tonality."

"But your grandmother wouldn't condone what you did at that pub, would she?" Mel said.

"She's dead. If I get to her age, I'll probably think different. But I have a lot of anger in me, and I'm not afraid to show it at the right time."

"How do you play jazz and rock stuff?" Henry asked, trying to ignore Mel's argument.

"Okay. But there are ways to show your anger, ways to channel it, without resorting to violence. You're never going to achieve your aims by violence against the State. They have the power, the resources. They'll always win, in the end."

"I've got a special pickup and magnetic microphone I attach to the bridge of my violin plus a whole lot of foot gear. Shit. Plum, remind me to pick all that up from Matthew. I've got cords and stuff over at his place. He's probably lost them all by now."

Plum nodded, although she was trying to follow the other conversation.

"I'd love to hear that."

"I thought that too when I was younger and a little naive. Now I know better." Wiremu turned to Clovis. He switched to a lighter tone, as if he had heard their dialogue and said: "Now what are you going to play for us?"

Mel stood up and announced they had to leave. She had a 6:00 A.M. start on Saturday. This saved Clovis from playing in front of the guests. A task he was in no mood for. Clovis and Henry swapped phone numbers whilst Mel invited them over for a meal on Monday night. Wiremu made a point of shaking hands with Mel as they said good-bye and looking her in the eyes.

Mel rested on Henry's chest. She watched a bead of sweat run down his bicep then stroked his pendant. The bed covers were at their ankles and they breathed heavily.

"It's cold."

"Tears are cold." Henry had taken the pendant out of storage and worn it for the first time on Friday night.

"He really reacted to this. Didn't he?"

"Yeah. I'd forgotten how much power this is supposed to have. I've been away such a long time."

"Too long." She moved her body up to his face to kiss him on the lips. "What power?"

"Didn't I tell you about the Tear of Tane?"

"No. You've been mysterious about this."

"Really?"

"Yes. You change the subject."

"Oh. I thought I'd told you? Well, here goes then. I will leave nothing out." He rolled Mel over and kissed her.

"You can leave that out until you tell me." She pushed him off, playfully but with enough force for him to realize what she could do.

"Once upon a time, before Maoris came here, Tane was the god of the forest. But the forest was in danger. Bugs were eating the roots of the trees, and unless something was done, the forest would die. Tane called all the birds together and asked for their help. The Kiwi bird was a bird of paradise and lived in the treetops. It was the most beautiful bird in the forest and very proud. When Tane told all the birds what was happening, none of them wanted to help to save the forest. Tane was in despair. None of the birds would volunteer or even offer a suggestion. There was silence in the forest."

"Well?"

"I'm pausing for dramatic effect. So, seeing that none of the other birds were going to do anything, the Kiwi stepped forward and said he would go and live in the undergrowth and eat all the bugs and save the forest. So the Kiwi became a fat, flightless, ugly bird eating bugs at night. It lost all its bright colorful feathers. Tane was so moved by what the Kiwi did that he shed a tear. Tane had never cried before. The tear fell to the ground and turned to greenstone and was lost for thousands of years until a Ngapuhi, a tohunga, found this piece of pounamu lying in the forest floor. It was black and covered in moss. No one would have recognized it. But the tohunga picked it up and immediately recognized it as the Tear of Tane. He cleaned it and put it around his neck. And with the power this pendant gave him he was able to guide his leaders to victories over other threatening tribes until the Ngapuhi were feared and respected throughout Aotearoa."

"That's a beautiful story. But if it's such a precious totem, I mean, it's really valuable, how come Wiremu gave it to you, a Pakeha?"

"The Tear was passed down to Wiremu's grandfather, and when he died he left it to his wife, Wiremu's grandmother, who gave it to Wiremu. She told him that, whoever saved him from something terrible, and he would know what this was, then he should without thinking pass the Tear of Tane to that person. No matter who it was. And this he did."

"That party and the police?"

"Yeah."

"I don't believe it. It's just too much."

"I think this whole night has been too much."

Mel went to sleep on his chest, her hand resting on the pendant. He went back to that party. He kept getting these flashes from his New Zealand past.

He was in a house packed with long-haired teenagers. Most of the men were drunk, and the women were dancing to very loud music. Land of a Thousand Dances. Uniformed police ran into the house waving their batons and forced everyone out into the street where there were more police and a large van, the Black Maria.

Henry, with very long hair and beard, had been talking to Wiremu in the kitchen. The police removed all the Maoris from the rest of the men at the party and lined them up against the wall. Henry had walked over to Wiremu and stood next to him. At first, with all the shouting, the police had not noticed him. Then they tried to grab him and separate him from Wiremu. Henry did not resist, but as two policemen held his arms tightly, another officer came up to him and addressed him.

"What do you think you are doing, boy?" the officer had shouted.

"I was having a conversation with this gentleman in the kitchen. I merely wanted to continue this," Henry began, in his most measured voice. "We were discussing the relative merits of Tamaki Grammar School's First Fifteen versus my Mt. Albert Grammar School's First."

"And?" The officer was hooked.

"Well. We beat them two weeks ago, and two of their players were sent off the field for foul play."

"That I can understand," the officer sneered.

"But we lost three men to injuries," Henry added.

"The score?"

"Twenty-one to three. They never got a try, and the penalty was a fluke, the referee saw one of our chaps return a punch."

"Hmmm, typical." The officer addressed the two holding Henry. "Let them both go and let's deal with the others."

Henry and Wiremu walked away from the police into the dark street.

Chapter Two

Plum trimmed Clovis's beard and hair the next morning. The front was too short so his hair stuck up. He was pleased with the effect and felt less hot. His violin sounded brighter when he had his final practice before the audition at one o'clock. Wiremu slept through everything, curled up on the floor in the living room. They could hear his snores coming through the thin wall. On his way to his audition, he returned the car to Rodney who was under his boat with the sander.

Clovis came back at 4:00, sweat pouring from his face. He had walked home from Parnell. It had been a grueling audition with the conductor of the Auckland Symphony Orchestra, Max Steinberg. The small cottage where Clovis auditioned was crammed with brass figurines and marble busts of the great composers. Not easily intimidated, Clovis had bowed his way through some tough sight-reading before the conductor had sat him down and begun the oral interview. Clovis used this to his advantage and, playing on the conductor's sense of elitism, casually remarked that he had just returned from New York where he had studied under a famous

Russian émigré called Vassily Kremer. Of course, the conductor was impressed, although he would never admit he had not heard of such a fellow. How could he have? Mr. Kremer was the caretaker to Clovis's sublet on St. Marks Place. Mr. Kremer could not tell a rondo from a rugelach.

"You did that?" Plum asked.

"Well, when I mentioned rugelachs, it sent the maestro off about his mother and Germany. They left in 1933 when things started to get bad. He was beaten up at school, something happened to his sister, so his father sat down with his family and an atlas and he found a country called Neue Zeeland that was the farthest they could get from the Nazis."

"How did they leave?"

"He said it took them three years to get here, and all their savings. They settled in Dunedin. Then one Sunday afternoon they were coming down from the hills and the entire town and the local constable were waiting for them. He said he was wearing his lederhosen and the locals were carrying torches."

"Like something out of Frankenstein."

"Yes! That was what I was thinking, but I didn't want to say that. Anyway, they were all arrested for signaling Japanese submarines. Can you believe that? And they spent the entire war interned on Somes Island."

"You mean a family of Jews was locked up for being German spies? That's like what happened to my relatives here. Makes no sense now, does it?"

"And that's how he practiced his piano and learned music; there was nothing else to do. His father died a broken man. But the maestro, well, he became the maestro. Then I told him about my great-grandfather, a horse thief in Bavaria. He fled in 1887 and using the same geographic logic as the late Mr. Steinberg, worked his way around the world until he came to New Zealand."

"You never told me this story. Were you making it up?"

"No. I swear it's true. It was just buried, you know? He became a shepherd in Taranaki and changed his name from Tiborsky to Tibet after he fell in love with a young Chinese woman he met in Wellington. He worked in Taranaki on sheep farms and finished up marrying the farmer's daughter."

"Where in Wellington? What woman?"

"I was never really sure. My father only told me this story once, and it is like a dream now. He mentioned something about the Sincere Laundry."

"Oh shit," Plum whispered to herself.

"After World War II, my father inherited a sheep farm, and I got sent away to a boarding school in Wellington and took to playing the violin as a means of escaping rugby practice. This sent the maestro off on another rant about rugby.

"'Ze vould commit any sin for their vorshipped sport but look how hard it vas to fund a symphony orchestra?' So that was when I knew I had the position."

Plum cooked an elaborate meal, with the meager cooking utensils she could find. Giant kumaras were baked in the oven, and she had marinated huge slabs of filet steak in a mixture of thick soya sauce, lemon juice, a pinch of cayenne pepper and beer. Wiremu, she explained later to Clovis, had pulled out a thick wad of twenty- and fifty-dollar notes from his sock and told her to buy as much food as she could carry.

In turn, Clovis did the same with beer, balancing a wooden crate of DB on his shoulders as he staggered down John Street.

"You realize, of course, Mr. Nepal," Clovis waved both hands in the air, intoxicated, doing his twelfth parody of the conductor. "That ve are zee very best orchestra in dis country. I might add zee entire Australasian continent, if not zee Southern Hemisphere. As such ve stringently adopt a rigid and professional bearing at all times. Do I make myself clear?" He paused for dramatic effect and looked down his nose at Wiremu (in his chair) and Plum (rolling on the floor). "I take it you hav tails?"

"Tails? What are you, a bunch of eels?" Wiremu roared.

"No. No. No. No. A penguin outfit." Clovis corrected.

"A penguin dressed as a tuna?"

Wiremu had scoured the morning and afternoon newspapers on Saturday and found some bargain furniture that he sent Clovis and Plum to pick up on Sunday. They came back in a truck with a long Victorian couch and two brown chesterfield chairs and a red kidney-shaped fifties coffee table. Wiremu could now slump in one of the chairs during the day while holding court. On retiring, he would sleep on the couch that Plum stayed clear of, claiming it smelt of tomcats.

"Loosen up more, Clovis. You have to feel it. Sway from the hips. The hips. Yes. Show that feeling by moving. Once you sway you set up your own internal rhythm. Real loose but tight. Yeah! That's it! You've got it!" Wiremu would act as coach, conductor and teacher, an appreciative audience of one. Clovis practiced all Sunday and Monday afternoon on his new orchestral parts. In turn, for added levity, during particularly ear scrapping passages when Clovis was trying to work out some new fingering, Wiremu would try to mimic Clovis mimicking the conductor. Only Wiremu's accent sounded like a very bad Oxford don who had lost his "w's."

"I must inform you zat zis is a truly, truly, truly first rate orchestra. Ve are at zee very peek of our perfection. As such ve look to zee highest possible standards, Mr. Himalayas."

Chapter Three

Monday

At noon, Inspector Bernard Grimble stood on the porch of a house at the bottom of Grafton Road. The floorboards creaked under his brogues. He was in his usual outfit when working unofficially, a grey windcheater with large outside pockets, dark pants and a white shirt with a clip-on tie. He could have passed for a building inspector. He gave the two-story house a quick scan.

Grimble took a brass ring of master keys from the side pocket of his jacket and, selecting a Yale key, inserted it into the solid oak door. He quickly took another key off the ring and unlocked the lower. Sergeant Cadd stood behind him, looking up and down the street, shifting his huge footballer's frame from one foot to the other. He wore a blue blazer and grey slacks with a blue shirt undone at the collar because his neck was so thick.

The inspector opened the door and strode up to a small metal box in the hallway by the stairs. When he had accessed the Wongs' file earlier on the Wanganui Computer, he saw that the Inland Revenue Department had itemized deductions for the Excalibur Burglar Alarm System with automatic police notification and the famous Excalibur 100 decibel audio alarm. Grimble was familiar with the model. He had one installed in his house, although he could not claim the tax deduction, he had noted.

"Come on, shut the door and don't look so worried. What can happen? Will the police arrest us? Are you counting?"

Cadd looked at his watch and nodded yes. Grimble took out a small screwdriver and some wires from his other jacket pocket and unscrewed the door of the box. Although he only had thirty seconds to complete his task, he was careful not to leave any scratches on the screws. The sergeant watched as Grimble placed two clips simultaneously on one set of red wires then two clips on the black pair. There was nothing hurried about his actions. The inspector had done this many times.

The burglar alarm that would automatically send a recorded message to the local police station was now short-circuited.

"Time?" Grimble asked.

"Er, nine thirty. Oh, no, about eighteen seconds."

"About? Too slow. Here, follow me and don't touch anything."

Was Cadd fooling him? Grimble wondered. It would have been easy for the inspector to obtain a search warrant from an understanding magistrate. He could have made up a story about stolen property or narcotics. But this would have taken too much time and paperwork, not to mention questions from his colleagues. The clandestine visit was more appropriate and, in keeping with the spirit of the commissioner's orders, no paperwork, nothing official. And this was a chance to try out Cadd, to see if he had potential. Not talent, potential. There was a difference.

The inspector did not suspect the Wongs of fencing stolen goods or smuggling class A or B narcotics into the country. Their martial arts mail order business, judging from their taxes of the last two years, was extremely successful. Even more so was their take-out shop opposite the Three Lamps pub. The Hungry Wok was an all-night burger and chips joint that also sold spring rolls and fried fish. There was no wok inside the place as far as Grimble knew.

Sergeant Cadd followed the inspector into the front room that was pitch-black from the closed blue velvet drapes. Grimble switched on the overhead light. On the wall opposite was a poster of Bruce Lee. The room was stacked with cardboard boxes. On one side there was a metal filing cabinet and a desk. In the center were opened boxes with nunchaku individually wrapped in plastic bags. Grimble picked up an unwrapped pair of these twelve-inch wooden rods and slowly spun the rod in a figure eight. The nunchaku hummed as the ball bearing swivel allowed the metal chain connecting the rods to spin with the minimum of friction.

"Lethal weapon, sir." Cadd stated the obvious.

"Yes. Imagine a small police baton against one of these wielded by an expert?"

The inspector carefully replaced the nunchaku and walked over to a filing cabinet and opened a drawer. He selected a large ledger book and laid it on the desk. He opened it and carefully looked through the book. On the table were a pile of wires, a remote-controlled toy car and a soldering iron.

"You're not missing anything, Cadd. Just keep an eye out for the Wongs, don't move the curtains and remind me about the clips when we leave. I don't want them to know we've been here. Understood?"

"Yes sir." Cadd edged his way to the curtains and kneeling down pushed a small corner aside.

"It's all clear, sir."

"Thank you, Sergeant. You only have to tell me if you see them."

The inspector leafed through another ledger book. The Wongs kept meticulous records. All he saw were numbers and codes.

Grimble had a problem. After golf with the commissioner, he had been assigned to work with a task force to help locate the suspected Maori who had fired a shotgun in the Jolly Rodger last Friday. The task force had tracked down the usual leads. But there were no firm suspects. Several Maoris had been held for the night but released the next morning because there was no evidence linking them with the shotgun. Grimble knew from his own sources that the Wilson brothers and their closest friends always drank at the Jolly Rodger when they were in town. Grimble thought the prime suspect would be Wiremu Wilson, who had disappeared. Rather than becoming angry that his target had vanished, he endeavored to uncover the elusive Wilson on his own. If Wilson was in hiding, the more likely he was guilty.

The Wongs had a lot of Maori mail order clients. So where was the list kept? Grimble found his answer in the second drawer of the file cabinet. He found the names of Wilson in a separate file. He wrote the two addresses down, one in Parnell, another in Hokianga.

"Wouldn't customs have had their dogs all over these boxes, sir? I mean, they must go through these with a fine-tooth comb. Being from the Orient."

"We're not here for that, we're here for this!" Grimble closed his notebook.

"Why can't we ban all this stuff? It all finishes up in violent crimes against us. Right, sir?"

"We live in a democracy, not a totalitarian state. People are allowed to use these for martial arts."

"I mean, we ban handguns and all barrels under twenty inches. So why not this too?"

"Cadd."

"Yes, sir?"

"Be on the lookout. You're not the Ombudsman for Kung Fu artists."

"I mean, remember last week outside that Chinese takeout on Ponsonby Road. Those bikies weren't cut up with knives or baseball bats, were they? They were…"

"Cadd!" He rushed to the door and ordered his vigilant student of break-ins to remain on watch.

In the back of the house were the kitchen, an open dining room and a toilet. The rooms were tidy with the minimum of clutter or dirt, apart from the breakfast dishes in the sink and a dripping tap. Two woks sat on top of the stove. They make their own muesli with dried fruit, he surmised; flakes of baked oatmeal and pieces of almond floated in two bowls in the sink. There were two packs of playing cards in a kitchen cupboard full of jars containing herbs, spices, nuts and exotic teas.

Upstairs the two brothers occupied a bedroom each, with matching antique queen-size beds. Their top covers were drawn back and T-shirts and jeans had been dropped on the floor. Looking through their drawers and closets, the inspector saw they were very basic dressers. He was about to open a restored tall kauri dresser with sterling silver handles when he heard Cadd yell out that they were coming.

Grimble tumbled as quietly as he could manage down the stairs.

"The lights," Grimble hissed to Cadd who was standing in the doorway not sure what to do next. He switched off the light in the front room.

Grimble raced to pull out the clips and screw back the cover to the metal box. They both heard the first key go into the lock and turn. Grimble finished securing the last screw and motioned to Cadd to go to the back. The second key was inserted and the door slowly opened as the inspector tiptoed behind Cadd into the kitchen. The back door had two locks. He twisted them open and let

Cadd go down the wooden steps, then he shut the door as quietly as he could. He could hear one of the Wongs stomp into the kitchen as he knelt by the windowless side of the house.

"We forgot to get tap washers!" Ricky Wong yelled to his brother who was turning off the alarm system.

"We have to get a better system or hide this box. It's not good enough."

The policemen smiled at each other as they heard this comment. They walked to the street and the inspector's Honda Accord. Only when they reached the bottom of the valley did Grimble turn on the ignition and let out an audible sigh.

"That was a close one, eh, sir?"

"Yes, Cadd."

Monday morning found Plum and Clovis dead broke. Despite Wiremu's largesse, they had sunk most of their money into the first, second and last months' rent plus a security deposit equal to two months' rent. Then there was the large fee they had to pay to the renting agent, the key money. Although they were suspicious of the legality of all the monies they had to come up with immediately, they had been desperate to find their own accommodation. The house was at least rat free and not as disgusting as the other flats and houses they had inspected.

Clovis did not want Plum to go to work right away. Since he would not receive his first orchestra check for a month, he decided he would try what he had done so well in New York City; busk with his violin. In order for Clovis to play in a public place, he had to have an Auckland City Council permit. He walked across Ponsonby carrying his violin case to the City Administration Building behind the Town Hall.

A clerk behind the city permit counter informed Clovis that it would take several weeks to process the permit as they were backed up. Having learned something from his stay in New York City, Clovis, with his eyes bulging and his face changing to his hair color, demanded the permit immediately, otherwise he would begin to play his violin right there and then. The small clerk disappeared behind a screen showing a poster "Don't take a chance! Use a condom!" The clerk appeared five minutes later with the permit typed out.

Clovis had other reasons to play on the streets. One was to escape from Wiremu's all hearing, all seeing ears. It was getting overbearing, yet Clovis could not bring himself to tell Wiremu to shut up. How could he? He was an extremely likeable guest, and a paying one. The other reason was more devious.

At five minutes past six, Clovis positioned himself outside the Ponsonby Women's Clinic on Ponsonby Road. He had spent the last three hours trying various locations along Queen Street, plying the passersby with his Irish gigues and Baroque partitas. He had collected $3.21. The public was not used to giving, Clovis reasoned. And he was asked four times by different policemen to show his permit. After a long and suspicious perusal of the permit and taking careful note of his name, which they all made the same comments about, they had asked Clovis to move on. Every time! Great! And he had an official permit! What more did he need? A letter from the Queen? Now he was in four different police reports labeled a public nuisance. As if having his colon inspected on returning to God's Zone was not enough! Welcome back to little old New Zealand, Clovis!

Clovis took his violin out of the case, placed the case in front of him (but within grabbing distance) and started to play an Irish gigue. The traffic sounds mixed with the violin to make Clovis nostalgic for Rockefeller Center or Columbus Avenue or St. Marks Place or anywhere where there were pedestrians with loose change and spare dollar bills. Nobody was on the street.

To complete the picture of the street musician, he wore dark glasses and had a sign in his case:

PLEASE HELP ME BUY
A BLIND DOG

After four gigues he had six cents in his case and a dozen Samoan children giggling and pointing at him, not fooled by the shades.

She came out of the clinic and turned right, to her BMW parked at the curb. She stopped in front of Clovis, looked at him, at the sign and at his face again.

"Clovis! You're not blind!" She uttered, astonished at his ruse and wondering what this was about. Clovis was playing "Women of Ireland" from "Barry Lyndon." He stopped abruptly and addressed her in a thick brogue accent, without looking in her direction.

"What has that got to do with it? I want a blind dog, not a seeing-eye dog. Who said I was blind?" he continued playing from where he left off. The children were laughing hysterically at his accent. The tall woman in the black dress and white shirt continued walking. The violinist speeded up the tempo and applied extra thick vibrato making the music very syrupy. The woman stopped, turned her head to one side then spun around.

"Do you want a lift?" she asked.

He lowered his violin, adjusted his glasses and smiled.

"Why, that would be dandy."

Clovis got into her car, his violin case on his knees, his dark glasses over his forehead nestled in his spiked red hair.

"Where can I take you?" Mel asked.

"Home." He gulped.

"How is our Maori chief?"

"Oh, he's fine. A little rowdy at night and he eats a lot, but he's paying for everything, so I can't complain."

"What do you think of him?" Mel had not turned on the ignition.

"I don't know, he's, formidable. Far smarter than he lets on. Cunning's the word, I think. I like him. But there's something else there I can't quite put my finger on. Maybe I'm too naive to work it all out."

"What do you mean?"

"Well, he said all he needed was a few more days, then everything would come together."

"Do you believe him, Clovis?"

She said this in such a way that Clovis's response had to be, "of course not!"

"Yes."

"I sense he's not telling you everything."

"Oh." Clovis had a sudden feeling of dread. He wanted to go home and hug Plum. Make sure she was all right. All the mysterious and attractive forces he felt for Mel had dissipated. "Are we still on for tonight?"

"Yes, of course."

Mel pulled up to Clovis's cottage. In the hallway, Clovis heard Plum sobbing. He burst into the living room to see her curled up in a ball on the sofa. Her face was invisible under her matted hair. Wiremu knelt beside her, trying to console her, making cooing sounds like he was luring a bush pigeon into a trap.

Wiremu stood up when he saw Clovis, his hands open in a gesture of helplessness.

"What happened?" Clovis asked.

"What did you do to her?" Mel addressed Wiremu, who was alarmed by her accusatory tone.

Clovis thought of all the times he had left Plum and Wiremu alone that weekend as he lugged beer crates and extra food home for Wiremu. Then there was the bitter memory of how he had found Plum in New York. And didn't he remember what Plum used to do in Auckland? The knot in his stomach grew tighter.

"It wasn't me!" Wiremu shouted. He was not used to being verbally attacked, especially by an angry Pakeha woman.

"Plum! It's OK. I'm here." Clovis hugged her as best he could. Her head was locked into her knees.

"Clovis. Clovis. You swore you'd never leave me," she mumbled through her hair.

He helped her sit up. She wiped back her hair from her wet face, too distraught to care about her appearance. Then she threw her face into Clovis's khaki shirt.

"He knows. He knows," she sobbed.

"Who? Who knows?"

"He came. He came to get me. He knows I'm here."

"Who?" Clovis lifted his face up to Wiremu.

"I think it was one of Terry the Turk's men," Wiremu offered.

"Who's that?" Mel asked.

"Terry the Turk. I saw one of his men through the window. He came to the front door, knocked for ages, then tried the handle. Went to the back door, then tried to look in the windows. Plum saw him. When he left she went hysterical. I've been trying to calm her down ever since."

"He knows. He knows." Plum lifted her head off Clovis's wet shirt.

"Just as well she locked the back door, otherwise I'd've had to blow him away."

Mel looked out the window at the street, then turned to Wiremu.

"Who is Terry the Turk? And what man?"

"Terry Turner. He owns a lot of real estate, a couple of massage parlors, a strip joint on K Road and the biggest used car lot over on Ellerslie Road. That's where he launders most of his money."

"I think I'm missing something," Mel said.

"Terry controls a lot of dope around Auckland, and he brings in coke, some hash and acid. Very diverse. And elusive. The cops have nothing on him."

"How do you know?" Mel shot back.

"I thought everyone did!" Wiremu was defensive. "Being in Para is like graduating magna cum laude at Crime University. I met just about everyone who went through there. In many cases we knew what was going on outside before the cops did. Everyone talked to me, because I had a certain influence."

He did not tell Mel that he graduated MA with first class honors in Psychology in the Waikato University outreach program. He had become a champion debater, the only way a prisoner could get out and visit other prisons, during debating contests. He failed to mention his older half-brother, Rawiri, who was also related to Hei Hei. Rawiri had not adapted to prison life as well as Wiremu, who became assistant librarian. The head librarian had been Terry the Turk.

"Terry did time for possession of stolen property. About the only thing he hasn't done. The cops set him up. Terry is basically into everything. Prostitution, false insurance claims, I've even heard he did some white slavery for some rich Arabs that passed through on their private 707. When there was a real bad oil shortage. Kiwi girls for oil. That's why the government can't touch him. I don't know about that."

"What about the man at the window? Was he armed?" Mel kept looking out of the window, moving from one foot to the other.

"That was Big John. He had a billy club in one hand. A big black American car, could be a Lincoln. Lucky I was here, Clovis. I wouldn't let anyone harm Plum. Especially that animal."

"Why would this man want to see Plum?" Mel asked.

"He's a bad man. I've had some dealings with him." Wiremu was unwilling to go into details in front of Plum. And was the man with the billy club looking for Plum or Wiremu?

"So now we're hiding from Peter the policeman and Terry the Turk." Clovis tried to make a joke. No one laughed.

"Don't worry, little sister. I'm here. I'll protect you." Wiremu laid his right hand on Plum's shoulder.

"Why don't we all pile into my car and we can eat and talk about this at my place. It is my official night off, so we won't be interrupted by my beeper. I hope."

"Yeah. Bring your violin, Clovis. You haven't had your practice today, and I'm really beginning to like that piece by Brahms. Have you a piano, Mel?"

"No. Do you play?" Mel was surprised at the question. When would she have had time to play the bloody piano?

"No. I thought you might."

Mel held her car keys in her hand. Clovis picked up his violin case. He hated being asked to play at other people's houses. It reminded him of when his parents were alive and he had to play in front of guests.

"Shall we put a sack over his head?" Mel looked at Wiremu then turned to the others in the hallway.

"You can hide my face, but you can't hide my body."

• • •

Terry Turner watched John Eustace sweep out the tiny room in the concealed side of his basement. His Victorian-built stone house was on a street behind Mount Eden on the Epsom side, with neatly mown lawns and flowering hibiscus shrubs.

John straightened his back to his full height. He ran one hand through his close-cropped white hair. His hands were like the paws of a polar bear.

"Reminds me of inside." He lowered his icy blue eyes. Terry noticed, not for the first time, how docile John could appear to him. Yet he had witnessed John kill with his bare hands, and the look on his bodyguard's face had been one of sublime enjoyment. How contradictory human beings are, Terry mused, as he bent over to adjust the sheets of the small cot he had set up in one corner. He stepped back to admire his handiwork. He wanted everything to be perfect for his guest.

"Do you think she'll like it here?" Terry ran his small left hand over his shiny bald patch, imitating John's gesture.

John went back to sweeping a ball of fluff out of the doorway, not sure if his boss was kidding him. Who likes to be kidnapped? Terry could ask some peculiar questions.

Mel lived in a two-bedroom house on Raurangi Road off Mount Eden Road. Her property extended to the reserve, Mount Eden, an extinct volcano nearly seven hundred feet high, once a Maori fortress with terraces and a pa site. The house's wooden slats were painted a dark green and the windows and shutters were a rusty grey. The front garden was filled with tall flowering shrubs, camellias, rhododendrons, frangipani and a grapefruit tree laden down with big yellow fruit. They could hear music, Split Enz playing "Stranger Than Fiction."

Henry was lying on the couch with his eyes closed and legs stretched out.

"Oh my god. You really got it?" Mel asked.

He sat up, beaming ear to ear. "Oh. Hello everyone. You all look so somber."

"You didn't get the food? You didn't go shopping? The list I gave you?" Mel asked.

"What list? Didn't have time. I had to wait for this delivery." Henry turned down the volume and hoped he had saved himself from one of Mel's outbursts.

No one mentioned the intruder called Big John or Terry the Turk as they sat at the dining room table and chewed their way through a tuna salad from cans with fresh summer vegetables and slices of large red beefsteak tomatoes, washed down with a cold Chardonnay.

"I don't think you can compare a Yankee to-may-toe with a Kiwi tomato. These are so much more yummy." Clovis savored a beefsteak exploding in his mouth.

Plum remained quiet. She slowly ate and observed everyone. Clovis kept looking at her, trying to gauge if she had recovered from her afternoon fright. He could not tell. She took everything in but let nothing out.

"I hear you're real skilled in martial arts," Wiremu asked Mel. Henry glanced at Mel.

"I used to teach women self-defense, but there was a case where a young Samoan woman, a student of mine, killed her boyfriend who was abusing her, and I was called in as a witness. Put me off teaching, but I haven't the time now anyway."

"You should come up to Hokianga and start a practice. There's a shortage of doctors up there," Wiremu added.

"Yes, we can move into the country, run a small farm. Grow organic food. Look at the stars every night."

"Henry's new theme song." Mel rolled her eyes.

"I grew up in the country, well, Pukekohe. It was green but no forests. I love forests. I can't believe we were in New York the same time you both were. We could've crossed paths," Clovis responded.

"Kiwis seem to find each other in faraway places," Henry said.

"New York isn't faraway, mentally." Plum looked across at Clovis.

"You know what I mean. It's different," Henry added "Different but the same."

"What was your dream in New York?" Henry asked Plum.

Here the dialogue split into two threads. They had finished the tuna salad, and Mel opened another bottle of white wine she got from the refrigerator.

"What did you think of New York?" Clovis asked Mel.

"What do you mean?" Plum asked Henry.

"Well, everybody who comes to New York has a dream. They want to conquer the city, prove themselves, be the best in their field," Henry replied.

"I found it rather civilized. Not what I expected. I've seen so many movies about New York. I think this place is more violent. We're not tamed here. It's like living in the savage garden. I see it all the time in my practice," Mel said.

"I want to be an actress," Plum declared to Henry. "I thought a New Zealand Chinese girl would be different there, but there were hundreds of actresses who looked just like me."

"No. I can't believe that. You're unique," Henry declared.

"That's what's so good about music. Even playing in the loudest rock band, there's a liberation I wouldn't trade for anything." Clovis's eyes went misty.

"I'm just relieved to be back here," Plum sighed. "I want to start my own theater troupe. I can do that here and get an audience. In New York it's almost impossible."

"You're playing in a pub?" Wimeru addressed Clovis.

"Not that one again?" Mel rolled her eyes.

"Why not join a drama company? There must be tons to join," Henry asked Plum.

"I know a lot of people who're interested. It's just a question of organizing."

"Couldn't find anyone to play with in New York. I really like the music scene here. Odd that. We're taught to look up there for the best of everything, but from what I've seen, we have it all here and better," Clovis said.

There was a lull in the conversation when the music stopped from the other room. Henry had turned up his new stereo system so that the music could leak into the dining room. The Split Enz album gave way to an old Animals album with "The House of the Rising Sun."

The delicious aroma of baking bread wafted into the dining room as they sipped coffee. Henry explained that his PhD thesis had propelled him into a top-secret research lab on Long Island. He resigned from the lab when he found out he was really working for an obscure section within the Department of Defense. All his research was for a new weapon. Because of his contract, he could not publish his paper.

"It's so secret I shouldn't even talk about it. What the hell! I'm here. On the other side of the planet. It's as if my work didn't exist."

"What was the research?" Wiremu asked.

"Pure, not applied. I was working on a universal algorithm, an equation that explains all matter and energy and how they work together. You know, Einstein's e equals mc squared? Well, it's an extension of that, the

Unified Field Theory. What I was proposing was..."
Henry caught himself. They looked lost. Mel was bored.

"What happened to you in New York?" Clovis asked
to break the silence.

"It's a long story. There were two groups of people
after me, American spies, I think, and Bulgarians, who
were trying to recruit me as a defector, you know, 'come
over to us and we'll give you all the resources you'll ever
need and you'll win the Nobel Prize in Physics and have
all the women and caviar you want.' No, Mel, just jok-
ing, only the caviar!"

He could not tell if Mel was scowling at him.

"They were either going to recruit me or destroy me.
They were found at the bottom of the elevator shaft in
my building. I only got to hear about that a few days
ago, when someone from the American Embassy came
over to interview me."

Mel kept that look on him. But Henry took this to
mean she was jealous about the Bulgarian women, even
though he had made that part up.

"Now, with all this going on, Mel flew into New
York. I had gotten back into my apartment and cleaned
it up. But then another couple of thugs broke in. They're
not Bulgarians or mobsters, they're Albanians! They
slap me around and start interrogating me. They go
through the remains of all my papers and notes. They
demand all my scientific work. Now Mel was coming to
see me. I had called her up. She said she was flying into
JFK. But I didn't know when. I found out later there was
an urgent telegram downstairs at my hotel from Mel.
But telegrams in New York are not what they used to be.
They worked in 40s' movies, but not now.

"So, while I'm tied up in my room being worked over
by these garlic smelling goons, she lands and is in a real
shitty mood. I wasn't there to greet her. There is no car
for her, no note, no nothing.

"Now picture this. I am passing out with fear and fatigue from these evil-looking guys in badly made suits. If you saw this in a film you wouldn't believe it! But I was tied to a chair, hands and legs.

"Then suddenly the door is flung open, no, it's broken down, and in storms Mel, really pissed. I mean, I have never seen anyone so pissed. Steam is coming out of her ears she's so pissed. She does not stop moving. She does a front snap kick to the oaf nearest her, then smacks him with a back fist so he's stunned, but he's so fat in the gut he doesn't fall over. The other guy who was just about to slap me again in the face swings around and brings out a long shiny knife. I yell at Mel to watch out, he lunges at her, and she sidekicks his knees out from under him then smashes her fists into his ears. And boy he had big ugly ears. Then she proceeds to pummel him until he collapses."

Henry stops to look at Mel. Mel has never heard Henry tell the story before and is surprised by his animated rendition.

"Now the other thug is coming around and is really angry. Only Mel is madder. She's beside herself with rage and launches into another attack on him. Fists, feet, elbows, the remains of the furniture. The fight seems to go on and on. And I'm still tied up. I mean, I cannot move, only yell and scream at them both. Mel finally knocks him down and gives him one last kick. Then she checks them, like she switches into Doctor mode, sees if they are okay. Of course they are not. They've had the beating of their life.

"Mel lets out a sigh and turns to me. She just stares.

"I said, 'Have a good flight then?'

"And she cracks up, bent over laughing, while I'm still tied up!"

"Well, I did untie you, eventually."

"Only after I promised to come back here with you."

"That seemed like a reasonable request, considering the circumstances. And you know what they say, you should always negotiate from strength." Mel laughed.

Wiremu was wide eyed. Bulgarians! Albanians! Huge knockdown dragged out fights in hotel rooms in New York! And they came back here to sleepy old New Zealand? No wonder they followed him out of that pub. They needed the action.

"You should turn that into a screenplay. Every other person I met in New York was writing a screenplay. Young people used to write poetry. Now they dream of selling a screenplay for a million dollars." Clovis looked across to Mel. "It's got action, adventure and romance. And scientific intrigue. What more could you want?" He wondered if there was more to the story. How could Henry have been apart from Mel for so long?

Wiremu shook his head and rose up from the table. He came back into the living room with another pot of coffee.

"What are your views of the universe, Clovis?" Wiremu asked.

"I don't know. All I want to do is play my violin, make music and bread and be left in peace," Clovis declared.

Wiremu eyed his new friends. Mel had her feet over Henry's knees with a faraway look in her eyes. Plum was sitting in between the legs of Clovis, who was massaging the top of her head. Wiremu thought he could hear her purring.

Mel glanced at her watch. "I have to be up at 6:00 this morning. Let me drive you back. We'll have to hear your violin another time, Clovis."

Chapter Four

Monday night

They were silent for the short ride back to Summer Street. Clovis squeezed into the back seat and cuddled Plum, the violin case between his legs. Wiremu sat in front.

"Keep on! Don't stop!" Wiremu commanded.

Mel cruised to the corner and turned down John Street.

"What was that?" Plum had bolted upright in her seat and tried to look out the rear window.

"The front door was open," Wiremu replied.

"Why don't you guys come and stay over at my place," Mel said, without stopping the car. "It's not going to be safe here." She wanted to get home to bed. She did not want any more drama.

"Let's make another pass and keep Plum out of sight. I'll check the house." Wiremu turned to Mel who doubled back.

"No. What if it's the police? I'll go," Mel insisted. "Clovis, come up front when I stop. You know how to drive, right?" Clovis nodded. "Honk two times if you see anything suspicious on the street."

Mel slowed down as they passed the house. She stopped four doors down. The front door was ajar. Mel turned off the motor and the lights. She adjusted her rearview mirror so she could see the dark house and waited. No one spoke.

"You sure you wanna go?" Wiremu spied up and down the street.

"Is your back door locked?" Mel turned to ask Clovis.

"Er, yes. Here's the key."

Mel shot a look at Wiremu, as if to say stay here or else. Then she got out of the car. She stood by the open door while Clovis climbed into her seat. Plum lay on the floor, her hands over her head. The seat felt hot to Clovis. For one guilty moment he relished the thought of Mel's ass having been in the seat a few seconds before.

Mel ambled up to the front gate, stepped over it and walked down the narrow path between the two houses.

"Why don't I go in as well?" Clovis suggested to Wiremu as he adjusted the mirror so he could see the house.

"No," Wiremu hushed. He rolled down his window to listen to the sounds of the street. He stared at the house as if he could see through the walls. "Shhh!" he hissed, as Clovis was about to console Plum in the back. The small noises in Ponsonby after midnight were magnified by the tension inside the car. Two cats were singing at each other across the road, a car accelerated down John Street below them. Wiremu thought he heard a Rolling Stones song. Horns were playing as he tried hard to concentrate on the house. The waiting seemed to go on forever. Wiremu jerked his head to one side. He sensed something was wrong.

"Watch the road both ways." He sprang out of the car and ran up to the front door.

"It's okay, Plum. I'm here. The street's clear," Clovis whispered checking the rearview mirror.

"You said this wouldn't happen. You said it was safe to come back. I was better off in New York."

• • •

Mel stopped at the back door. She could see through the side window an overturned chair in the kitchen. She listened for any sounds in the house as she waited for her eyes to adjust to the dark. Although it could have been her imagination, she thought she heard a faint shuffle of a boot inside. Rising to her feet, she put the key in the lock, turned it and twisted the brass doorknob. She slowly opened the door as quietly as she could. Mel slipped in, keeping very low and cross stepping to the corridor along the wall. No one was in the kitchen.

She advanced so that she was opposite the first door on the right and squatted, ready to pounce. If anyone were inside, he would be in one of the front rooms, with access to the windows and a view of the street. He would be waiting for her behind a door, listening. Or, she reasoned, he could have ducked back to this room and waited for her there, having seen her enter the front gate. Damn. She should have gone over the back fence from the adjacent property.

Mel edged step by step down the corridor, being careful not to touch the cracked wallpaper. Crouching, she peeked through the half open doorway into Clovis and Plum's bedroom. The streetlight shone onto the outlines of an unmade bed. Clothes were strewn across the floor. Moving her head back and forth, Mel could not see anyone in the room. She turned again and stepped back to face the living room door that was open a couple of inches. A dog barked outside, once. A car squealed around a corner in the distance, making the silence in the house even more intense. Mel took a slow deep breath and changed the position of her feet. She sprang into the room, taking an extra step away from the door and spinning around so she could launch an attack.

It was still a shock. A large figure raised a softball bat and plunged it down on Mel's skull. With the extra step she was out of range. The bat whizzed past her face and she spun around with a flying back kick to strike the figure in his unprotected solar plexus. Winded, he dropped the bat and stumbled forward, trying to grab Mel. She kicked him again, a high front snap that did not reach his face, only grazed his chin. Mel stepped forward and threw three punches at him; one in the face, landing on his left cheek, one in his solar plexus and one in his groin. That was the one that made him bend over in pain. The kicks and punches had been delivered in such quick succession that he had had no time to react, let alone consider that his attacker was a woman more than a hundred pounds lighter than him.

With one hand clutching his genitals, he desperately tried to hit his assailant, anywhere. But she already had control of his free wrist. Twisting his wrist inward, Mel rapidly forced him to the ground, snapping another kick to the kidneys as his face hit the floor with a loud thud. She threw his trapped wrist up behind his neck and knelt into his lower spine. She mounted him and slid her other forearm under his chin, exerting a sharp pain across his trachea as she used her knifelike forearm to cut off the flow of blood through his carotid artery. He could not move, he could not cry out. He tried to grasp for air and struggle with what little strength he had left, but her knee pressed deeper into his back like a dagger. He had lost all control, and this made him angry. She clamped her right palm behind his skull with her fingertips against the back of his left ear and she applied pressure from both forearms until he gave up struggling. His arteries were temporarily sealed. She counted to seven, then slowly released the pressure, feeling his faint pulse in his right twisted wrist. He was unconscious.

Mel stood up and threw her hair back. Despite her kicks and blows, he was not badly injured. She had broken no bones, and the sleeper hold would wear off in a few minutes. He could not have seen her clearly. He probably would not even want to admit that this had happened to him. These thoughts flashed through her mind as she stepped back to look at the man. He was a giant.

Hearing footsteps, Mel drew back into a defensive position again, to see Wiremu coming bounding into the room.

"Mel?" he yelled.

"Be quiet," she snapped.

"Did you kill him?" Wiremu knelt down beside the assailant. "That's John Eustace. Big John. A real dangerous bugger." Wiremu noticed the softball bat then searched through Eustace's pockets. He took out a wallet, a piece of paper with a phone number on it and a set of car keys. Wiremu pocketed these.

"Are you sure that's right?" Mel asked.

"You're asking me? You just about killed him."

"Let's get out of here."

Wiremu followed Mel back to the car. Mel was untouched, but Big John was lying dead to the world. How had she done that?

Clovis slipped into the back of the BMW to be with Plum. She was still on the floor, trying not to shake with fear. Mel freewheeled to the bottom of the road, adjusting her mirror before starting the motor and turning into John Street. Wiremu kept his eyes glued on the street behind them.

"No one following, Bruce," Wiremu broke the silence. These Pakehas were not enjoying this. Where was their sense of adventure? Did they not relish a little dash of violence?

Plum surfaced from the floor and came up to Clovis's knees. "Bruce? Bruce?" she asked.

"I was trying to make a joke," Wiremu sighed.

"Let's talk when we get back to my place. I need a strong cup of tea," Mel uttered.

Wiremu asked Mel to stop at a corner on Mount Eden Road. A phone booth was on the other side of the street. Checking to see that there was no traffic, he ambled over to the phone and started to put coins in the phone box. Mel watched him. He seemed to make several calls. The last one was the longest. She saw him hang up, then checking the street, place something on top of the booth before trotting back to the BMW.

"Isn't that a little risky? He'll regain consciousness any minute," Mel asked him as she turned into her road.

"My boys are pros." Wiremu sat back and kept a straight face.

Mel gave Plum a couple of strong sleeping pills so she would sleep better on the living room couch.

Clovis lay on the carpet staring at the ceiling. He always slept better after making love to Plum. This was not a good time to approach her. Instead he thought about New York and why he had bought her back. Had it been such a good idea? Could they have survived there together? His eyes refused to close.

Wiremu stretched out on the sofa in the living room. He had promised Mel that he would guard the sound system from any thieves in the night.

"The only thieves I know out at this time are your friends stealing a car on Summer Street," Mel had replied.

Once he heard the house grow quiet, Wiremu stepped out onto Mel's back porch. He sat on the steps and wondered about the first call he had made. He had dialed the number on the piece of paper he had found on the body. A young Maori woman had answered. Her voice was familiar and hesitant, as if she knew who he was. She had not given him her name. And she had hung up abruptly. What was that thug John Eustace doing with the phone number of a sweet young Maori girl in his pocket?

Mel climbed into bed to find Henry awake. He rose up on his elbows and managed to slide on top of her without any resistance.

"What took you so long?"

"If you had got up when we came back you'd've found out."

"We?" Henry adjusted his weight on his elbows so he would not crush her.

"I bought them all back. There was someone in their house."

"I suppose you Kung Fu'd whoever was in there. Right?"

"Yes."

Mel pushed him over so she was on top. She kissed him forcefully. She knew one way to get rid of the tension in her body.

Hei Hei huffed and groaned behind Moana who could not get to the sofa in time. Her angelic face, buried in the cushions, did little to mute her protests. Jesus, Hei Hei thought, those soft round buttocks and little drooping breasts drive me crazy, and the more she whimpers the more turned on I get. Her body, even hidden in those shapeless floral smocks she had brought from Hokianga, also drove him crazy. Hei Hei had a hard-on whenever he was near her.

"No! Don't put it in there! It hurts!" Moana moaned.

"Bitch. Shut up and love it! AHHHH!" Hei Hei was trying to get his penis inside her, anywhere, as he struggled to get his feet out of his jeans. They were caught around his ankles. Then the phone rang. The sound threw him off balance and he fell sideways. Moana crawled out from under him and ran to answer the phone. When she picked it up she was shocked to hear a voice she not heard for a long time. All she had said was, "Hello." That had been enough.

"Wrong number," she said without turning to Hei Hei, who would, if she had looked him in the eye, know she was telling a lie. Wrong number! Bah! More like wrong man, she thought as she saw Hei Hei playing with himself. His penis did not extend beyond the outline of his stomach. They never kissed. There was no foreplay. There was no romance. She wanted long soft kisses. Not onion breath from behind and a damp beer belly pressing into her back.

Hei Hei got his jeans off and beckoned Moana to come to him on the sofa when the phone rang again. He held his erect penis in one hand and picked up the receiver with his other. He stared at a nervous Moana as he breathed into the phone.

She had no idea that she could leave. She could not imagine returning to her family in Hokianga. They did not care about her anyway, she reasoned.

Hei Hei stood with the receiver pressed to his ear. He remained silent, waiting for the other party to speak. He had seen this on an American TV soap opera. The powerful tycoon picked up the phone and waited for the caller to speak first. Although on TV the American did not wave his penis around. He listened to the heavy breathing on the other side of the line. This standoff went on for several seconds before Hei Hei got bored and hung up. Moana sat on the sofa with her hands between her legs, her smock covering her knees. Her face, to Hei Hei, seemed to say yes and no at the same time.

"That's odd." Hei Hei stood by the phone and scratched his head. He did not realize how ridiculous he looked, naked but for his unbuttoned shirt and socks. One month ago, the last time he was in the Hokianga checking up on the State-grown marijuana plots, he had found and enticed her back to Auckland. Free room and board in return for taking care of him and as much reefer as she could smoke. She had been too naive to realize she had to share his bed as well, but that was all part of the process of educating her in big city life.

The apartment Hei Hei so graciously shared with Moana was at the back of a crumbling two-storey wooden house at the bottom of Bassett Road in Parnell. It consisted of one tiny bedroom, a living room that led into an open kitchen and a bathroom with a door that would not close properly. It always smelt of damp rotten wood. Down the road, Wiremu and his brother Hone Wilson camped out, when they were not up in Hokianga.

Hei Hei was a self-confessed close friend of the Wilsons, having grown up in the same marae. Wiremu and Hei Hei had spent too many years together in D block.

"Perhaps it was your new Pakeha friend?" Moana said, sweetly sarcastic. "Checking up on you."

"Nah. That was no Pakeha breathing. Shit! They could be onto me."

"How?"

"Dunno." Hei Hei finally realized that Moana had worked out what he was up to. He had not told her anything. Another smart Wilson. He would have to be more careful around her. Though she was part of the plan. Damn those Wilsons. All their spirits will be flying off from Cape Reinga soon enough. All those fucking degrees and they're still not clever enough. Shit! Anyone can use long words and sentences longer than prisons. They're academic cons. Not like little Hei Hei who they think is a dummy. Hei Hei waddled over to the refrigerator and pulled out a flagon of beer. He took a long swig. "They're in for a surprise."

He eyed Moana with that look she knew too well. She was saved again by the phone. He picked up the receiver and said, "Yes?" He had no time for power techniques now, and he had lost his erection.

"This is Tina calling from the Flamingo. Is Moana there?"

Moana came over to Hei Hei and spoke a few words into the receiver, looking at him nervously.

"I start tomorrow night. Eight o'clock. At the Flamingo Paradise."

"Great!" Hei Hei rubbed his hands. He wanted to dance around the sofa but controlled himself because of Moana's mournful expression. He needed to send her out to earn money. What better plan than to send her to the place owned by his new ally?

"Cheer up, sweetheart. You won't have to do anything you don't want to. I checked it out with John. You'll be quite safe there." He started to play with his penis again.

Hone held a glass of brandy in a snifter in one hand and balanced a large volume of Edward Gibbon's *The History of the Decline and Fall of the Roman Empire* in the other. Johannes Brahms' "String Sextet No. 2 in G Major" played on the stereo. His absolute favorite; the Amadeus Quartet with friends, on Deutsche Grammophon. He was rereading the passage on the belief in the immortality of the soul. Evenings did not get much better than this. Hone was in love with Gibbon's voice; the clean, well-rounded string of sentences that effortlessly spun into long seductive paragraphs. Every word was essential but bore an authority that reminded him of great Maori oratory. He sighed as he read another passage again, slowly. Great music, good booze, a great book. What more could he wish for? Not much, maybe brandy that was not so rough and a record that did not crackle.

Gibbon could understand the irrational in history. Few historians could grasp this profound fact. Men fucked up. Even great men made mistakes. And history was full of them; mistakes, that is. This was Hone's inspiration, to write a definitive history of Maori from the 17th century to the present. He understood what an enormous task this was, especially as there was no real written material, no texts to base his research on before the mid-19th century, and even then they were inaccurate and rife with biases. This was about the time Brahms was writing this sextet. What an incredible juxtaposition: the build up of the Pakeha and their lack of culture in their self-confessed colonial wasteland and the finest chamber music being created on the other side of the world, in Germany. The true intellectual giants came from the 18th century, like Gibbon, Hone mused. And there were some definite parallels between the current state of Pakeha society and late Imperial Rome.

He was thinking about Wiremu when the phone rang. With his hands full, he was reluctant to answer, but he had a feeling only his brother would disturb his perfect evening at home.

"What took you so long? You okay?" Hone heard Wiremu's distinctive voice.

"Yeah. What's up?"

"Plenty. Tell you later. This phone good?"

"Sounds clean." Their ears were attuned to the bugging devices the police had connected to their phone lines at the local switching office.

"Right. I'm at the corner of Parnell Road and Newmarket. You know the phone box?"

"Yeah."

"On top I've put car keys. The car is at the bottom of Summer Street and John. It's a black Lincoln. New looking. You can't miss it. Roll it down the hill and then start it. Leave it somewhere safe, off the road. Check with our friend in Traffic so we can get the registration. I've got the owner's wallet. We'll work out everything later when I reach you. Okay?"

"Yeah."

Hone put down his heavy book, after carefully replacing the marker, a pressed flower in a plastic sheath from Haifa. He had not heard Wiremu sound so excited in a long time. Whose car? Whose wallet? What plan?

Hone poured the rest of the brandy down his throat, squeezed into his Dr. Martens and trudged out the back door, up a damp narrow path to Basset Road. He would need Hei Hei to drive him across town. Hone did not have Hei Hei's new phone number. He secretly hoped Hei Hei was not doing anything to Moana. Hone did not mind Hei Hei bringing her down from Hokianga, but Wiremu, if he found out, would go crazy. All those years in prison had made Wiremu into a celibate prude.

"She's tangata whenua. If she comes down here she'll get fucked up, mentally and spiritually. I've seen it so many times. She'll get pregnant with someone she's met once. Then it's all downhill. No. She stays with her grandmother, up on the land. If her parents don't want to look after her, her grandmother will. There's plenty of things for her to do up there. If she comes down here all her values, all her sense of Maoritanga will wither." Hone could hear Wiremu's argument in his head. Only

Moana never went to her grandmother. Hei Hei got to her first.

What a mad brother. Fancy firing a shotgun over the heads of cops. It made no sense. Yet Hone was not angry at him. Hone realized what prison life and endless persecution had done to Wiremu.

Hone knocked on the front door. He could clearly hear Hei Hei's sound system pounding out "Bungle in the Jungle."

Hone knocked again, louder. Hei Hei peeked through the side window and quickly opened the door. He was careful not to show Moana cowering on the sofa.

"I didn't hear you," Hei Hei yelled over the Jethro Tull track.

Hone noticed Hei Hei had not buttoned up his jeans.

"Get the car keys. We're going out. Hurry."

Hei Hei scrambled behind Hone to the car, a 1963 light blue Morris Minor. Hone noted how tense Hei Hei was.

"Hey. What's up with you?" Hone asked.

"Fuck! They hate to fuck, and when you do fuck 'em they pretend to not like it so when you leave and don't fuck 'em, they hate that too! We're fucked! You know? We're fucked! Shit! Fuck! We can't fucking win!"

The thought of Hei Hei being interrupted amused Hone.

"What a car." Hei Hei grinned. "Top speed thirty-five. Gears so worn you don't have to use the clutch. Probably banana skins in the transmission."

"Yes, Hei Hei. A real drug dealer's car. That's what I like about you. You've got class. Not like the Mongrel Mob and their Yankee limousine. You're real inconspicuous."

• • •

Plum fell asleep as soon as her head touched the pillow on the sofa. Clovis lay out on the carpet in front of Plum with a cushion under his head. He shut his eyes, but could not sleep. His mind was racing. He felt too hot and agitated. Here he was back in safe little New Zealand, and he could not stay in his own place. Was Plum the target, or were they after Wiremu? Perhaps he had made the wrong decision in letting Wiremu stay with them. Would they have been safer in New York? Here they had Mel to protect them. But he had successfully auditioned for an orchestral position, something he would not dare to have contemplated before he left for New York.

He stretched out on the carpet and recalled how he had found Plum Blossom in New York. He had made a phone call, to a 976 number he saw in a magazine, 976-FUCK.

After he had heard her voice eight times, he went out and rummaged through every softcore porn magazine he could find. He was dressed in an army surplus overcoat, with a fur-lined hat; it was so cold and windy out on the streets.

"If you don't buy it you can't look at it!" the little man in the last shop had yelled at him from behind the counter. It was in that shop that Clovis found who operated the 976 number he had been dialing all night, Spunk Productions, owned by the legend of porn, Sammy Goldstein.

The next afternoon Clovis strode up to the offices of Spunk Productions. It was on West Twenty-Fourth Street, a bleak sunless canyon of tall warehouses. Small mounds of black ice were left over from the last blizzard, stuck in corners that would not see the sun until May. Dog turds and pieces of garbage were imbedded in the ice.

Clovis had stated, in his best Kiwi accent, to Goldstein over the telephone that morning, that he was a journalist from New Zealand writing about "girlie" magazines in New York. He was especially interested in the "976-phone-sex-phenomenon." Could he see him today? His magazine had such a small budget he could not afford to stay at a hotel overnight. He was catching a flight to London that night. Mr. Goldstein was too much of an egotist to refuse having himself written up in New Zealand, especially a national publication as illustrious as the *New Zealand Women's Weekly*.

"What is that? Some kind of lesbo mag?"

"Not really," Clovis parlayed. "It is very butch though."

"Yeah. I can imagine," the President of Spunk Inc. retorted. "I've met some of the women from down under. Oh boy. Have you guys got problems." He laughed.

Clovis laughed. The interview was set for three that afternoon. Ten minutes max.

After waiting thirty-six minutes in a nondescript reception area that could have been a dentist's office, if it had been cleaner, Clovis was ushered into the inner sanctum of the Spunk Empire: Mr. Samuel Goldstein's office. It was an oversized living room gone wrong. The walls were covered from floor to ceiling with framed photographs of women, naked or near naked, in various anatomically revealing poses. Mr. Goldstein half rose from an oversized vinyl-covered executive chair to reach over his oversized desk to give Clovis a wet, limp handshake. Clovis pricked his finger on the president's diamond-encrusted pinkie ring. He briefly glanced at the glossy color photographs spread over his desk and gave a genuine impression of being overawed by the amount of pink labial flesh exposed to him from all sides. Next to the phone was a row of progressively larger rubber dildos, lined up like soldiers on parade.

On an oversized coffee table in front of the desk were stacks of 8mm films and magazines. A television set stood in one corner; in another were racks of stereo equipment with huge black speakers, the size of coffins. The president gestured to the oversized stained couch. Clovis seated himself and realized his interviewee, a man in his late forties with balding hair and a stomach that bumped up against the desk, was at least twelve feet away. Clovis observed that the pale overweight man had far too much energy and vitality for such an unhealthy individual, with sparkling eyes, gesturing hands and a head that appeared loosened from the neck.

"This is where it all happens. Where all the work gets done." He chortled. "The buck comes here!" he declared, not for the first time, Clovis assumed. Clovis took out his new notepad and pen and sat on the edge of the sofa as far away as he could from the stain. What would a real journalist do now? Start asking dumb questions, dummy!

"No tape recorder?" The president sounded disappointed. He had never seen a journalist write anything.

"No. We're old fashioned down under. Do it by hand," Clovis replied.

"Oh! I get you." The president laughed, seeing a joke where Clovis intended none. The interview proceeded painlessly, Clovis remembered. He dutifully wrote out the statistics of dialing porn. In New York City alone, men dialed to hear the Spunk girls one million times a month. With the money collected by the respectable New York Telephone Co., Goldstein was grossing $150,000. Every month.

"Hey! Let's face it. I'm a nice Jewish boy. My mother wanted me to make a lot of money. She wanted me to be a doctor. So instead of putting them in stirrups and staring at their pussy and charging 'em $100 a visit, I became the doctor of porn. And I pay them to do the same things. Do I feel guilty? Do I need a psychiatrist's couch? No way, Isaiah! This is an ethical way to do business and, believe it or not, it's all part of the women's liberation movement. These women are getting paid far more to do this, which is essentially harmless, than work as some goofball's secretary and make his coffee and pick up his dry cleaning and all that shit. Now that is degrading.

"We're at the forefront of the post-revolutionary liberation for women, and all those hard line bitches, god bless their unfucked pussies, don't understand this. I'm really a radical feminist. Tell the lesbians in New Zealand that. That'll give 'em something to choke on."

Clovis tried to write down everything the man behind his desk spat out. But there was a magazine on the coffee table in front of him, entitled *LONELY TEENS*. Where was that girl, in pigtails, putting that broomstick? She looked not a day over thirteen.

It was unbearably hot in the office, a wet 90 degrees. Clovis could feel the sweat dripping down his armpits. He did manage, however, to find out that all the audiotapes for the phone messages were recorded at the Silent Studio, one block away in a basement.

"You'd be surprised. Some of the ugliest people we auditioned have the sexiest voices. So I made a policy decision. Beautiful bodies, beautiful voices. You like it? It worked. Look at the figures."

Trying to find out who was the saleswoman in the men's trouser department proved impossible. Goldstein did not seem to hear the question, or for that matter any question, unless it pertained to himself and what a great businessman he was. On leaving, Clovis obtained the phone number of Jose Fibilitis, the manager at the Silent Studio.

Clovis called Jose from the corner payphone and booked an immediate appointment with him. "Hey!

Any friend of Goldspunk is a friend of mine. Come on over." Jose sounded too loose, too happy.

The studio consisted of two small rooms in the basement of a brick three-storey building wedged in between two tall industrial lofts that were being converted into co-ops by artists and attorneys. From the street, Clovis was buzzed in through the steel door. He felt his way down a damp creaking staircase to another steel door with a red light outside. This door clicked open and he found himself in a small carpet-lined waiting area facing another solid door. Jose slipped through the door and looked confused. He did not know who Clovis was. Clovis reminded him of the phone call a couple of minutes ago. Jose started to grin, grabbed Clovis's hand and shook it violently. Clovis was ushered into the control room, a brightly lit space with a clear glass panel on one wall looking out to darkness.

Jose was a small Puerto Rican with a big bushy beard and long curly black hair. He had dark shining eyes that never stopped on one place long enough to focus. Clovis noticed he wore high-heeled cowboy boots as he stepped up to the control board. Several tape machines were stacked on the opposite wall. An engineer with thick headphones was remixing an audio track for a radio commercial and muttering under his breath.

Clovis noticed a cereal bowl that looked full of sugar. They must drink a lot of coffee, he thought.

"Want some?" Jose smiled, his eyes glazing over.

"Coffee?" Clovis guessed.

"No. Coke." Jose rolled his eyes.

"Gosh." Clovis tried to be cool. "I've never seen that much. I mean, I don't even use that much flour when I'm baking bread."

"Oh, we're a bit low at the moment. Help yourself. The agencies drop it off in bags." Jose shrugged. It was just like the seltzer delivery.

"No, er, thanks. Not when I'm on the job. I haven't even seen it." Clovis began to think he could write an article and send it back to New Zealand. Maybe the *Listener* would publish it? But would anyone believe him?

He explained to Jose, in what he thought were professional journalist terms, what he was doing with his article and asked a few questions about recording the phone fantasies. Currently three or four girls came in and taped a week's worth of sixty-second spots. The spots counted out to thirty-five to forty-five seconds, with a twelve-second plug for a live sex call on another phone number, if they had a credit card.

Credit card call? This was getting more and more bizarre. He had missed this detail when he listened to Plum Blossom. Then he remembered the pages and pages of advertisements in the girlie magazines with girls sprawled out on satin sheets wearing garter belts and high heels with their fingers between their legs and a telephone pressed to their ear. Live phone sex, they claimed. How could you have live sex with someone over the phone? And masturbate whilst having it charged to your credit card? Clovis thought this concept absurd, like performance art with no audience.

"You gotta see it from here, man. These chicks are hot. The way they move over that microphone. Unbelievable. Then we get them ripped, so juiced up, they're amazing," Jose continued. The engineer snorted and grinned at Clovis.

If Clovis asked Jose outright about a woman who resembled Plum Blossom, he would get suspicious. Jose was that kind of guy, Clovis surmised. Stroke his ego, ask him flattering questions, and he would love you to death, but throw him a pointed question or slip in a snide remark and he would turn against you faster than you could say Wolfgang Amadeus Mozart.

While Jose went into some technical detail about the eight-track tape machine they used, Clovis pretended to take notes. He moved around the small room trying to locate a list of women's names, phone numbers, some contact sheet that Jose had amongst the debris littering the control room.

"How do you find new talent? I mean new voices. You must get new talent occasionally."

"Goldfuck. He selects them. He gets them to sit on his couch, stands right over them and puts a tape recorder to his zipper and auditions them." Jose tried to keep a straight face, but the engineer who had taken off his earphones broke out in knee slapping laughter.

"He uses a small microphone so his dick looks bigger," the engineer gushed in one breath.

"You mean he doesn't say anything? Or even point?"

It took several minutes before Jose could calm down enough to continue the interview. In that time, Clovis managed to see a clipboard with a list of girls names lying half under a carton of cigarettes. At the top of the typed sheet was the title "SUCK TAPES."

"Tell me about some of these new girls."

"Well, last week, or was it the week before. Shit. I dunno. We got the cutest little Asian."

"What a bitch in heat!" the engineer let out.

"Very quiet. Very professional," Jose continued, his pupils expanded and contracted as if connected to a weight machine.

"She wouldn't do it for twenty or all the coke she could snort," the engineer piped in.

"You mean they do it for you?" Clovis was incredulous. He felt sick to his stomach at the thought of Plum being propositioned.

"Whaddaya think? They've been working over that microphone for hours. They've already creamed their pants. Now they want the real thing." Jose puffed up his chest.

"Perhaps she was an actress" Clovis tried.

"Yeah. They're all actresses," Jose retorted cynically. He reached over to the clipboard by Clovis. "This is her. Plum Blossom. What a name!"

"You're pulling my leg." Clovis reached for the clipboard. "Let me see."

Clovis memorized the phone number and put down the clipboard. He quickly wrapped up the interview and promised to send them copies of the published piece.

"Hey! If you've got any New Zealand chicks you know, send them to us. We'll give 'em an audition. And we'll give 'em some toot!" Jose threw out at Clovis, who could not leave fast enough. He felt blood pounding in his head like a drum track speeded up.

At the corner payphone, Clovis dropped a quarter and dialed the number. After twenty rings, he hung up, collected his quarter, redeposited it and dialed again. He was in a trance, connected to Plum again by a telephone line, yet unable to reach her. A bike messenger screeched to a halt by the payphone and brought Clovis back to the world. Clovis jumped, hung up and walked away, leaving the quarter in the coin return for the messenger to grab.

Clovis could not understand how Plum had progressed from working in a massage parlor in New Zealand to recording sex tapes in New York. This was not furthering her acting career.

Clovis tried the number again, at his apartment. A young woman answered with a heavy Texan drawl.

"This is UPS here, ma'am. And we have a delivery for a Ms. Plum Blossom. It's been returned from her address, could you tell me the exact street and number, please?" Clovis spoke from the back of his throat in his best South Bronx accent.

The woman gave him an address in the West Village. Clovis thanked her and hung up. That trick would never have worked on a New Yorker.

In thirty minutes, Clovis had set himself up outside the apartment building. He was wrapped in his overcoat with his fingers exposed to the below zero degree cold and his violin tucked under his chin. Please don't let the cold temperature snap my strings, he said to himself. He launched into a Hungarian Czarda, trying to warm up his body with a quick foot stomping tune and fast bowing. It was so cold, no one was on Charles Street, and if they were, they would think Clovis insane, madder than the usual New York variety.

How many times did he play that fiery dance? It was dark when he spotted Plum Blossom walk around the corner. She was wearing jeans under a sheepskin-lined coat and had her pageboy haircut exposed to the elements. Clovis kept playing. Five steps from him she stopped, her mouth wide open.

"Clovis Tibet! What are you doing here?" she exclaimed.

He stopped and smiled, his violin in one hand, his bow in the other. "Don't I get a hug? At least." Her smile, her accent, the way she clipped her "t's" and stuck one hand on her hip (that was hidden under her thick coat), were too much for Clovis. He ran up to her and passionately embraced her, almost breaking the bridge of his violin in the process.

She invited him up to her apartment. Her new roommate was at her waitress job, Plum explained, as she double-locked the front door. Any inhibitions they had about each other melted, once they had taken off their coats. The passionate embrace Clovis gave Plum was returned with equal ardor as she wrapped her legs around Clovis's back and clasped her hands behind his neck. He could feel himself become erect instantly as Plum ground her hips into him. She steered him into her tiny bedroom.

Very quickly, they undressed and fell into bed with the covers thrown off. He noted immediately, with added pleasure, that she was so tight inside and so horny on the outside, that she had to have been celibate in New York. He could feel it. There was no other explanation. No matter what he had told her six months ago; the ultimatum that she had to stop working at the Flamingo Paradise as a masseur, that she had to get a decent job to support her acting classes, all those bad emotions melted away in her bed. Clovis realized how much he cared for her.

After they had made love twice and had slept for an hour, Plum nestled in Clovis's arms and they talked about what they had done in New York. Clovis informed her about Juilliard and his street busking, and Plum was candid about her part-time work doing fantasy recordings.

Clovis tried to convince her that what she was doing there, cutting X-rated phone tapes to pay for her exorbitant rent and food, pouring over *Backstage* and waiting on line every day for the countless auditions she would never be called back for. Well, this was not the way to progress as an actress. She could learn her craft, perform more roles, maybe even form her own fringe theatre group, back in Auckland, where she had the freedom to lead a decent life.

Clovis was very persuasive. Or perhaps she was blindly in love with him like she had never been before. She had to come to New York to see another way of life before realizing what Clovis wanted and what he stood for. She told him this in her own physical way.

Clovis booked two seats back. He had had enough of the bitter cold. He had learned something about life and music and reassured Plum that Auckland would be safe and full of promise.

Inspector Grimble had parked his car opposite the Wilsons' Parnell address shortly after nine o'clock. The car was between streetlights, and there was no moon tonight. Grimble was prepared to wait until midnight, but he was not going to tell his assistant. Cadd would keep checking his watch. When you were on a stakeout you never looked at your watch unless you were writing a report. It made the time go even slower. Cadd kept quiet, much to Grimble's relief. He did not need a comic foil. He wanted to mull over everything he knew so far about the Wilsons, which was precious little.

Grimble caught some movement out of the corner of his eye. He turned to make out the large form of Hone Wilson amble up the street. Hone disappeared down another driveway. He reappeared a few minutes later with another shorter Maori. They got into a Morris Minor that backfired as it slowly crawled up the hill.

The inspector followed them at a distance in his Honda.

"Don't exactly go for Ferraris, do they?" Cadd said.

Grimble stopped at the top of Parnell Road. He turned off his lights as the car ahead pulled up to a phone booth. The two policemen slid down in their seats as Hone got out of the Morris.

"Why make a call there? We're not tapping them now, are we?"

"Be quiet and watch. You might learn something," the inspector whispered, as he watched Hone Wilson in the phone box. There was enough street light for Grimble to see Hone feed some coins into the phone box, hit it with his fist then hang up. Grimble thought he saw Hone raise his hand above his head, grab something and walk back to the Morris.

"Mmmm. Interesting," Grimble muttered as he eased the Honda into first gear.

"Yeah. It was a signal. They're meeting someone. Maybe we need backup?" the sergeant proclaimed. His superior kept a respectable distance from the slow Morris Minor.

Hei Hei stopped the car at the bottom of a narrow street full of parked cars.

Grimble pulled over at the top of the street with his lights off. He could barely see Hone walk back, casually turning his head. There was no one else out, not even a stray dog. Hone walked into the shadow of a dead streetlamp and stopped.

Grimble wound his window down and poked his head out to see Hone bend down and open a car door. He disappeared from Grimble's vision.

"The Morrie's gone." Cadd's voice sounded like a shout in the strained atmosphere of the car. Grimble looked at his watch, grunted and sat back. He waited for the car Hone had slipped into to move. But the car remained where it was. Cadd tried not to fidget and kept his eyes on the street. Grimble waited for something to happen and Cadd realized that if he asked what this was he would be yelled at.

"Damn!" Grimble sighed. "He should've pulled out by now. Walk down this side, past the car. If something is wrong, cross the street, don't look back at me. If it's okay just keep walking and I'll pick you up around the corner. Got it?"

"Yes, sir."

As the sergeant got out, they both saw someone as big as Hone step from a parked car and walk down the street. The man was about the same size as Hone, but it was impossible to identify the large figure in such dim light.

Cadd was almost level with the car when he saw a black Pontiac at the bottom of the street. It slowed to pick up the unidentified man. Then it disappeared from his view. Cadd crossed the road opposite the car where Hone had stopped and waved his arms frantically at Grimble who had already reached for his ignition.

Grimble roared down Summer Street in second gear and skidded to a halt next to the Lincoln. Cadd stared through the side window. Grimble stood next to him and peered into the car. Hone lay flat on his back across the front seat, his eyes wide open and his tongue hanging out to one side, like a grotesque Maori carving.

"I couldn't see the other joker clearly. He was big, like a Maori."

"Was he?"

"I don't know."

Hei Hei drove straight home as Hone had instructed him. But he did make one quick call; to a number he had for John Eustace, at the corner of John Street and Ponsonby Road. A man with a high voice answered the phone and took the message. Hei Hei told the voice that he had dropped off Hone Wilson who had been carrying a set of keys to a black Lincoln.

"Good work. Go home now and make sure no one follows you. We'll look after you for this," the voice had instructed Hei Hei.

When Grimble opened the car door, Hone's head rolled back. There was a thin red line around his neck. He checked the body's pulse. He tried to shut the bulging eyes. But the eyelids would not move nor would Hone's jaw close. The tongue hung out of his mouth, dark purple and bloated.

"We'll take him inside." The inspector grabbed the corpse under the shoulders. Cadd caught the legs and they dragged the heavy body up to the house and through the front door that opened to Grimble's kick.

"Did you get the number of the car?"

"The one that picked up the big guy?" Cadd asked. "No. Just saw it side on. Black Pontiac, late model, four door, with white rims. Why are we doing this?"

They propped the corpse against a wall in the living room.

"Whoever did it will panic when they find the body missing." The inspector kept an eye on the street from the window, as he answered Cadd. "If it's another Maori, they'll go hysterical. They're suspicious about these things. Keep a lookout here, will you. Call me if you see anything. Don't stand too close to the window." The inspector left the room to search the house.

Cadd could not take his eyes off the corpse. Two big brown eyes stared at him. He tried to move the head with his foot, but the eyes kept their deadly stare on him. Poor sod, he muttered to himself, as he watched a young Samoan girl dressed only in a wraparound on her lighted porch eat a piece of watermelon. She was unaware of Cadd's eyes on her voluptuous dark body.

There was no furniture in the front bedroom. Grimble found a suitcase on either side of the mattress on the floor. He opened the suitcases and found two passports. One belonged to a Mr. Clovis Tibet, the other to a Miss Plum Blossom. He stared at the two photographs. He was going to look through the rest of the house before going outside and securing the Lincoln when he heard Cadd.

"The car!"

They almost knocked each other over in the corridor as they rushed to the front door to see the Lincoln sail down Summer Street and disappear around the corner. They ran across to the Honda and jumped in. An old Holden station wagon, full of large Samoan men who had been drinking all night, was double-parked adjacent to them, blocking them in. Grimble honked his horn as Cadd yelled at them. But the partygoers ignored the two Pakehas. Grimble threw the car into reverse and backed out of the spot.

He steered as fast as he could, screaming in reverse, back up Summer Street and narrowly missed several cars and a van that swerved into a driveway to avoid the insane Honda driver.

The sergeant held onto his seat as Grimble swung the car around at the top of the street and gunned it down Ponsonby Road.

Grimble cursed himself for not having the sergeant outside in a car with a radio. Why didn't they have radios? Because the Wilson case was unofficial. It was a silent operation and he was working on his own, on the commissioner's orders. If the inspector produced results, no one would question him. That was Grimble's style. Arrests, convictions, results, by any means. If the bad guys played dirty, why shouldn't he? If he had had two additional cars with radio contact he would have caught everyone involved, it would have been simple. It would have been over but for the paperwork. But neither he nor the commissioner had expected this sort of thing to happen. It was too late now.

"Keep a lookout. They should be coming this way." The Honda swerved to the right to narrowly miss a scooter making a left turn. He calculated he had less than twenty seconds to get to the other side of John Street that ran into Jervois Road. He should then be able to meet up with the black Lincoln. When they reached the corner there was no sign of the big American car. There was no traffic at this time of night. The inspector continued to race down Jervois Road, but it was hopeless. The car had slid down one of the myriad little streets in Ponsonby.

"Tell me you got the plate?" Grimble asked. Cadd nodded.

He pulled over to a phone box and told the sergeant to call in the license plate.

Grimble sat in his car, trying to make sense of the dead Maori, two getaway cars and two passports fresh from short stays in the United States. He felt disgusted with himself. He thought he could outmaneuver anyone.

Clovis heard someone on the back porch as he walked into the kitchen. He tiptoed to the back door and quietly opened it. He was hit by the sweet smell of honeysuckle.

"Nice out, isn't it?" Wiremu spoke softly.

"Yes. Mind if I join you?"

"Be my guest." Wiremu was sitting cross-legged on a wooden bench facing the dark outline of a grapefruit tree. Wiremu could see the Southern Cross and Mars.

"It's a beautiful night."

The houses on either side cut out the glare of the streetlights. Beyond the garden was the black mass of Mount Eden.

"Up in Hokianga, I spend a lot of time up on a hill, the whole night. It's special. You know?" Wiremu turned to face Clovis. He could feel Clovis's anxiety.

Wiremu wore a khaki shirt Clovis had lent him.

"If anything happened to Plum, I don't know what I would do."

"Don't worry, Clovis. Tomorrow we'll go back, clean the place up and get you another home. They'll never find you again."

"Did they really wreck the place?"

"Not much really. Just looking for stuff. It could've been a robbery. Like Mel said."

"She was trying to placate Plum."

"Yeah. You're right. I think it had to be Terry the Turk."

"Is he after you or Plum?" Clovis asked.

"He wasn't after me last week. So why this week? He seems to be after Plum."

"Who is he then? And why would he want Plum?"

Wiremu sighed and stretched out his legs. He stared into Clovis's eyes. Clovis was unsettled. Wiremu's eyes did not lend themselves to any sustained investigation.

"Clovis, you have to tell me everything about Plum and Terry the Turk. Begin at the beginning."

Clovis first met Plum when she was nineteen. They shared a house with some friends in Parnell. Plum was attending University, studying drama. Clovis was finishing his Masters in Violin at the Conservatory.

Once Plum graduated, she could not, Clovis explained, find any work. So she answered an ad in the paper for a masseuse. She had always given great massages to Clovis. She began working at the Pink Flamingo on Newmarket Road. The interior was converted to resemble a Finnish sauna. Plum was a bona fide masseuse. Clovis did not realize what she was doing for several weeks, until he visited the place. Clovis wanted her to leave. She insisted on staying. It was good money. Better than picking lettuces with her cousins in Pukekohe or being a girl Friday in an office downtown. Those jobs paid less and were far more degrading. At least in this job she could earn decent money and did not have to take her clothes off.

Clovis was not impressed. He gave Plum an ultimatum. Leave the masseuse's job or he would leave her. She called his bluff. She stayed. Clovis, heartbroken, flew to New York to see if he could apply for a post-graduate course at the Juilliard School of Music. He was turned down. He finished up playing on the streets and made, what was to him, a lot of money. He bumped into Plum when he was playing on a street in Manhattan. Just like that, Clovis told Wiremu. It was a small world. Plum told Clovis that Terry Turner, her boss, had fired her because she would not do what he wanted her to. He wanted her to do bad things. Clovis believed her.

They fell in love again and flew back to Auckland. They rented a house in Ponsonby and went to celebrate at the Jolly Rodger. Wiremu knew the rest.

Wiremu shook his head. There was more to it than what Clovis had said. He sighed and thought there was time enough to question Plum about this at a later date. Clovis could cling to his innocence. For what it was worth.

Wiremu then began his story about Terry the Turk.

"His real name is Terry Turner, immigrated from London, the East End, back in the early sixties. He had a vegetable barrow, you know, sold veges. He married real young, his childhood sweetheart, and came out here. He tried to run a greengrocers in Auckland but found the Chinese and Indians controlled everything, so he sold his shop, although he did have some dealings with the Chinese.

"He set up Terry's Burgers in Newmarket. Ran it himself with his wife and two helpers. He took the midnight shift. When no respectable citizens would be out. Let alone eating a greasy hamburger. The bikies got to know and love him. This was when the cops first got interested in him. He acts like he wouldn't hurt a fly. Which is true, because there were always lots of flies around the food.

He's tiny and going bald, with a squeaky cockney voice, though he had greasy long hair back then. He'd get anyone to do anything for him.

"The cops wanted Terry to squeal on the bikies; what he overheard, what they told him. Stuff like that. Be an informer. Bikies back then rode huge motorbikes with deep-throated engines like Triumph Thunderbirds and Bonnevilles and Norton Commanders. They wore their leather jackets with patches, had their own private code and kept to themselves. Just like the cops. That was why the cops took a fundamental hatred to them."

"Oh come on, that's a little farfetched," Clovis interjected.

"Okay. Cops wash and shave. So Terry, being a man of principle, refused to cooperate. They kept on trying. Then they found this kid with a hot TV set and threatened to throw the book at him unless he set up Terry. The cops busted the bikies as they were stripping a house in Remuera one night, and the kid told them it was Terry. Terry was the informer. A week later BOOM! Terry's Burgers was blown sky high. No more burgers. Almost no more Terry. It was his night off. A helper was killed. Terry just went back and rebuilt it.

"Years later Terry came across this kid in Para. The poor sod got impaled on an iron pipe ripped out of a shower. They never found out who did it, but we knew it was Big John. Who was going to tell on him? We'll come to him later. Well, Terry won the bikies over to his side again with his greasy burgers.

"One night, an old friend from London comes to him with a van full of stolen TVs. He wants to park it in Terry's garage for the night. Terry says no. The thief pleads and pleads and pleads. Terry still says no. Then the thief hints he can find out who set up the kid who set up Terry. So Terry, in a moment of weakness, says yes. Just till the morning. That night the cops raided Terry's house and found the TVs. He got the maximum sentence.

"He took to prison real well. A natural organizer. His cockney humor, funny voice worked to his advantage. He could talk his way out of any situation, and he soon got the protection of Maori gangs inside. They actually vied for his brain. He was running all the drugs coming into Para. He only served five years on account of good behavior. Funny when you think about it. A guy that small usually becomes someone's old lady real quick, but not Terry. The man who controls the drugs in there, controls everything. And he was the librarian! The screws loved him or were paid by him. He perfected smuggling drugs into prison. I never found out how he did it. He's still doing it."

"How do you know all this?" Clovis asked.

"I was inside with him. I worked with him. Not for him, mind you. I wouldn't want to make an enemy of him. Not outright. Not with someone who had John Eustace around.

"Anyway, when he came out, the police were waiting for him again. Protection for information. Only the police didn't understand that the game had changed. They needed protection from Terry now. The cops didn't know that. His wife had aged whilst he was inside, and his kids had left school and drifted away. He felt he had been robbed of the most important years of his life. He felt an outsider in his own family. So he did what he did best. Organize. He had graduated with a doctorate from the University of Crime and now it was time to really get into business.

"The funny part was he opened up another hamburger joint. Twenty-four hours. That was his cover." Wiremu wound up his voice to approximate Terry's high-pitched cockney intonation.

"'Leave me alone. I'm just a little old man framed by the fuzz. I just want to live in peace and look after my sick wife.' Now he controls a fucking empire!"

Clovis had never heard Wiremu swear. "How come he can get away with all this?"

"He owns property, lives in a nice house, doesn't act rich. He's audited every year by the tax people. The cops bug his phones. They probably have stacks of intelligence on him. But he's always a couple of steps ahead of the law. Usually a couple of miles.

"And I'll tell you something else, Clovis. I don't think Terry would come after Plum like that, if that was all she did. Either she's hiding something from you, or ..." Wiremu shrugged. He never wanted to underestimate someone like Terry the Turk.

It was so peaceful outside that Clovis could not move. But he had no desire to come under Wiremu's scrutiny, so he got to his feet and tiptoed back to the front room to check on Plum. She should be sleeping like a baby, he thought. It was only three o'clock. The silence was such a contrast to the perpetual din that had assaulted his ears back in New York.

Plum was not on the sofa, and her blanket was gone. He ran out to the kitchen, not daring to think what had happened to her. Wiremu, who was about to fix himself a sandwich in the kitchen, immediately stopped buttering his slice when he saw Clovis's ashen face.

"She's not there!"

Clovis ran out onto the front porch and yelled at the top of his lungs.

"Plum! Plum!" He gripped his head with both hands and tried to scan the street. There was no sign of her. He ran back inside. Mel appeared in the hallway, in her long pink robe.

"Plum's gone," Clovis uttered, as he felt his whole world collapse around him.

He came to a few minutes later, on the sofa where Plum had been fast asleep. Mel was sitting beside him with some smelling salts. She addressed Wiremu.

"You can't expect me to believe there's this super villain who's masterminding all this against Plum Blossom! Whoever it is, is probably after you, Wiremu." She paused, waiting for Wiremu to respond. He kept his sullen expression, though he had no guilt, no sheepishness about him.

"I think it's better for all of us if you went back to your people so we can go to the police and report Plum missing. We'll leave you out of everything."

"Mel! Where have you been?" Wiremu raised his voice. "What good will reporting Plum missing do? You know what they'll say. 'She's over twenty-one. There's no body. No evidence of foul play. She probably left of her own free will. Now bugger off, we've got better things to do!' That's what they'll say."

"Like track down this Terry the Turk," Henry muttered from the doorway. He was dressed in his purple polka dot boxing shorts and was rubbing his eyes. "Mel and I will go back to your house, Clovis. You stay here with Wiremu in case she comes back or someone phones."

"No. I should go," Clovis insisted. "Perhaps she has taken a walk." He knew this was not true. She would not wake up. And if she had gone for a walk, she would have told him. No. She would have been afraid to go out alone.

"Okay. Suit yourself. I was just being heroic." Henry shuffled off to the kitchen to make a cup of tea.

Mel changed into black tights and a black short-sleeved top. At another time Clovis would have wolf whistled. He followed her to the car as she checked the street for anything unusual. They were in Ponsonby in a few minutes with Clovis scanning the deserted streets, trying to spot Plum walking back to their house. He did recognize the driver of a bread delivery truck, from the bakery he used to work in as a student. They had seen only two cars, going in the opposite direction.

Mel suddenly swung into a driveway. She turned the lights off, shut off the engine and grabbed Clovis's shoulders. She put her lips to his cheek.

Clovis froze. Her abrupt action sent him into a panic. He could not understand what was going on. Then he tried to kiss her.

Mel pushed him away. "You pig! You put your tongue in my mouth!" She was disgusted.

"But you started it!" Clovis yelled back, now more confused than ever.

"Didn't you see the police car?" She was embarrassed.

"No."

"Oh god. Any car out at this time they take note of. Especially a BMW. I saw that trick in a movie once. It must've worked." Mel backed out of the drive before switching on her lights. She wiped her mouth and glanced at her shocked passenger. "You okay, Clovis?"

Clovis could not speak.

At the top of Summer Street they saw a fleet of fire trucks, police cars, crowds of people in their bedclothes, an ambulance and a traffic police car blocking the top of the road. With all the red and blue and white strobe lights bouncing over the small compact houses, it was difficult to see where the fire was.

Grimble had two missing cars, a dead body and a break-in. Then there was Plum Blossom and Clovis Tibet. What sort of names were they? Courier names? The house was another mystery. Not a trace of a controlled substance. He would have to go back and check.

Cadd opened the car door and collapsed into his seat. He held his notebook and faced his superior. He took a deep breath.

"The Lincoln's owner died last year and it now belongs to a Mr. B. Golacinski at 137 Ayr Road, Parnell."

"And there's no such address."

"Yes. That's right!"

A fire truck roared past with its siren cutting through the night.

"Shit!" he uttered. "The house!" When things start to go wrong, they go totally wrong. Why did he drag that Maori into the house? At the time it seemed a smart idea. Now it could backfire on him. He swung the car around and followed the flashing red lights back down John Street. At the bottom of the street there was another fire truck with firemen unwinding hoses as they ran up Summer Street. The inspector came to the corner and parked the car facing the wrong way.

He walked quickly up the street till he came to the fire truck nearest the house. The house where he had placed the body of Hone Wilson. The wooden structure was engulfed in flames. The fire had already reached the roof. Grimble could see the red heat dance across the overhang like a curtain of flames. The front windows exploded from the heat, as the firemen started to direct high-pressure hoses onto the house.

"Oh shit!" he whispered to himself as he felt the heat of the flames on his face. He turned to Cadd. "We better keep this to ourselves. Understand?" Grimble screwed up his eyebrows as he scanned the sergeant's face. He could see the red flames flickering in Cadd's blue eyes.

Mel pulled over at the top of Clovis's street. A traffic officer sat in his car, his red lights on, blocking the way. Mel took out her doctor's bag from the trunk and the officer automatically let her pass. Clovis trotted behind her. Down Summer Street there were three fire trucks lined up and miles of entwined hoses, like giant spaghetti. Clovis and Mel passed Polynesian men and women in their nightgowns and children in various states of undress. The entire street had got out of bed to watch the fire.

Mel's walk slowed down and her body stiffened as she realized where the fire was. Clovis grabbed Mel's arm for support.

"My house is gone."

One sidewall stood, together with the brick foundations and the back wall. Charred twisted pieces of corrugated iron, the remains of the roof, hung from the center brick chimney. Firemen in silver fire boots were wading through the smoldering black hunks of wood that had turned into ashen sludge. Water from their hoses poured down the road, overflowing from the drains and flooding the bottom of the street.

Clovis was scared that Plum had been in the house. Perhaps deliberately burnt by her abductors. Then he remembered Mel's story and how she had left her attacker in there. He saw that Mel was treating an older woman in a nightgown who had collapsed in the street. He could not think clearly. He walked away from the crowd of neighbors he was standing by and approached two men who were obviously plainclothes policemen.

Clovis Tibet addressed the older detective who looked Clovis up and down.

"How did it happen?" Clovis asked.

"That's what we'd like to know. Where were you?"

Clovis wondered how the detective knew who he was.

"I was with some friends."

"Why did you come back now?"

"We were up talking."

"Do you live with anyone else?"

"Yes. A young woman. Plum Blossom. She was with us, but left." Clovis's voice trailed off.

"Is that her real name, and could you describe her to me?"

"Small. About 5'2", looks Chinese but she was born here, and her name is Plum Blossom. She changed it by deed poll when her parents died."

"Stay here." The detective walked across to the group of policemen who stood in a huddle near the battered down fence and layers of limp hoses. A plain black van drew up from the bottom of the street, guided by a traffic officer. There were now dozens of spectators. The detective came back to Clovis.

"Mr. Tibet, I must ask you to come back to the station for questioning."

"What? What for? I mean, what's going on?"

"Oh, just routine." The detective smiled.

"Am I under arrest?"

"Ah. Should you be?"

"What about Plum? I've got no idea where she went."

"Did you have an argument?"

"No. Not at all."

"Well, come on. No use standing here."

Clovis followed him to a Honda Accord, the other detective close behind. Clovis tried to find Mel's face in the crowd, but he could not see her. He wondered if he should yell out to her, but thought better of it.

The detective carefully drove the car between the fire trucks and police vehicles.

"Terrible things, fires. Happens so quickly. I hope you were insured."

"No. I'm not." Clovis sat in the front seat, wondering what was going to happen to him.

"Pity. Been living there long?"

"About a week."

"Where were you before?"

"New York. We just got back."

"Never been there. They say it's a wild place."

"Not as wild as here. I never had anything happen to me like this."

"Any valuables there?"

"Yes." For a second Clovis could not breathe. He thought his heart had stopped. Then the attack subsided. "No. Only clothes and books. And I'd just bought some furniture. Thank god! My violin." Clovis gave out a big sigh. "I took it over to a friend's house."

"Oh. You play?"

"Yes. Just got a position with the Symphony Orchestra."

"The Auckland Symphony?"

"Yeah."

"Ah." The detective did not show he was impressed. He thought he was dealing with a drug courier hippie, not a classical violinist. "My elder daughter plays in her school orchestra. Been playing since she was eight."

Clovis was in no mood for a chat about violins with a detective who had not introduced himself and with the silent policeman in the back seat who was taking notes. The detective drove in silence to Auckland Police Headquarters at Cook Street. It was a hostile fortress-like building, made taller by its position on the crest of a hill. Cold and forbidding, Moscow modernist architecture was how Clovis remembered someone describe it.

Clovis was left in a small room with bare green walls. He sat opposite two metal chairs and a table on which rested a form he had to fill out.

"Thank you for coming here, Mr. Tibet." The detective entered the room and shook his hand, as if they had just been introduced. Clovis discovered he was talking to Inspector Grimble. The name rang a bell, but he could not place it. Grimble sat opposite Clovis and picked up the completed form.

"Who were you staying with tonight?"

"I already told you, with friends."

"Yes. But who?"

Clovis saw the inspector was holding a computer printout and was comparing it with the form Clovis had filled out. It was the Wanganui computer! They knew more about him than his mother, who was dead anyway. Tax, overseas travel, money in the bank, police intelligence files (if they existed for him, which he doubted), who had employed him, that he had applied for an outdoor musician's license and was written up by every policeman in downtown Auckland. It was that complete! He should never have read Kafka when he was fourteen. It made him paranoid. *The Castle*. *The Trial*. They were nothing compared to New Zealand bureaucracy and the police. He felt guilty, even though he had done nothing wrong. Well, apart from hosting Wiremu.

"Was anyone else in the house when you left?" Grimble was exhausted.

"No. We live alone, I mean, with Plum."

"What time did you leave Summer Street?" The inspector looked at Clovis's wrist again. Not even a tan line for a watch, just some big freckles.

"Oh, about six. I'm not sure. I arrived with Dr. Johnson and picked up Plum and we went to their place for dinner."

"Did you notice anything unusual on the street? Any parked car with someone inside?"

"No."

"What time did you leave Dr. Johnson's?"

"I don't know. But we came straight to my place."

"What time did Plum Blossom leave?"

"I don't know, I was outside on the terrace."

"In the front?"

"No! In the back."

"Were you talking to Dr. Johnson?"

"No." Clovis fought to stop his face from turning red. How could he deceive this detective?

"Where was Plum Blossom?"

"In the living room. I think she fell asleep. Er, she was definitely asleep." He felt his face return to normal.

"What do you mean?"

"Well, she had a headache and Dr. Johnson gave her some aspirin and she put her feet up."

"Was anyone else in Dr. Johnson's house?"

"Yes. She lives with Henry Lotus."

"How long have you known him?"

"About one, almost two weeks." Clovis told himself he had not actually told a lie, he had just left out certain key facts. "He's a physicist. Real interesting to talk to."

"And Dr. Johnson is his wife?"

"No. I don't think they're married. But they're in love."

"Did you have anything valuable in your house?"

"Well, my Post Office Savings book, all my music! Oh my god!" Clovis let out a moan, all the sheet music that had taken years to collect. And his orchestral sheets all burned. How could he explain that to his new boss, the conductor?

"There were clothes, all Plum's clothes. But I'm worried about Plum. It's not like her to disappear. Once she falls asleep she never wakes up till morning. I'm really worried about her."

"Can you think of anyone who would want to rob your house? Burn it down?"

Clovis did not realize how close the inspector was to the truth. Grimble thought that Clovis was mixed up in a drug conspiracy. The inspector did not need any intuition to realize Clovis was not telling the truth. His sweating red face and earnest facial expressions were an open book.

"No. No one." Clovis was afraid his eyes would betray him.

The tall detective came into the room. He handed Grimble another computer printout and stood behind him.

"I'm going to need a list of everyone you've met since you got back. And I want a full description of Plum Blossom, including what she was wearing."

"Okay. But my address book and diary, everything was lost in the fire."

"Well, do the best you can. See to that, Sergeant. I'll be back shortly, then I'll take you, er, do you have anywhere to stay?"

"Yes. But what about Plum?"

"File a missing persons report. Get it for him, Cadd. Show it to me when he finishes. Oh, by the way, how old is she? And did she graduate from University?"

"Twenty-two. Auckland University, a year ago."

"Good. Cadd, get a photo from the Registrar's office. First thing this morning. What about her parents. Where do they live?"

"They don't. They were killed in an explosion about twelve years ago, maybe more, in Pukekohe."

"Explosion?" The inspector pressed his eyebrows together.

"Yeah. A septic tank blew up over their car. So the police said." Clovis gulped. What was he saying? He was talking to the police.

"Oh." The inspector looked at Cadd. "Who's next of kin?"

"Her whole family lives down there. I've met her grandfather, Sam Look. He was her legal guardian. I don't have his address, but he's still down there. Plum talked to him on the phone when we came back from New York."

"Cadd. Call our friends in Auckland South and get them to visit this Sam Look right away. I want a report on my desk by two." He left the room, scratching his chin. He was too old for these all nighters.

Inspector Grimble came back into the room twenty minutes later. Cadd was going over the papers in front of him. Clovis could barely keep his eyes open.

"Are you sure nobody else was in the house or was coming over or could just walk in?" Grimble asked.

"Quite sure."

"How tall did you say Plum Blossom was?" Grimble remembered her height from the passport, but he wanted to play this out, gauge Tibet's reaction. Tibet was not telling him everything.

"Five foot two."

"That's odd. Very odd. There was a body in the house." Grimble scratched his chin and casually observed Tibet who was about to burst into tears.

"It was very charred," he continued.

"No!" Clovis stood up. Grimble could see the sweat stains on his shirt.

"Calm down, Clovis. Let me finish. The corpse is at least six foot tall. We'll check dental records, but other than that, it's ..." He wanted to say "toast."

"That's bizarre." Clovis held his head in his hands. He was genuinely relieved that Plum had not been in the house, but he knew that the detective was playing with him. Clovis was so wound up he did not know how to react. He let everything show on his face. He thought of Mel and the story she told of how she had knocked out the big man and left him on the floor. How could that house have burnt down? How could it be an accident?

"Yes. It is. Looks like arson and murder. I'm afraid we're going to need to talk to you later. Please don't leave town. You will be valuable in our investigation. Cadd, see he gets to where he's going." Grimble checked the missing person's report for Clovis's contact address. "Who is this Matthew Bounder?"

"Fellow musician."

"Good. We'll put an APB out for Miss Blossom. We're most anxious to talk to her about this."

"You have to find her. She just wouldn't disappear like that. This is a total mystery to me."

"Likewise."

Chapter Five

Tuesday

The police car dropped Clovis off at a small wooden house, near the Domain on Park Road. Clovis had not seen Matthew Bounder for seven months, but he was there to answer the doorbell and stare suspiciously at the departing police car. There was a smell of cremated toast, cigarette smoke and cats coming from the kitchen. Matthew had been the singer and leader of the group Dogs Breath and a later group the Cat's Pajamas. Clovis had played electric violin with him.

"Clovis! Fancy seeing you. I thought you were in New York! Are you a cop now or an informer?"

"Are you going to invite me in?"

"Fuck! Come on in. I'm serving the breakfast of champions." Matthew leered at Clovis.

Dishes were piled in the sink, waiting for a miracle. Four cats meowed on the cluttered Formica table waiting for a separate miracle, whilst the toast sent smoke signals from an Art Deco pop-up toaster that refused to pop up. Clovis found the telephone and quickly dialed Mel. Matthew poked the blackened toast out of the toaster with a large serrated knife.

Mel answered on the first ring. She could not go to work until she had heard from Clovis. She had not been able to sleep, haunted by the sight of the body bag. Clovis let out a big sigh when Mel told him that the police had not contacted her yet.

"They're not coming back here, are they? I mean, Clovis, this is so irresponsible of you. You were always like this. Shit! This fucking toast." He looked at Clovis with wild eyes. The kettle on the gas stove began to scream. "I've plants in the back and god knows what else around here. Shit! They'd put me away for life!"

"Sshh! I'll explain in a minute." Clovis cupped the receiver and glared at Matthew, who was pouring water into a filter bag of recycled coffee grounds.

"It's okay." He went back to talking to Mel. Wiremu had disappeared up Mount Eden as soon as Mel had returned. He had left a message for Clovis saying he would do everything he could to find Plum. Mel thought he meant it. He had thanked Henry for all the food and hospitality before departing. There was nothing Clovis could say to console Mel about the body. He did not want to tell her, but felt he had to, in case the inspector sprang it on her.

Breakfast with Matthew Bounder helped Clovis put some perspective on his situation. Matthew still wore his curly blond hair past his shoulders. His hairline had receded, and his once golden locks were now plain mousy. Six foot four and thin as a beanpole, he had taken to wearing horn-rimmed glasses. Years of dropping acid, smoking homegrown weed and singing his songs in front of an over amplified band had done things to his brain that were reflected in his appearance. His eyes were glazed. His mouth was half open with an occasional glob of saliva hanging from his lower lip. And he had a constant sniffle that never developed into a cold.

Matthew still had an excellent voice, despite or because of all the abuse he had heaped on his body. With a range of three and a half octaves, he could fly into a searing soprano or come down to a deep gravelly blues voice from lungs that had inhaled far too many legal and illegal substances.

"Hey! Why don't you play with my new band?" Matthew's eyes lit up as if hit by a Buddhist reawakening. He was about to pour some light brown coffee into a cracked pottery mug for Clovis.

"What's it called?"

"Particle Board."

"Sounds solid."

"Yeah." Matthew grinned. "Wall of sound. My voice has never been better. We might have Billy. You remember Billy? He'll play if he's not inside. And your buddy Rua. Why don't you join us this Friday? We're playing in a pub in Ponsonby." Matthew had spilled most of the coffee over the table in his excitement. A large ginger cat with only three legs hopped over and started licking up the mess. Trust Matthew to have a caffeine-addicted cat, Clovis observed.

"I'm a little superstitious about pubs in Ponsonby right now."

"Why? You don't like coconuts?"

"No. It's a long story. Thanks for breakfast. But I need a car to get around today. It's really important."

"Uhh?" Matthew had his mouth full, with the remains of what was edible from the table that the cats had not eaten. The thought of Clovis doing something important was alien to Matthew.

"Someone burnt down my house last night."

"Wow! Heavy!"

"So I need a car." Clovis thought that sort of stoned logic would appeal to Matthew. He underestimated his host.

"Why? Did you drive around in your house before?" Matthew saw that Clovis was about to burst into tears. "I didn't know you could drive."

"Plum taught me."

"Are you still hanging around with her?"

"Well, we were together, but she disappeared last night."

"Fucking shit. You do everything at once. Is this some kind of police mystery? I mean, that was a cop car that dropped you off, right? It wasn't the Mongrel Mob with a stolen car. And Plum is Chinese. I mean, really Clovis. You can't fool me. I mean, I've been around, and I've survived."

"They wanted to talk to me about my house, that's all. Look, it's really important I get going. You've still got your Studebaker, haven't you?"

Matthew nodded.

"Well. I've given the cops your number, in case they have to reach me. I'll call you this afternoon. Is that okay?"

"What? I've got a whole nation of plants out the back. You know, there is a drug war going on. Maoris, bikies, the drug squad, everyone and his mother. They had a bad crop last year and now there's a drought, and with prices going sky high, it's got out of control."

He eased out of his chair, somewhat exhausted from so many coherent words spewing from his mouth at one time and reached over to the car keys hanging on a nail. "Don't get caught up in all this shit. Otherwise you'll be mown down in the cross fire. Remember Willie the drummer in Dog? Well, he was a courier. They found him tied up, bits of him missing. The good bits. And three bullet holes in the head. Three! Fuck! He was brain dead when he was alive!"

Matthew threw Clovis the keys. "Bring it back by six. You owe me a guest gig. Okay? Friday night."

"Of course. Thank you, Matthew. And I'm not caught up in anything like that. I promise."

"Just be careful with my fucking car. It's like a wife to me."

Clovis tried to block out all negative thoughts of Plum as he steered the '58 Studebaker down the Southern Motorway to Pukekohe. The dashboard was covered in fake leopard skin that had faded in the sun. A plastic skeleton hung from the rearview mirror. The fuel gauge was stuck on full.

Clovis had not seen Grandpa Sam for a year. He drove up to a large wooden house that looked abandoned. When he turned off the motor, Clovis was overcome by the isolation and quietness of his surroundings.

He walked around the back of the house on a gravel path. An old man was squatting next to a small patch of parsley, weeding, his back to Clovis. Clovis stood ten feet away at the edge of the path. There was a chicken coop nearby and a row of glasshouses, full of gigantic tomato plants.

The man stood up slowly. He turned around and stared at Clovis with a face that showed no sign of recognition. He wore a spotless white shirt with the sleeves rolled up to the elbow, black trousers and rubber sandals. With his clear light skin he could have passed for a young sixty, but he was well into his seventies. He gave Clovis his blank stare.

A young detective from Auckland South had visited Sam Look that morning to inquire about Plum Blossom. Talking too slowly and too loudly, the detective had asked Sam if he spoke English. The detective left, convinced the old man was deaf, mute and unable to comprehend even the simplest English phrases.

"I've come about Plum Blossom."

"Why did you bring her back?"

"Can we go inside and talk? This is very serious. She's missing."

Sam Look motioned to Clovis to follow him into the house. They sat in the dining room. The wooden furniture, everything about the house was very old, but still functional and clean.

In the dark interior, an older woman shuffled around in what Clovis took to be the kitchen. She appeared at the table briefly to pour tea into two bone china cups. Then she disappeared. Ancient lace curtains blocked out most of the sunlight. Sam sipped his green tea. Clovis cleared his throat and began at the end; the burning house, the disappearance of Plum, the tall man waiting in their house, and the appearance of one of Terry the Turk's henchmen that sent Plum into hysterics.

Sam finished his tea.

"She called me a week ago to say hello. Why did you come back here with her?"

"Why not" Clovis felt uneasy.

"Because Plum was tied up in some very bad business with that man."

Clovis was shocked. This was the first time he had heard Sam raise his voice.

"But that blew over, didn't it?"

"Something like that never blows away. It blows up!"

"I don't understand."

Sam allowed a small muscle in his face to twitch as if to say that was the stupidest statement he had ever heard.

"This man, Terry Turner. I know him. He came here a few years ago. He sat right where you're sitting now. He talked about making a deal."

Clovis sat motionless.

"He wanted me to grow some plants for him. He offered me a good price."

"And?"

"The next year he wanted to grow more. Much more. The price was better, but I said no. My youngest grandson dropped out of University. He was an addict. He almost died. I bought him back here. He is better now, but I never see him.

"We had our opium in the old days, but it was in moderation. For ourselves. It was different then. Now everything is too fast. Everyone wants everything immediately. It's a no waiting world. They are greedy. So along come these people like Turner and use this weakness and get rich. I do not want anything to do with that."

"But what about Plum? How does she fit into this?"

"This man came to see me. He came with another man, with a face like a bulldog but eyes of a little rabbit. Light blue, like ice. Then Mr. Rabbit Eyes came alone one time. He threatened me. They had convinced some relatives over in Mangere to work for them, so he said. And they never admitted it, but I can believe it. There was a lot of money at stake. There is little money in cabbages and onions compared to that. Easy money has a very high price. You get nothing without paying for it."

The old woman appeared again and silently refilled their tea before shuffling off. Clovis could not make out if Sam was staring into his eyes or over his head. The gaze, like Sam's voice, transfixed him. He no longer thought he was sitting in a rundown house in the middle of nowhere. He felt he was in the center of the universe and he was about to receive some secret that would unlock this whole mystery and he would be able to find Plum Blossom, safe and sound.

"Plum found this out the hard way. That man lured Plum into working for him, giving him a chance to get back at me. I forbade her, but she would no longer listen to me. She thought she was smarter."

"What can I do?"

"To find her, you have to go and see this man. Better yet, get someone else to check on him. You will mean nothing to him." He shrugged his shoulders slightly. "You have to convince him without him knowing, that he can use you or your friend. You understand?"

Clovis felt he had been handed a riddle. He would need time to think it through. "How can I do that?"

"Have you got a strong friend?"

"Yeah! Wiremu. He's a leader of some Maori gang and carries a shotgun up his trousers."

"Ah." Sam allowed his face to break into a slight grin. "Then this is the man you want on your side."

"But he's in hiding. From the police."

"So much the better." Sam stood up, picked up his cup and saucer and disappeared into the kitchen. When he reappeared, Clovis followed him out onto the back veranda. Clovis squinted his eyes at the bright sunlight.

The old man raised his head to the sky and gazed at the high grey clouds.

"It's going to rain tomorrow." He walked back to his parsley patch.

Clovis did not hear the peculiar noise the Studebaker made as other cars roared past him on the way back to Auckland on the Motorway. All Clovis could think about was what Plum Blossom had not told him.

He pushed down on the accelerator. The Studebaker lost speed. Clovis wrestled the rack and pinion steering so he could stop on the shoulder. The fuel gauge indicated three quarters full. He got out of the car and could not find the release for the hood. Clovis knew nothing about cars. First his girlfriend goes missing, then his house is burnt down with someone inside and all his sheet music and his orchestral parts go up in smoke, and now the car he has borrowed breaks down in the middle of nowhere! How could Matthew keep such an unreliable car? He had to hitch a ride. He put the car keys under the front seat and slammed the door shut.

Clovis stuck his thumb out. A gang sped past in a blur of black leather, deafening him with the roar of their Kawasakis, Hondas and Harley Davidsons. When the dust settled, Clovis saw a giant blob of spittle on his trousers.

For half an hour Clovis talked to the cars and trucks that sped by him.

"Look! I'm harmless!" he shouted. "All I want is a bleeding lift back to Auckland! Just because I've got red hair and a beard and I'm over six foot and two hundred pounds doesn't mean I'm a bleeding murderer. For Christ's sake, I'm a classical violinist!"

An old black Mercedes sedan screeched to a halt in front of Clovis's raised thumb. A tall gawky man in his late thirties climbed out of the driver's seat.

"G'day, mate! Trouble with ya car?" He bounded over to the hood, caught the release and lifted it up. He stuck his balding head inside the engine.

"Turn on the ignition. It's in neutral right?"

Clovis did as he was told. The motor turned over but did not catch.

"Any petrol?"

"The gauge's stuck."

The lean man grinned and strode over to his trunk. He pulled out a tin can of petrol and emptied most of it into the Studebaker's tank. Leaning over into the engine again, he poured some petrol into the air filter. He poked around with his hands and nodded to Clovis to turn on the ignition. He then reached into the engine. It turned over several times with no effect.

"Looks like yer fuel pump's crook. Wanna lift into the city?"

Clovis found out his savior's name was Lance Beef-eater. Lance the only son of a gentleman farmer, preferred to drive at 80 miles per hour. He had left his father in a ranch near Taupo.

"It's for soaks trying to dry out. He goes in, gets cured, comes home, gets bored out of his brains, hits the bottle and gets bombed out of his skull. Misses mother. She blew her brains out last year. Lived in Hamilton. They call it Suicide City. She had a TV in every room, three cars, a maid, went bowling twice a week, and she still couldn't hack it. Makes you wonder, don't it? I mean, what's the point? If you've got everything?"

Clovis was at a loss as to how to talk to Lance Beef-eater. Words came out of his mouth like warm milk squeezed from a cow's teat. As they approached the Epsom exit, Lance interrupted his monologue.

"So where can I get a good time? You know, girls and stuff." He winked as he changed lanes narrowly missing a Post Office van.

"Oh, if you want girls, I know just the place." Clovis rubbed his hands.

"Yeah? Really?"

"Oh. This is some place."

"Come on. Where?" Lance Beefeater sounded too eager.

"I'll take you right there. It's the numero uno massage parlor in Sin City called the Flamingo Paradise. You get a sauna, a massage and anything else you want."

"Hot diggitty! This is fair dinkum?"

"You bet!"

"Holy shit! That's what I need. A nice young Maori girl. A virgin. Oh boy! I don't care about the massage bit. You know … it's the extras that count!"

Lance Beefeater followed Clovis's directions and dropped him off opposite the Flamingo Paradise. The house was ordinary but for the giant unlit neon flamingo and its name scrawled across the roof in a seven-foot-high illuminated sign.

"Matthew? It's me Clovis," he began sweetly from a payphone on Newmarket Road.

"Where are you?"

"Nearby. I just wanted to check in to see if I got any phone calls."

"Phone calls! Fuck! And they're outside waiting for you. Two of the meanest fuckers you ever laid eyes on."

"You mean the police?"

"Who else? Fucking hell! Clovis, aren't you forgetting something? Like my fucking car!"

"Oh. I was getting to that, Matthew. Now sit down and take a deep breath. I've some bad news, but it's not that bad."

"Oh shit. I knew it. You can't drive. You can't fucking drive! And you've gone and totaled it, haven't you?! Shit! Tell me it's not true, Clovis! Clovis?" Clovis was glad he had decided to phone the news in.

"Calm down, will you? It's not as bad as it sounds. The car broke down on the Motorway just past the Pukekohe exit. It's quite safe. Hold on. Don't flip your lid. The keys are under the seat. Get someone to tow it to a garage. The fuel pumps beat. Nothing I could do about it. You're lucky it happened to me, not you. Now don't tell anyone I called. Okay?"

"Pukekohe? Pukekohe?" Matthew yelled in disbelief as Clovis hung up. He did have a terrible temper. Like the time Matthew screamed at the leading Commedia Del Arte player in Mission Bay Park. That was when

Clovis first met Plum. No. That was the first time he talked to her. He had first seen her at a Children's Insane Asylum, two days before Christmas.

Matthew had arranged for a group of musicians to play at the Oakley Mental Hospital for the Children's All Star Christmas Show. Matthew was dating a nurse there, and Clovis had correctly assumed Matthew's motives were more inspired by carnal desire than Christmas cheer. The acoustic group consisted of an overweight tuba player, Nick the Greek, Clovis on violin, with his long red hair and beard, and a guitar player, Billy Whitehorn, who was almost on home territory. He had checked into the adult wing to unscramble his acid-addled brain twice in the last three years. Now, he believed his Gibson Les Paul was a prophet and spoke to him in screaming blues notes. Matthew, as singer and tambourine player, headed the group. Cavorting in front of screaming, overexcited children, he thought he was Mick Jagger at Altamount singing "Sympathy for the Devil."

Plum Blossom played the duchess in a troupe of Commedia Del Arte players from the University. Matthew had persuaded them to perform at the Mental Hospital.

"What a perfect place to meet someone as beautiful as you. In a madhouse for kids!" were Clovis's opening words to Plum when he bumped into her off stage.

"Hah!" she had exclaimed, keeping up the mocking character of the duchess. "You have more hair than brains and more stomach than hair!"

When Clovis entered the main building of the asylum, he saw rows of little white canvas straitjackets bolted to the wall, two feet off the floor. They were empty. Clovis imagined them full of yelling kids, wrapped up in white canvas, some of them with their legs not reaching the ground and their eyes crossed, mad with rage and fear at being tied up like hogs about to be slaughtered.

Opening the door to the auditorium, Clovis was assaulted by the sound of one hundred and three children, between four and fifteen years of age, jumping up and down, screaming at the top of their lungs. They were witnessing the long-gowned 16th century Italian Dentist, with a ridiculously long nose and a huge pair of pliers, chase a small Chinese girl, dressed up as a 16th century Italian duchess, around the small stage. Clovis was immediately enamored with the duchess and her ability to project her realistic screams over those of her involved audience. Half the children looked as if they came from the same family, but they understood the story. Perhaps they had a similar dentist at the hospital.

Pulling teeth was a hard act to follow, but Matthew had arranged a medley of songs he knew the children would respond to.

Clovis, playing a simple melody, watched in awe as the children displayed an enthusiasm for madness that he never knew existed, as the group wound up "The Ying Tong Song!"

The "Ying Tong Song" went on and on. Clovis's fingers were on automatic as he played his amplified violin and watched Matthew in his high-pitched goonish voice intone the insane lyrics over and over. It was like an anthem to all the children assembled before them. Even the Commedia Del Arte troupe came out onto the stage and danced around the musicians, infected by the energy in the air. Plum Blossom circled the sweating violinist three times, eyeing him intently with her haughty duchess look.

The audience, despite the anarchic ecstasy, did not misbehave or throw anything. The form seats were bolted to the floor. Many of the children were heavily sedated so they could not stand up without falling over. But they exuded a spontaneous happiness that moved Clovis. He could not enter their physically narrow world nor peek into their unknown mental life to touch their fantasies or dreams. It was beyond his comprehension. Their lives, enclosed in that institution, were neatly sealed off from the outside world by a brick wall. When they were adults, no one would come and sing them "The Ying Tong Song!"

Clovis knew he would meet Plum Blossom again. They were booked to play alongside the Commedia Del Arte troupe the day after Christmas at Mission Bay Park, with Rangitoto in the background. Rangitoto was like a giant pine covered breast that pointed straight to the heavens. It was an extinct volcano, an island that, because of its circular shores, appeared the same no matter where you were in Auckland. It always reminded Clovis of Plum's well-rounded and pointed breasts. Plum Blossom, the volcano about to erupt.

At another phone booth, Clovis called Mel. She arranged to pick him up on the right side of Epsom Road, as he walked away from Newmarket.

"What did you find out?" Mel greeted Clovis as he slid into the seat next to her. Clovis informed her of his meeting with Shanghai Sam.

"An Inspector Grimble came and questioned me at work. I don't think anyone came forward and informed them of our first visit. Your neighbors aren't exactly the crimewatcher type."

"What about the body?"

Mel's face fell as she turned right off Mount Eden Road and pulled over to the curb. She left the motor running as she turned to Clovis. Her eyes misted up and she squeezed the steering wheel.

"I didn't kill him. I didn't. His pulse was regular when I left. There's no way he could have died. Although he could've gone into cardiac arrest. But ... God! They can't even identify him. I'm sick. Sick! If I killed him, I mean, if that was the same man and, well, I'd give up. Resign. I would no longer have the right to call myself a doctor. Shit! Some healer. I feel like, like some vigilante idiot. I'm confused by it all, Clovis! Its all my fault." She kept her grip on the steering wheel.

Clovis was both shocked at Mel's state and secretly flattered that she had taken him into her confidence. With tears falling down her cheeks, she was even more beautiful to him.

"Listen. You don't know if it was the same man. Whoever torched my house must've entered it first, right? Therefore, they must've seen him. Perhaps they swapped bodies. Or he regained consciousness and came back with some others and put another body there. So you'd think you killed him. You see, there are lots of rational explanations. But the guy you hit is not one of them. I mean, he's still alive. You said it yourself. He couldn't've died. Right?"

Mel bit her lower lip as she stared straight ahead. She did not say another word but turned the car around and parked by the next payphone. After a quick call to Henry, she drove down one block over from her house and parked.

"Just in case, we can walk through that garden there." She checked her eyes in the mirror and got out of the car as if nothing was the matter.

Henry greeted them at the back door with a pained expression.

• • •

When the big red and white car disappeared, Sam stood up from his parsley plants and walked to the house. Using the phone in the kitchen he dialed his grandson's number.

"Bruce. Come over. I want to see you. Yes, now!" Sam replaced the receiver and went to find his wife. He needed another cup of jasmine tea; his throat was dry.

Bruce kept the phone to his ear until he heard the dial tone. Grandpa Sam had not sounded like that in years. That was when Bruce remembered his aunt and uncle had been blown up, an event that had changed his life. He had been fourteen. After school he would organize and stack the trucks that carried the vegetables to the market in downtown Auckland, from Sunday to Wednesday. With the loss of his uncle, he became the farm manager and was responsible for running the family business. He married his second cousin and now his three children would inherit this land, if he did not get caught.

In fifteen minutes Bruce could drive to his grandfather's house if he took the Land Rover over some of the rougher roads. He would not take the white Volvo station wagon he had spent two hours waxing that morning. Bruce jogged around the three-car garage and up the small hill behind his house. Nestled in a valley were four glasshouses, hidden amongst protective rows of poplar and yew trees. The glasshouses had been built twenty-five years ago.

The sun and rain had peeled off the primer coat on the wood structure. Bruce could see Chuck's 1000 cc all black and chrome Kawasaki motorcycle parked under a cypress tree next to the nearest glasshouse. On the front leg shield was the name of the bike, stenciled in neon crimson.

Chuck Look inspected the last of the plants that were hanging up to dry in the glasshouse. He had already completed all the bud harvesting over the last few weeks and they were now dried and cured, ready to be packed up into one-pound bags. The afternoon sun shone through the dusty panes making Chuck appear a maroon color. He inhaled the sweet aroma of the resin and was happy. He stood up and wiped the beads of sweat from his forehead.

The mature buds of the Looks' sinsemilla crop would be sold for top prices. Auckland was in a late summer drought. The local supply from last year had dried up. Maori gangs blamed the police for the shortage and their efficient find and burn campaign, "Operation Weedout" from last year. People were crying out for quality marijuana. They would pay anything for it.

Instead of fetching $130 an ounce, or $250, the current price, this crop of highly potent sinsemilla would fetch over $300 an ounce, wholesale. Each plant had delivered at least twenty ounces of THC choked buds. With four hundred plants, this would equal $2,400,000, not including the leaves they had dried and would pack into hundreds of one-ounce plastic bags for distribution at a later date. Not bad for a cash crop that was tax free, even if the money had to be split so many ways.

There were other costs involved like the $20,000 to be paid to the staff sergeant at the Pukekohe Police Station. Another $50,000 was earmarked for each of the Wong brothers for supplying the seeds. At least Turners and Growers were not getting their high commission that they collected for all the produce that passed through their downtown auction house. How many lettuces would it take to get this amount of money? But the police did not seize lettuce and put you in jail. That sergeant in Pukekohe was now saying he needed another $20,000 to keep his mate cool in Otahuhu in the South Auckland Drug Squad. Could they believe him?

Could they afford not to believe him? What was another $20,000?

Chuck took a step back into the gravel pathway in the center of the greenhouse and executed a high round-house kick. He let out a yelp as he clutched his left thigh. He cursed himself because he knew he should always warm up and stretch before practicing. Then he jumped as he caught sight of a figure behind him.

"You should've called out. You gave me a fright!" Chuck brushed dirt from his jeans.

He motioned to Bruce to come nearer the trays of buds that resembled furry cobs of green corn. "The amount of THC in this is ten to fifteen times greater than the usual Kiwi green. We could charge even more for these clusters."

Bruce frowned. He was short and stocky with thick black hair. His shirt stuck to his barrel chest. The dry heat and the overpowering smell made Bruce forget what he wanted to see Chuck about.

"Last year we were beginners, but this season we're going to clean up. We're ahead of the main harvest, and we're ready to unload in the middle of a huge drought. The local cop and the Drug Squad are in our pocket, we can't lose!"

"Guess who just called me," Bruce replied in a dead-pan voice, unaffected by Chuck's sales pitch.

"That slut Plum." Chuck threw up his hands, they were green, the color of money.

"No. Why do you call her that?"

"She just is. She went to work for that man and, you know, did stuff." He moved his hand like a hollow fist next to his mouth and puckered his lips.

"She didn't know who owned the place. He was a sleeping partner."

"Yeah. She probably did that as well."

"Plum is still part of the family. Even if she ran away to the States. Maybe we could've helped more. I still feel bad about what happened."

"She was so naive she could've finished upside down in the Albert Park fountain with a dagger in her pants."

"Do you think her parents were murdered?"

"There was only one witness."

"Yeah. Grandpa. He called. He wants to see me right away."

"Shit. Do you think he knows about this?"

"He couldn't. And if he did, he wouldn't say anything. Not now. He's too removed. Has been since the accident." Bruce breathed out deeply.

Chuck pulled his eyes back with his fingers and leaned forward with a grin. "Inscrutable Chinaman. Read Confucius and do Tai Chi every morning before bleakfast. Don't tell him anyfling!" Chuck said. He did not see Bruce lean over and vomit into a plastic bucket outside the glasshouse.

He pushed the Land Rover as hard as he could over the dusty back roads to Sam's house, the original family home. Sam straightened his back and brushed his hands in front of him. He stared hard at Bruce as his grandson walked up to him.

"Plum came back last week and now she's disappeared. Her boyfriend was here. Very upset. And the police were here first thing this morning. Asking about her. What have you got to do with this?"

"I, I don't know what you mean." Bruce gestured with his open hands.

"Plum is missing. There is a reason. It must be because of our family. What we're doing or not doing. You are the head of the family now. You must know."

• • •

Something was wrong, Bruce sensed, as he approached his driveway. The front door was closed and the garage doors were open, as he had left them. He felt someone had been there. He parked the Land Rover away from the Volvo so dust would not settle on the clean surface. He turned off the engine of the Land Rover and listened. There was an odd stillness and a faint sizzling sound. Then he noticed the paintwork of the Volvo. It was no longer an immaculate white. The car's surface was bubbling. It was alive. He could see paint lifting off, turning black and yellow as the colorless acid ate into the metal. An acrid smell assaulted his nostrils. He saw the windows had been smashed and acid was eating into his taupe leather upholstery. As he approached the car, he could see the tires had been slashed. On top of the car were the barely discernible letters M–U–L–P Etched in acid! They had spelt her name backwards!

Bruce screamed.

Chuck was shutting the door to the glasshouse when he heard the scream. He ran over the hill as fast as he could to the house. He first saw the car, smoldering. Then he saw Bruce on his knees with his fists clenched and his eyes screwed up. Smoke began to pour out of the exposed engine as the heat from the acid set off a chain reaction and ignited the oil and grease around the manifold.

Chuck felt strangely detached as he dragged Bruce into the house. He left his brother on the white shag pile carpet and stood in the doorway to watch the car. Flames were lapping up the upholstery. A black pillar of smoke rose up from the engine. Chuck was reminded of the car explosion they had been talking about that morning. Bruce dry retched on the carpet.

. . .

Clovis wiped the dirt off his boots as he entered Mel's kitchen. Henry was at the door to greet them. He threw a quick smile to Clovis and a scowl at Mel who followed Henry into the bedroom. Clovis, as instructed, set about brewing tea for everyone. He tried not to hear their raised voices in the next room.

"This is totally insane! We've been dragged into some bizarre plot over which we have no control, let alone knowledge. I mean, do we know what's going on?" Henry paced across Mel's carpet. She sat on the bed, watching him.

They both heard Clovis call out that he had made a pot of tea. Mel went into the kitchen, followed by Henry.

"Excuse me, Clovis, but I came back here to work and think in peace. Instead of which ..." He threw up his hands. "Any news?"

Clovis told them about his trip to Pukekohe to see Shanghai Sam. He also informed them about Plum's previous employment at the Flamingo Paradise and why he and Plum had broken up.

Henry went outside and returned with the afternoon paper, the *Auckland Star*.

They're still there, pretending to be asleep." He turned to Mel.

"Must be waiting for me to return."

"MAN BURNT TO DEATH IN HOUSE," Henry read the headline. There was a picture of the remains of Clovis's house underneath. He read the lead article whilst Mel and Clovis crowded around him.

"Firemen early this morning dragged from a blazing house in Ponsonby the charred remains of a man. The fire was brought under control by 4:00 AM in a five-fire tender alarm that kept the residents of Summer Street nervously awake all night as firemen fought to stop the flames from spreading to the nearby wooden houses.

"The tenant of the house, Mr. C Tibet, was not in the house at the time, although the *Auckland Star* has ascertained that he had no insurance.

"'This whole area of Ponsonby is like a tinderbox,' Fire Chief Brian Fitzpatrick said at the scene of the tragedy. 'One spark and the whole neighborhood could have burnt down. We got here just in time.'

"Police later identified the remains of the burnt body from dental records as Hone Wilson, a well-known Maori Land rights activist.

"Jesus shit! That's Wiremu's brother. We saw him at the pub! Christ!" Henry interrupted himself.

Mel felt a taut wire in her stomach snap. She was as white as a sheet. She collapsed into a seat with her hands over her face.

"Then they did switch bodies," Henry muttered.

Mel was the first to sit up. She took out a lace handkerchief from her trouser pocket and wiped her face then blew her nose so loudly she laughed nervously whilst stealing a look at Henry.

"I'm so relieved it wasn't that man. But, I feel terrible for Wiremu. He must be devastated."

"We need a lawyer. I know just the man. We should have involved him sooner." Henry flung down the paper and stood up. "You two have to talk to the police, but only after you've met with my lawyer. We're going to find Wiremu' then we're going to smoke out this Turk and find Plum. Okay?"

Henry turned to Clovis who was trying to mouth air. Eventually Clovis spoke in a low whisper.

"If they did this to Hone, what would they do to Plum?"

• • •

"Perfect! I love SPIBBIES!" declared Alan Crispfeldt, who was dressed in a traditional three-piece pin-striped suit, shiny black Bostons and a red striped tie with a gold pin and a gold watch chain. Mr. Crispfeldt was an expert in the currency export laws that the New Zealand government had devised to stop money leaving the country. SPIBBIES stood for South Pacific Investment Bank that had branches in Auckland, Nauru, Hong Kong and Panama. He represented the Maori Land Rights Council and an odd mixture of wealthy investors and poor Maori activists.

"I understand entirely. You needn't say more," Alan Crispfeldt declared on Henry's first visit to Crispfeldt's chambers. "I have clients who want to send money out of the country, and you have money you want to get in. They are restricted to taking out $6,000 a year, each. You can bring in as much money as you like, but you will be taxed by the New Zealand government. You've already paid enough tax over there, so why be victimized with double taxation?"

He adjusted his gold-rimmed glasses and measured the effect of his words on his new client.

"Please be aware that as your lawyer I aim to obey all relevant laws. There is a huge difference between tax avoidance and tax fraud. The process I have developed is both elegant and legal. Although, with all the shell companies we set up and the shifting of money from New York to Nauru, Hong Kong or wherever, it becomes hopelessly complicated for a little government clerk to understand. So, through a shell company here, we assign your money, which is still in New York, to my client in Hong Kong. We do the transfers through SPIBBIES. They're very cooperative. My client gives you, through another shell company we set up here, his original money. It's really magic. So he hasn't exported any money and you haven't imported money. He has already paid taxes on that company's earnings, or should I say losses. So no ones been naughty and you both get what you want. It's like a shell game with no pea!

"Of course, we take a 2 percent administrative fee off the top, and we get the best currency exchange rates. And there's my 3 percent fee from the original sum." Crispfeldt slipped this in. One cabinet minister and the other politicians he dealt with always objected to these fees. How could they complain? Crispfeldt thought to himself. They were robbing the country anyway. Why couldn't he rob them? Henry Lotus seemed to be taking this all in good humor. He was not haggling at all. He must have stolen it.

"Then we can arrange for your money to be put into a money market fund here that's lent out at twenty-five to twenty-six percent interest. So it's quite profitable. You almost double your money when it comes down here, and you double it again in three years. It's almost as good as printing it!" He laughed at his own joke. Henry kept a straight face.

"I was thinking of keeping it liquid so I could buy some property."

"Oh yes, yes. Of course. We can arrange that too. Anything you like. Short-term loans can fetch even higher rates. Twenty-eight percent is no problem. At the moment."

Henry sighed. Crispfeldt was his kind of lawyer. Ultra respectable on the outside and completely unscrupulous on the inside. What you would call, in New York, a total sleazebag. Or was it scumbag?

"Should've done this sooner," Henry muttered.

"You've a lawyer?" Clovis tried not to be surprised.

"Of course." Henry noticed Mel was rereading the article on the fire.

Henry was unsure how much experience Crispfeldt had in arson and homicide cases, but he knew the lawyer had a shrewd mind and the right connections. He dialed the number.

"Crispfeldt speaking."

"This is Henry Lotus."

"Oh yes, yes. How are you Henry old boy?"

"Fucked, Alan. Fucked. Have you read the *Star*?"

"Yes."

"Well, I'm involved in that fire."

"Do you know the Wilsons?"

"Yes."

"Say no more. Come over right away." Crispfeldt hung up. He had lost one client today. Hone's photo was on the front page of the afternoon paper. It was a bad sign.

Tony Look drove to Bruce's house. Chuck opened the door. Bruce sat upright in his rocking chair, his face immobile. Chuck paced up and down the shag pile carpet. Tony stood in the middle of the living room with his tongue out and his tie loosened. He watched Chuck's feet wear down the pile.

"No. You're wrong, Tony. We can't burn it now. If we back down we'll never be free!" Chuck reasoned.

"Chuck's right." Bruce spoke at last. "They'll force us to grow their dope on our land on their terms. We can't give in. And aren't we forgetting Plum? Her name was on the car? It's no coincidence that she disappeared and Sam's been visited by the police."

"My wife says Plum is a whore and she will only bring misfortune on our family," Tony muttered.

Chuck remembered catching Tony and Plum behind a shed after school. Plum was barely thirteen and Tony had her knickers down and his hand up her skirt.

"Remember Plum's parents? How they died?" Bruce glared at Chuck and Tony.

"What do you mean?" Tony shot back. He jumped as the phone rang.

Terry Turner washed his hands in the back of the workshop, a dirty concrete building behind his large used car lot on Ellerslie Road. He flung the blue rubber gloves into a plastic crate next to some auto spray equipment and turned to John Eustace.

"You can't say I don't have an acidic sense of humor." Terry spoke in his soft high-pitched voice. John allowed himself a grin. He did not have to answer. He had heard the same pun twice on the drive back from Pukekohe.

"I hope they got the message on the hood." Terry wiped his hands on a towel. "They can read backwards. I only hope it sunk in."

John's grin broke into a wide smile.

"They're trying to be hoods, anyway. And they'll get burned! Clean up that car and we'll get outta here. Don't leave a speck of dust on it. It's gotta look like it never left the lot."

Terry the Turk gained a couple of inches in his Frye cowboy boots tucked over his black trousers. He wore a black cotton shirt open at the neck to show a Krugger-and gleaming from a thick gold chain.

Terry waited by the Lincoln. He watched John change the license plates back. John drove Terry to a phone booth off a side street in Panmure. He never made any important phone calls from his car lot or the Flamingo or his home. He even assumed the nearby payphones were tapped.

Terry dialed the number he had memorized and fed enough coins into the phone box for his call to Pukekohe.

Bruce pressed the receiver to his ear but did not speak. Terry, in a Maori voice, spoke slowly, as if addressing a child.

"We cleaned your car today, boy. We'll clean up your crop too if you'se don't listen carefully. You're to load it up in a truck. We know you'se have harvested it and it's ready to be bagged. Put it all in big plastic bags. We'll call you'se on Sunday evening to tell ya where to deliver it. No Kung Fu stuff."

"Who are you?!" Bruce demanded. "I want your name!" Bruce stood up, his eyes half closed.

"Wilson," Terry spat out. "That's all you're getting, boy. Call you Sunday, at five, when the sun sets over your cabbages!" Terry hung up and let out a high-pitched chuckle.

Bruce replaced the receiver. He recounted the exact words of the Maori to Tony and Chuck then collapsed into his chair covering his face with his hands. Chuck paced across the shag pile carpet while Tony stood in front of the painting entitled Stag at Bay.

"It's not possible. It's just not possible."

"Perhaps it's a trick," Chuck stopped in front of Bruce.

"It's not business, it's extortion, and he didn't even mention Plum. Right?" Tony added.

"I didn't want to mention her name to him. So where is she, if she's involved in this?"

"How many Wilsons are there?" Tony was trying to think rationally.

"Hundreds. And we don't know where to look first. Auckland? Otahuhu? Here? It's Tuesday night. We have less than five days to do as he says, or," Bruce took a deep breath, "or something."

"Four, and we've got to find Plum. She must be behind this," Tony insisted.

"She doesn't even know we've been growing this," Chuck retorted. "She could have walked out on her boyfriend and gone off with someone else."

"I don't know, Chuck. If the police are so interested in talking to her, we should be too. It's too much of a coincidence she's missing."

"I agree," Tony added.

"OK. How?" Chuck gave in. He had forgotten how forgiving his two brothers had been when they checked him out of Oakley Hospital after his heroin overdose. How they took him back to the farm and supported him whilst he went through another nerve-racking withdrawal. They had never mentioned it to him. "We have to save the crop as well."

"Or destroy it." Tony was thinking the unthinkable. It would be better to see it burn than hand it over to someone else who could come back next year and force them to repeat the process.

"Remember we used to dream of having a gang?" Bruce looked at his two brothers. He wanted their full attention.

"As kids we used to go charging down to the milk bar in Pukekohe on our 100 cc farm bikes."

"You only had a 50 cc," Tony reminded Chuck.

"Well, we should put that together now, tonight."

"Most of our relatives are too stick-in-the-mud. Besides, we can't tell them about our crop." Chuck dampened Bruce's enthusiasm.

"Martin and Rick know about it," Tony added.

"Yeah." Bruce began to smile. "We only have to tell them Plum is kidnapped, and they'll move heaven and earth to find her. You know how they really like her."

"I don't think 'like' is the right word," Chuck added.

"They can help dig out this Wilson and find Plum."

"Okay. I'll go to see the Wongs." Chuck went to get his helmet and leather jacket.

"We're in this now till the end. I said we'd bitten off more than we could chew when Chuck planted the seedlings. Well, we have. We're in this all the way." Tony stood up and embraced Chuck who already had his black helmet on. Bruce stood up and hugged them both, knocking his head on Chuck's visor. They were silent as they held each other.

"Henry Lotus and Clovis Tibet. Sounds like something out of a Gilbert and Sullivan opera." He begun to hum a melody from one of their operas but stopped when he noticed his guests were not amused.

They sat on red leather chairs and looked at the oak paneled walls with watercolors of 19th century sailing ships. Henry tried to explain the series of events that brought them to Alan Crispfeldt's office, but Mel and Clovis interrupted him. Alan sat behind his large kauri desk and eyed his cocktail cabinet opposite.

"You have to start from the beginning. I'm lost," Alan said as he chewed on his gold-rimmed glasses.

Henry excused himself to use the bathroom. He had spotted a tall wooden filing cabinet where Alan's secretary sat, and he now tried the first cabinet but it was locked. He opened a desk drawer and found a set of keys. He opened the cabinets one by one until he came to the client files marked "W." He took a scrap of paper from the desk and wrote down Wiremu Wilson's addresses, one in Parnell and one in Northland.

Henry walked into the office and closed the heavy wooden doors behind him then ran his wet hands through his hair as Mel gave him a quick questioning look.

"Well, the only thing to do is go and see them, then we'll clear this up. You've done nothing wrong. And Plum Blossom might be a clue to this entire regrettable episode." Alan sighed. He hated going to Police Headquarters. "I'll go with them and see that everything goes right, and we'll settle up later?"

The black Rover 90 crawled out of its parking space in the basement of the Albert Street garage. Alan Crispfeldt tried to cheer up his three morbid-faced passengers. Henry turned from the front seat to give Mel a quick wink.

"Drop me off here, Alan. I'll get a cab home. Bye, love. Clovis, just be cool and let Alan do all the talking." He turned in his seat to shake hands with his lawyer before slamming the door too hard. Alan winced and drove to Cook Street.

The first thing Clovis saw when he stepped up to the main counter were a stack of 8 x 10 black and white photographs of Plum Blossom on the counter, reproductions of her University of Auckland ID photograph.

Crispfeldt had phoned ahead and the duty sergeant expected him. Mel and Clovis stared at the photograph. The three visitors were escorted to an unmarked office on the fifth floor. It was a small room painted pale blue.

Alan Crispfeldt felt like a regular at an exclusive restaurant who had been made to wait too long for a table. He hoped Inspector Bernard Grimble would not be heading this investigation. Clovis had not remembered the name of the detective who had questioned him. Alan knew Inspector Grimble had a vendetta against the Wilson brothers, and Crispfeldt, because he represented the Wilsons.

The door flew open. A tall man with thick eyebrows entered and stared hard at Mel and Clovis. Clovis not only recognized him from earlier, but also felt he was back in school, about to be interrogated by the headmaster.

"Evening. I'm Inspector Grimble. Glad you came in. I want to take statements from both of you," he said in a soft deep voice, smiling at his captive audience. The inspector ignored Crispfeldt. The lawyer stuck his thumbs in his waistcoat pockets and puffed up his chest.

"Ah! Mr. Crispfeldt. Forgot about you there." Grimble wore a light grey suit, a little worn around the elbows and knees, but presentable for a senior policeman.

"What did Plum Blossom actually do at the Flamingo Paradise?" The inspector rephrased a question he had asked earlier. They were not telling everything, which was very common in his line of work, but for two well-dressed professionals, it was annoying.

"She was a masseuse."

"Come, come, Clovis. Do you expect me to believe that? Our men routinely raid the place. Vice is always prosecuting girls there who'll do anything for a price."

"Well, Plum didn't! Okay?"

"Did she say that to you?"

"Yes."

"What were her exact words?"

"Inspector, I must protest. The man's already told you this twice. She's missing. Give him some room, will you? Can't you see he's disturbed about her disappearance? You're treating him like a common criminal, yet he wants to help you." Crispfeldt stared down the inspector.

"Thank you, Mr. Crispfeldt. Point well taken." The policeman turned to Clovis and changed his tone. "Excuse my curiosity, but I have to know everything. There might be a clue, a hint of something you might have forgotten, something that could be vital to me. It's painful but necessary. I trust you understand?"

Clovis nodded. The last two sentences were identical to what he heard at the airport before he got the gloved hand treatment. How much understanding did he need?

"Now, Clovis, did Plum Blossom ever mention anything about a Terry Turner?"

"No. She never said that name to me. Who is he?" He was not lying. Wiremu had been the one to tell him about Turner, and he could not mention Wiremu's name.

Crispfeldt silently fumed. He would have something to say to Commissioner Thompson, when they met at the next Governor General's garden party, in two Sundays. The inspector had pioneered the use of the "no search warrant-forced entry" tactic on known anti-apartheid organizers on the basis that all such dissidents were drug users. "It stands to reason that these people who do not respect the rights of others to enjoy sport without politics are also the same people who indulge in illegal narcotics." Crispfeldt still remembered the inspector's quote from an interview in *New Zealand Woman's Weekly*. He hoped one day to throw the quote back in the cop's face before a hostile jury. But he had other matters to take care of now, including the abuse of his client, Mr. Tibet.

"So you were sitting out on Dr. Johnson's patio by yourself and your girlfriend, whom you are very close to, just disappeared from the front room? She got up, went outside and poof! Was gone? And you didn't hear?"

"Yes. Exactly. That's what I've told you three times already." Clovis was trying to control his temper. Crispfeldt made calming gestures behind the inspector's back.

• • •

One hour before midnight the Flamingo Paradise came alive. Locals thrown out of pubs, country boys visiting the big city and one speculative physicist came to the massage parlor.

A giant in a white ten-gallon hat and red cowboy boots was ahead of Henry.

"Geeve me a gurl with biig tiits! I'm from Tex-ass and I wanna gurlie with biiig tiiits!"

Henry thought this a hard act to follow as he signed in at the front desk under the name Stephen Hawkins. He had met the physicist after a lecture at MIT. What would Hawkins make of all this?

Oiled pine planks had been nailed over the existing walls to give the appearance of a Scandinavian health spa. A red lightbulb hung from the ceiling. Two thin women wearing white towels and too much mascara chewed gum behind the counter. They had looked blankly at Henry when he signed up for a sauna and towel, $10, followed by a back massage for $46 plus tip. The Texan in front of him had opted for the personal bubble bath, $60 plus tip, and a full deep massage for another $60, plus tip. The two girls watched Henry's tight buns in blue jeans disappear round the corner to the dressing room. They put him down for a quick hand job, $20. What a waste. The unposted rates for extras were: $40 for a blow job, no swallowing, $60 for coming in the mouth and $100 for full insertion. French or Greek was negotiable, depending on the girl. She kept half the money and gave the other half to the manager, the big scary guy.

Henry folded his clothes up and locked them in a rusty locker. He put the key on an elastic band around his wrist. There was a group of three farmers on the other side of the locker room who were having trouble wrapping the towels around their waists. The towels were not big enough. The Texan had his back coyly turned away as he unfolded the rolls of fat from within the confines of his polyester leisure suit. He was singing "The Yellow Rose of Texas," probably to give himself courage, Henry thought.

Henry wrapped a towel around his waist and walked out into the corridor, turned left then right and pushed a heavy wooden door open. He found himself in the sauna. The pine slatted hot box had an electric sauna unit in one corner with dry stones on top of the red elements. He was relieved the three country boys and the Texan did not join him. He wanted some time to himself to think about the last five days. Why had he joined Wiremu and his back door escape? Even if he had gone back to Clovis's house without Wiremu, he would still be mixed up in Plum's disappearance. Nothing made any sense to him.

He did know that Plum used to work here, so he planned to casually ask the masseuse about her. If she did not know, perhaps another masseuse would. He could spend the rest of the night getting his back rubbed and handing out unearned tips. They'll think me a pervert, he mused, or a cop.

Two men clutching their small towels around their distended bellies burst into the sauna. The air became thick with beer and onion smells. Henry sat on his towel and looked down at his penis. At least he could see it. He had a flat stomach, because he hardly ate. His New York diet had consisted of bagels with cream cheese, coffee and moussaka at the local Greek deli. He tried not to stare at the two men opposite as they eased down onto the hot planks.

"Fuck! It's hot," the first one said.

"Asshole. It's a suana!" the second replied.

The intercom crackled and Stephen Hawkins was summoned to Room 9. The two men nudged each other. One of them winked at Henry as if he was going to a rather uncomfortable medical examination. The other whispered good luck. What was the big deal? Henry thought. Mel could do things that most of these girls had not heard of.

Henry wandered through the narrow labyrinth of pine-slatted corridors until he came to the room marked "9." He knocked and walked in. A Maori girl stood to one side with her big brown eyes cast down. She had long straight hair past her shoulders and a narrow straight nose. She wore the mandatory towel wrapped tightly around her that pressed down her small adolescent breasts. Oh no, Henry thought. Who is going to initiate whom? She was standing by the massage table, a brown vinyl slab six foot long and at least two feet wide, at waist height. He could hear through the thin walls a muffled voice declaiming: "I wanna guurl with biiig tiiits!" How did the Texan fit on this? Did it break?

Henry unwrapped himself and leapt onto the table. He lay on his stomach and put the towel under his chin. He would, he decided, enjoy this. He introduced himself as Stephen Hawkins. The girl did not reply. She was still recovering from her first client on her first day at the Flamingo; an oaf called Lance who would not take no for an answer. She could still hear his whiny Pakeha voice in her ears. "Come on, girl. Your type loves it. Let Lance give it to you for free. It's unlike anything else you've had. The girls in Hamilton can't get enough of it."

She poured some baby oil into the palm of her hand. She carefully began to rub it over his back, leaning into her hands with a smooth slow rhythm. At least this Pakeha had not tried to jump her or wave his penis at her.

The smell of the oil bought back memories to Henry: of Saturday nights parked on top of Mount Eden in his little car, trying to unwrap a condom and struggling to remove the girdle of a drunken sixteen-year-old girl. To think girls wore girdles then. The lubrication of memory!

Henry's mind was jolted back to the present when the young Maori ran her hands down his thighs. He was ticklish there, and she had bypassed his exposed buttocks. As she pushed her palms down his thigh biceps and over his calves, Henry wanted to reassure her that he had no intention of coming on to her. He had a girlfriend, a steady girlfriend. What was the right term? Lover? Paramour? Housemate? Here he was, naked, facedown on a vinyl massage table under a dim red light in a tiny room in the Flamingo Paradise, deep in thought about Mel as the Maori pushed her thumbs into the back of his calf muscles.

She massaged Henry's feet. He turned his head slightly and smiled at her. She smiled back, her towel still tightly wrapped around her.

"What's your name?" he managed, as she pulled at his big toes so that they snapped.

"Moana."

"Ah. Ouch! The ocean. That's a nice name. What tribe are you?"

"Ngapuhi."

"Got some good friends you might know." Henry felt her hands come up to massage his back again. She ran her fist up his spine, not too hard, but the sensation was thrilling. He thought her hands might communicate more than her eyes.

"Do you know Wiremu Wilson?" he asked as Moana worked his left shoulder. Her hands stopped for a second. Then she switched to his right shoulder. She did not answer. It was the last name she wanted to hear in that place, on her first night.

Henry was now concentrating so hard on how to draw out his reticent masseuse that when he rolled over, he did not display an erection, despite his thoughts about Mel.

"Oh. Excuse me," he mumbled, embarrassed. He took the towel and draped it over his hips. Looking up, he caught her eyes. She was staring not at his limp penis, but at his greenstone pendant. She caught herself putting her left hand to her mouth.

"Where did you get it?" she uttered.

Henry sat up on the bench. Careful to keep himself covered, he held the pendant in his right hand as she stared at it.

"Wiremu Wilson gave it to me a long time ago. I helped him out. He was in a bit of trouble."

"It must've been some trouble." She could not keep her eyes off the greenstone.

"But not as bad as what happened last week."

Moana took a step back. Her facial expression changed to one of hostility.

"Who are you?"

"I told you, Stephen Hawkins." He realized he could not tell her his real name now.

"Are you a cop?"

"Don't be silly. Do I look like a cop?"

Moana examined him up and down, as if this was the first time she had seen him.

"You don't smell like one."

"Well. That's it then. Isn't it?" Henry was upset that there was even a remote possibility that he would be taken for an undercover cop.

"I'll tell you why I'm here. Okay?" He watched Moana's face calm down. "Wiremu is a friend of mine. His brother was murdered and placed in a friend's house in Ponsonby. That friend is Plum Blossom. She's now missing. Probably abducted. She used to work here. For Terry the Turk."

Moana tried to hide her shock. She had vivid memories of Hone when she was younger and he would visit from Wellington, the great Maori scholar who was unaffected by Pakeha ways. There were so many confused thoughts and feelings struggling to come out of her. She did not know if she could afford to cry. All she could do was stand there, speechless, trying to control her cheeks from moving.

"I need your help, Moana. I need to know where Plum is," Henry whispered. He tied his towel tightly around his waist. "It will help Wiremu. It's absolutely necessary."

She lowered her head and whispered, "Okay."

"I'll have my phone number on the money I'll give you. Call me." He walked to the door. "By the way. You give a fantastic massage."

Showered and dressed, Henry walked up to Moana at the front desk with the two other women. He slipped her a $50 tip in tens without the others seeing. On the back of one $10 note was his phone number. Moana tucked this between her breasts. Then he openly gave her another $30. She, in some small way, was about to help Wiremu in seeking utu, revenge, for his brother's death. And the money helped. She would hide the money in a secret place where she lived. One day she planned to return to Hokianga, rich.

Moana had to declare all her earnings to the older woman who sat behind the counter and watched everything. The woman had only to look at Moana to send a shiver of fear down her spine.

As he walked down the front steps, Henry bumped into a small bald man dressed in a black and white houndstooth jacket, accompanied by a huge man who glared at him. Henry tried not to draw attention to himself as the two men walked into the Flamingo Paradise as if they owned it.

"See, we're attracting young professionals. It's all in the marketing," the short man said.

Henry found a taxi at a stand two blocks north and headed to the address he had from Crispfeldt's files. At the top of Bassett Drive he walked down a few houses before he came to the right address. The house was down a right-of-way, overgrown with weeds. There was no car in the driveway, no lights on in the house. He knocked twice. The door cracked open letting out a strong musty smell. Henry walked into the hallway and noticed a faint light coming from the door to the front room. He leaned against the door.

"Wiremu? It's me, Henry," he whispered as the door moved. He could see a tall beeswax candle burning on the floor and behind, the face of Wiremu slumped in an armchair, staring into the light.

Henry entered the room and sat opposite Wiremu. Wiremu held a branch of kawakawa leaves in both hands that he would rustle every few seconds to the secret rhythm of his mourning. He did not acknowledge Henry.

Wiremu recited a waiata tangi. His voice was low and soft. The words rose from the back of his throat and were joined by tears as he sang for his lost brother.

"Te Po nui, te Po roa, te Po kerekere, te Po uriuri, te Po tangotango."

"Te Po nui, te Po roa, te Po kerekere, te Po uriuri, te Po tangotango."

(The great night, long night, deep night, dense night, dark night.)

Henry fingered his jade pendant. The waiata, repeated no more than three notes in tone, mesmerized him. He was filled with sadness. The kawakawa leaves rustled like dead bones.

"He's gone." Wiremu spoke in a low monotone. "We started this together. For a cause. We made the Pakeha high. We got rich so we'd buy back our land." He drew in a deep breath and sighed. The candle flickered, sending Henry's shadow across the far wall.

"There was a lot more at stake. Even if we didn't recognize their laws. They are not our laws. We had no say in drafting them." He paused but remained motionless. "Money. Greed. The god of Manon. That's the cause. That's why Hone was taken."

Henry watched the candle flicker.

"It had to be Hone." Wiremu turned his head to stare at Henry who gave a start. "I sent him to his death. I phoned him. Told him where the keys were. Hone went to the car. To his death. They thought he was me. They wanted to kill me."

Henry would have to recount this to Mel before he understood what Wiremu had confessed.

"He's on a slab now. Being dissected by the cops. That's the final insult. No dignity for a dead Maori."

Wiremu bowed his head and repeated the waiata.

"Te Po nui, te Po roa, te Po kerekere, te Po uriuri, te Po tangotango."

Henry stayed with him, watching the candle burn down.

"Te Po nui, te Po roa, te Po kerekere, te Po uriuri, te Po tangotango."

• • •

Mel opened her eyes wide when she heard footsteps in the hall, lighter than Henry's. She gripped the sides of the bathtub prepared to leap out of the water. What if it was the man with the baseball bat, come back for vengeance? She heard the footsteps continue down the hall to her bedroom. The light was switched on, then the feet came back to her bathroom door.

"Is that you, Mel?" Henry whispered. He opened the door.

"You gave me a fright." Mel sighed.

He took his clothes off in a hurry and slid into the bath. The water flowed over the sides onto the linoleum floor. She eased down to meet his submerged body and feel him press against her. He kissed her and held her as close as he could. More water slopped onto the floor.

"Henry? What's got into you?"

"You look so magnificent."

"Have you something to hide? Or clean?"

"Something to tell you, actually. A lot's happened tonight."

"You're telling me."

"No. Really. I saw Wiremu."

"And?"

"You know all that stuff I said on the plane coming over," he started.

"What stuff?" She did not understand what he was talking about.

"You know. About how we should live like free human beings having an open relationship. And we shouldn't feel fettered, you know, tied to each other."

"Oh. That stuff."

"Well, I've been thinking. It came to me in the Flamingo Paradise."

"I hope it wasn't organic."

"No, no. You're ruining it," he whispered.

"Ruining what?"

"Er, this."

"This?"

"My a-approach." Henry found this more difficult than he imagined.

Mel's expression kept changing.

"Well, I understand why you came to New York to see me. If you hadn't've flown in, I don't know what would've happened."

"Postcards from Romania."

"I'd be in a cell in Albania."

"They're all the same. Dingy."

"Anyway. You're not making this any easier. Really. I'm serious now. I came to this revelation tonight about myself and you. And I..." He stopped.

"Yes?" Mel dared to smile.

"Could you add some hot water? It's getting cold."

Mel twisted around to open up the hot tap and push the water back to Henry. His jeans and shirt were soaked on the floor.

"Is this too uncomfortable for you?" she asked.

"I think I sowed some seeds there."

"Seeds? You said sowing seeds?"

"I should get a call from a young girl working there. Although I have no idea why a relative of Wiremu would be working in Terry the Turk's place."

"Working girl? You know I see them in my practice. What did you do?"

Plum ate the hardboiled egg and white toast that Terry had left for her on a tray inside her cell. She ate off a plastic plate with a plastic knife and sipped cold milky tea from a polystyrene cup. She felt sick. She finished her toast and burped. She could not get out of her mind the man she had seen outside her window in Ponsonby.

She knew that Terry the Turk had abducted her from the couch she had slept on in Mel's living room. Had the others been awakened? What had happened to them? What were they doing to find her? What had Terry planned for her?

Her captor had designed the space carefully when he had his basement excavated three years ago. The real basement was only accessible from a door in the long carpeted hallway upstairs on the ground floor. The doorway led to a concrete stairwell. A concealed door in a small closet on one end wall opened into another part of the basement that had been excavated beyond the house's original foundations. In the hidden basement was a small cell that contained a cot, a chair and a bucket.

As soon as John had regained consciousness, he had walked back to his Lincoln and radioed to Terry. Terry ordered him to torch the house and drive back. Then John reached into his pockets and found that his keys had been stolen and money taken out of his wallet. Terry, after being contacted again, improvised his new plan and told John to wait in the back seat of the car with his handheld radio next to him, once he had set the candles.

Back in the house, John had gathered together all the spare paper he could find and neatly stacked it in a small closet near the kitchen. He had taken the wax candle from the front room, not the beeswax, and cut it in half. He lit both of them atop the papers. It would be textbook arson. The light from the two candles could not be seen through the closet door and no draft would blow out their flames. He estimated he had about half an hour before the candles burnt to their base and ignited the papers. The house was so dry it would erupt into an inferno.

John went back to the car and lay down in the back seat. In the darkness he relaxed even though his neck hurt. He waited to hear from Terry. He could only wish that his victim, greedy for the American car, would appear. He hoped it was the person who had assaulted him. In his hands was a thin strand of high tensile wire that had a small wooden handle at each end.

What a bonus, Terry mused as he looked through the peephole glass to see Plum Blossom sitting on her unmade bed, running her hands through her unkempt hair. John had not only burnt down her house, but he had scorched a Maori, Wiremu Wilson's brother. What luck! A war was brewing between Maori and Chinese. How did that fat Maori get into the house when he was already dead? Could Maoris do that sort of thing? No. John had told him he had seen the two cops do it as he was hiding around the corner, waiting and listening for Terry to appear. One of the cops was Inspector Grimble, John recalled.

"Oh lovely!" Terry had explained. "That's all we need. That bugger on our backs!" Since when were they in the business of moving bodies from the scene of the crime? What was Grimble up to? Perhaps Terry should complain to the police commissioner through one of the Samoan neighbors, an independent witness coached and paid for by Terry. Then he thought better of it. You could be too smart. Grimble was one cunning cop. The police were a law unto themselves. Terry shook his head. What was the country coming to? Who could you trust these days?

And what luck to have Hei Hei call at precisely the right moment to tell him of Hone's plan to steal the car.

Terry could not have gone wrong. He had ordered John to grab the keys and to get out of the car as soon as he had finished with Hone and wait around the corner. Terry circled around the block to make sure there were no police staking out the house, then he got John to walk back around the corner and pick up the black Lincoln. Right under the cops' noses, he found out later from John. The cops were inside the house! Probably playing with the dead body. Maybe Grimble was dancing with it or measuring its prick! And they hadn't spotted the candles in the closet! And these were their smartest cops!

Terry had the Town Car broken down into spare parts that night, in his Ellerslie garage, to be shipped to Australia where it would fetch more than it would in one piece in Auckland.

Acquiring Plum had been a stroke of luck. One of John's older masseuses had spotted Plum Blossom at the new Women's Clinic in Ponsonby. Knowing that John and Terry would pay a high price for information about her appearance back in New Zealand, the girl had found out Plum's address from the doctor's front office. Her file had been left on the counter. Terry gave her fifty dollars with the promise of another fifty if she tested negative for any sexually transmitted disease.

He dispatched John to scout around Plum's house. He found her at home with the doors locked. He caught a glimpse through a window of a large Maori. John had waited in his car for hours until a BMW drew up and a tall woman and a red-bearded man walked into the house. Later, he followed the car to a side street off Mount Eden. In fact, it was the other side of Mount Eden from Terry's house. He had seen Plum Blossom, the red-bearded man, the tall woman, another man and Wiremu Wilson slip into the house.

"Curiouser and curiouser. Now why would she come back after all this time? Does she think I've forgotten?

I never forget or forgive. Hah! And she's got protection of some Maori gang? What is going on?" he thought aloud, after John delivered his report. "The trouble with cops is they don't think creative. When I go to work, I have a plan, then I have another plan, and then I have a backup. It's not that things go wrong as they go different. The universe is a weird place, and it would be foolish if you thought it always conformed to the way you think it should.

"Now take this. It's a miniaturized handheld radio that uses a radio frequency unused in this country. It's from Aussie. They can't listen in on us. But we can listen in on them with this older scanner."

John smiled. He enjoyed the performance more than the substance. But it was better if he played dumb.

Chapter Six

Wednesday

Henry rolled over onto his side. He looked at his watch in the light of the bedside lamp. Five AM. He did not feel tired. He turned to kiss Mel who was flat on her back. Her eyes were wide open as she stared at the ceiling. She could not move. The bed linen had been pushed onto the floor. The light made her skin pink.

He put his other arm around her and held his lips to her right cheek. His pendant swung over her shoulder and tickled her. She playfully bit him. Why was she so happy, yet so afraid?

Terry started his business every morning at the breakfast table with John. The house, made of stone and native timbers, was on a cul-de-sac, surrounded by a seven-foot-high wall.

"Goddammit! Look at this. Will you look at this!" Terry put down his bone china teacup and stuck his right index finger at the front page of the *New Zealand Herald*, which showed Plum Blossom's photograph.

John carefully lifted the last two pieces of toast out of the pop-up toaster. He knew Terry would yell at him if he made too many crumbs. He moved his sore neck to scan the front page. His body ached from the assault two nights ago.

"Saw it on the way over. All the cops have her picture, Terry."

"Really? Who told you?"

"That new joker at your burger place. Told me last night, after I dropped you off. Went over there to check on the place and get a Hawaiian."

Terry drained his cup and eyed John.

"You're going to get fat. All those late night calories and no exercise."

John grinned as he helped himself to more marmalade.

"You haven't been back to that doctor's house, have you? I thought we agreed that revenge would come about in a different way. The idea is to eliminate the opposition. Yes?" Terry stared at John to make sure this had sunk in.

"How is she?" John asked, to break the silence.

"Oh, fine."

"Did she say anything?"

"Nothing."

"Do you think I should go in and talk to her a little?" John grinned. "You know. The good cop, bad cop routine."

"No, John. It's very sweet of you to offer your services. Even if they give up their crop, we might have to dispose of her, because of this." Terry pointed to the front page again. "This has complicated everything."

"Then it doesn't matter then, does it? What I do?"

"Save it. We might need her yet. In one piece. There's no knowing what they might do. They're amateurs, and they're desperate. Don't look so glum. Make us some more tea.

"Tomorrow we'll go down to Pukekohe and check out those greenhouses. They couldn't possibly do it all by Sunday. If they haven't started packing, we'll have to get creative."

John Eustace put the kettle on. He knew exactly what his boss meant by the word creative.

Sergeant Cadd reported to Inspector Bernie Grimble's office promptly at 8:00 AM.

The inspector's office was an organized mess. Computer printouts, fingerprint cards and thick manila folders were piled up on his grey metal desk. The inspector had his own terminal on another small table that gave him direct access to the centralized police files at the Wanganui Computer Center.

A giant map of Auckland filled the other wall. Different colored pins were stuck in key locations.

Grimble was engrossed in the late edition of the *New Zealand Herald*. He was frowning. Large photographs of Hone Wilson and Plum Blossom were on the front page with the banner headline: MAORI ACTIVIST BURNT TO DEATH. STUDENT BEAUTY MISSING. Thank heavens the *Herald*'s editor, also a Mt. Albert old boy and a friend of Bernie's, had assigned an alcoholic to this case, a reporter who, close to retirement, would be content to read police reports and be hand-fed shreds of information labeled exclusive.

"There you are, Cadd." Grimble peered over his paper.

"The thing about Grimble," Cadd had said to his girlfriend, Donna, whilst they were reading in bed the other night, "is that he's invariably right. He doesn't give a hoot about public opinion or what that liberal Jew mayor says."

Grimble would have been surprised to know Cadd read. His current book was about tunnel warfare in Vietnam. He regretted not having volunteered to go over. It would have been good on his record, more so than playing rugby for the Auckland First Fifteen.

"What about the Three Kings murderer, you know, whatshisname." Donna looked up from her book. They were a respectable couple, squeezed shoulder to shoulder in his double bed.

"Well, that might've been the wrong man. But he got a conviction. That's what counts."

"You admire him, don't you?"

"Of course. He might not be perfect, but…"

"Do you want to be like him?"

"Yes and no. I mean, no. He's like a warning. What not to become. Sometimes he goes too far. You know?"

"No. I don't," Donna replied, worried.

"Look at this!" Grimble motioned Cadd to take a seat as he flung down the paper. "They're playing up Wilson as a peaceful intellectual. What tripe. They're growing dope up north. I've talked to Wally in Vice, and he reckons with the short supply right now, the Wilsons, I mean Wilson, will try to sell it down here for top prices. Wally also thinks this is a sure sign a major drug war is brewing."

"Who's the source on that?"

"Wally wouldn't say. You know how they are over there. Wally's a good cop, but he's always two steps behind. Anyway, he wants in on this. Which is good because we need all the manpower we can get now. And he talked about Terry the Turk." Grimble's voice trailed off.

"Oh him." Cadd had no idea who Terry the Turk was.

"Plum Blossom filed a tax return before she left the country and got a refund based on her earnings from the Flamingo Paradise." Grimble tapped a computer printout next to him. He had accessed this information himself last night after finishing his interview with Dr. Johnson and Clovis Tibet. Simply by dialing up and entering his password, he was able to call up the Inland Revenue Services tax records on all three of them.

"Do you think it's a coincidence they came in with that lawyer Crispfeldt? Him representing the Wilsons."

"Good question." Grimble knotted his eyebrows. "Could be. Maybe Wiremu will turn up at the tangi. I doubt if he'll come to collect the corpse from the morgue. The report came in from South. A police dog could have done a better job. Plum Blossom's grandfather did not know she had come back from New York. But he wasn't exactly loquacious. We're going to go down there ourselves. We can pick up some cheap vegetables as well. Does your girlfriend cook?"

"No. Like this."

Ricky Wong threw the five-pointed ninja star at the wall. It sunk into Bruce Lee's black hair.

"Sorry, Bruce." He saluted the poster. Fifteen other throwing stars were stuck in the poster, eleven in Bruce. The rest were on the floor.

"Okay. Let me." Martin Wong took the remaining star, made it disappear in his right hand, flung his hand back and flicked his wrist. The star pierced Bruce Lee's right ear.

"Hey! Bruce Van Gogh!" Martin shouted.

Boxes of martial arts supplies shipped from Hong Kong by an uncle were stacked in the room. The Wong brothers had overcome a new law that required that these weapons be used solely in a dojo. They supplied a preprinted and signed letter from a martial arts instructor stating that such weapons would never leave the dojo. They had sold hundreds of these letters for $14.95. A new shipment of twelve-inch long nunchaku had arrived.

"How many Maori boys in Mangere have knocked themselves out spinning chucks over their heads? Er?" Ricky broke open another carton.

"Bruce is really going to get nailed with that dope he's growing down there," Ricky added.

"Why? Why are you saying that now?" Martin squatted by the poster and picked up the stars. They had acted merely as a conduit between an eccentric plant geneticist and the Looks. The geneticist had graded all the seeds at the University with a new electron microscope.

"There's word out that a war's brewing between Maoris and Terry Turner. Something to do with a fire Monday night. One Maori got burnt to death."

"What has that got to do with Bruce and Chuck?" Martin flicked a star at the poster. The point connected to the wall then fell out.

Ricky had unwrapped a nunchaku and checked the swivel. He held a chuck in each hand then slowly started to rotate one.

"They're going to be drawn into it whether they like it or not because of what they're growing and who they are."

Ricky held the chucks aloft.

"Stand back," he muttered. This was unnecessary, as Martin had moved to the farthest point in the room.

The chuck moved so fast in the air that Martin could not see it. He did hear the deadly whooshing sound as it swiveled and twirled around Ricky's body.

Ricky caught the spinning chuck above his head and bowed to Martin.

"Let's spar," Ricky countered. "Only, no contact."

Ricky threw the chucks back into the box and went into a side double-fist pose. There was a loud knock at the front door. Martin peeked through the curtains to see Chuck Look holding his helmet in his hands. "Shit," he muttered. "Something must be wrong."

The Wongs listened in silence as Chuck told them what happened to Bruce's Volvo, the disappearance of Plum Blossom, the police visit to Sam, how Sam had summoned Bruce and the threatening phone call.

"You sure Bruce recognized that Maori voice?" Ricky asked. They sat at the kitchen table drinking green tea out of bowls.

"He says so."

"Why would they take Plum?" Martin could still remember how he had put his hand up her skirt when he sat next to her at a New Year's Party in Pukekohe, ten years ago. She had been a precocious eleven.

"I didn't know she was back." Ricky sighed. "Didn't she leave the country because it was too hot for her to work at that massage parlor?"

"Yeah." Chuck bowed his head.

"Then why did she come back?" Ricky asked.

"We have to help find her," Martin filled in the silence. "Maybe we can do something. I heard something tonight, in fact." Martin raised his eyebrows at Ricky.

Sam stood on his back veranda and watched the rain water the rows of parsley and spring onions. An unmarked police car drew to the edge of the gravel driveway.

The car reminded him how he had allowed Plum's parents to grow opium poppies on such a big scale. The second larger crop was what had killed them. Sam was certain of that. But he was not sure who the killers were. There was a septic tank nearby. The septic tank did explode and covered a wide area with foul smelling shit. But the parked car had exploded as well. An expert from the Department of Scientific and Industrial Research had surmised that a leaking carburetor and the hot engine had caused the methane, then the petrol in the car, to ignite. There was never a full investigation into the cause of the explosion. There was never any conclusive evidence regarding the possibility of a bomb because no one had looked for a bomb.

But the police did have Sam as the prime suspect. Sam could not understand such logic. They had accused him of blowing up the septic tank. But it was his tank. Why would he blow up his own tank? He never told them his suspicions nor did he tell them about the poppy plants at the other end of the family property. Back then the police did not know opium came from poppies.

Inspector Grimble and Sergeant Cadd stood on the veranda and introduced themselves to Sam Look. The old man spoke of the weather, the rising costs of fertilizer and how it was difficult to do everything he wanted to each day. He knew nothing about Plum Blossom returning to New Zealand, and he could give no reason why she had come back and not called him. "The young generation. They don't listen to the old ones anymore. They think they know it all." Sam, being talkative, had given them what they had wanted to hear, but he had not told them anything they wanted to know.

As they drove back, Grimble turned to his sergeant.

"He wouldn't say anything," Cadd stated the obvious.

"Not for all the tea in China."

• • •

Bruce towed the remains of his Volvo to a junk heap at the edge of their farm. He left the burnt out chassis and wheels next to the rusted remains of Plum's parents' car. He did not think about the juxtaposition at the time.

.

Chapter Seven

Thursday

Chuck called at ten o'clock. He had camped out at the Wongs'. He recounted to Bruce what they had told him.

According to Martin, there was a large shipment of marijuana about to come down from up north courtesy of a Maori gang. They hoped to capitalize on the current shortage and the resulting high prices. A huge Pakeha with pale blue eyes had told them this at their shop. They believed him because they knew he was well connected in the underworld. Ricky had also heard that there was a lot of Maori pot about to appear soon. "Everyone tells us little bits and we piece it all together," Martin had told Chuck. "Like our spring rolls. The whole is greater than the parts."

"So it could be possible that these Maoris have kidnapped Plum in return for, whatever?" Chuck had asked Martin.

"We know it's about the pot in your glasshouses. That's okay." Ricky nodded. "We're going to find her. You just tell us what you know and we'll fill in the missing pieces."

"Yeah! And if we don't, we'll have something worked out where we will," Martin added.

Chuck Look told Bruce that he would stay in the city. The Wongs were to talk to some of their Maori friends and report back to him.

"Okay," Bruce agreed. "Tony is doing some research at his office today. We'll know more tonight. Then we'll have to meet and decide if we pack it all up. It's a big job."

"Yeah. I know." Chuck spoke with no trace of irony. "I planted them. Remember?"

Hei Hei had fallen asleep on top of Moana. She was naked on the carpet in the living room and she could smell his breath very clearly as his chin dug into her shoulder. His stomach pressed into her groin, but his elbows and knees took some of his weight off her. She could feel his semen oozing down the inside of her thighs. She had no privacy, no freedom and a new job that terrified her. Each new man who walked into her tiny massage cubicle was another drunken nightmare.

She heard footsteps coming down the path. Moana squeezed out from under him. He grunted and his face sunk into the carpet. There was a loud knock on the door as she put on her dress.

Hei Hei grunted again and rose up on his elbows.

"I'll answer it," he muttered.

There was another loud knock. Hei Hei, his jeans were around his ankles, attempted to walk towards the door. He stumbled but caught himself. He pulled up his jeans, pushed back his shoulders, stuck out his ample stomach and marched to the door. He flung it open to see two well-built Chinese men burning holes in him with their eyes. Hei Hei looked from one to the other then down at his jeans. He realized his fly was undone and he tried to zip it up with both hands without them noticing. The two young men wore light nylon jackets that were open to show black T-shirts. They waited for Hei Hei to open his mouth.

Hei Hei raised his eyebrows, which elicited a response he had not anticipated. A front snap kick hit him in the solar plexus. If he had not possessed such a large stomach he would have collapsed in the doorway. Instead he was propelled back to the sofa where he slumped down. He had not been winded since playing front row forward in his high school rugby team. He tried to regain his breath while eyeing the two strangers. He seethed with anger that someone had dared attack Hei Hei, the great Maori poet.

The two men stepped inside and one shut the door behind him and noticed Moana. She covered her mouth with both her hands and retreated slowly into the background.

"Where's Plum Blossom?" Ricky Wong, the kicker, addressed the gasping Hei Hei. He was bent over, holding his stomach with one hand, stunned. His other hand hung down from the sofa almost touching the carpet.

"Who?" Hei Hei replied.

"Plum Blossom. You'se know where she is."

The wounded Maori rubbed his stomach and tried not to show his pain. He reached down under the sofa with his right hand and pulled out a four-foot long chain. He unfurled it as he leapt up and swung it over his head. The chain caught Ricky's elbow as he tried to step back. He let out a yell. Martin came forward, one hand inside his nylon jacket.

Hei Hei thought the chain would scare them off and impress Moana.

The younger visitor drew out a pair of nunchaku. He twirled the wooden baton above his head then executed a figure eight in front of him as he advanced on the Maori. Hei Hei was transfixed by the speed of the nunchaku. Then he leapt to one side and thrashed out with the chain.

Hei Hei planned to strike the weaponless one in the face with his next chain lash then whack the other across the room. Who could withstand an attack from him? He felt the chain whip through the air and graze the wooden handle of the spinning nunchaku. The young one threw the chuck above his head, spun around and aimed the edge of his right foot into Hei Hei's chin. The Maori staggered backwards as the attacker put both feet forwards and swung his nunchaku across the side of Hei Hei's face, catching his left ear. He dropped his chain and collapsed to his knees, his face in agony. The inside of his head made so much noise he could not scream.

Moana, terrified by the violence, let out a piercing cry. Martin, poised with his nunchaku raised with both hands above Hei Hei, waited to deliver the final blow.

"Don't!" the other yelled, clutching his elbow in pain. He walked over to the fallen Maori and rested his shoe on the Maori's heaving chest, causing enough pressure on the sternum to make Hei Hei grimace even more. He spoke very slowly.

"I want you, to tell the others, that we want, Plum Blossom back. You understand?"

Hei Hei moaned. His left ear, his entire face throbbed in pain.

Ricky turned to Moana and motioned her to the door. She picked up her canvas shoulder bag with her purse in it and stood by the door.

"You're coming with us. Don't be afraid. We won't hurt you." The one with the nunchaku stood guard over the Maori, the chain between the batons rattled in his hand.

Hei Hei tried to move when he saw her led out of the apartment. His attacker walked over to the telephone and ripped the cord out of the wall. He threw the telephone at Hei Hei, hitting him in the stomach. The telephone bounced off and spread across the carpet in pieces.

"Call up your friends and tell them to bring us Plum Blossom," he yelled before slamming the door. Hei Hei's head fell back as he passed out.

Moana walked quietly to the car. Her arms were folded across her chest. She did not want to be touched by them.

Ricky drove them up Bassett Drive. She sat in the back seat of their white Holden. Her two unknown assailants were in the front and seemed to ignore her. Never in all her dreams did she imagine she would leave Hei Hei like this.

Moana could not keep her eyes off the back of Ricky's strong neck and his wide shoulders. She caught glimpses of his clear face in the rearview mirror as he drove through Newmarket.

Ricky parked the car by one of the few remaining Victorian houses on Grafton Road, shut off the engine and turned to face the perplexed Maori girl. Moana squirmed in her seat and suddenly realized she was not wearing any underwear.

"Wong House."

It was a family joke. Ricky and Martin never failed to laugh, and they did now, despite the confused look of their passenger.

"There's some tea there. Pour yourself some and then I'll cook you some eggs. You had quite a sleep."

"You know, Mel, I don't want to exploit your sense of charity, but I must look for a new place today, get my bank account in order and move out, I mean."

"Just stop there." Mel stood up and raised her hand. "I invited you to stay. Your first priority is to find Plum. We'll help you. I'm off work for a few days. So how do you want your eggs?"

"Over easy. Thank you."

"I better be going over to see Wiremu. He's going to the tangihanga this afternoon," she said as she served him.

"Where?" Clovis asked.

"Mangere. That's the nearest marae. Wiremu didn't want his brother transported up north for some reason and thought he should be laid to rest here where all his followers are."

"How do you know Wiremu's address? He never told us."

"Retired physicist's secret."

"Tell him," Mel shot out.

"Okay. I got it from my lawyer."

"He never told you."

"Not in so many words."

"You mean you got it when you went to the bathroom?"

"Yeah." Henry smiled.

"I thought you were gone a long time. Your own attorney!"

"Well, I couldn't put him in a situation where he'd have to breach a confidence. And I don't want him knowing what we're up to. Because then he might breach our confidence."

"Before I forget, Matthew, that's the guy who lent me his car that I left on the Motorway. Well, to cut a long story short, I'm going to play on Friday with his new band, Particle Board, at the Gluepot on Ponsonby and Jervois Road. You know the pub?"

"Yes. Three Lamps. I'm a little off pubs lately." Henry pulled a face, more of a grimace than a frown.

"The reason I want to play there is there's always lots of Maoris and some rough characters hanging around. I want to talk to some people, see if I can get wind of anything."

"That's good. We'll go too and hear you play. What do you think, dear?" Henry watched Clovis wipe the plate clean with the last of his bread.

"Let's go." Mel got up from the table and turned to Clovis. "You better stay here."

"But I spent six days with him locked up in my house. When it was standing," Clovis protested.

"Someone might call. You never know. And you can do the dishes. We'll be right back."

Henry sat with his arms folded as Mel drove through the late morning traffic across Mount Eden to Parnell.

"Are you quiet because you're not driving?" Mel asked as she maneuvered between a Toyota truck and an old Ford flat top.

"No. I like being driven, reminds me of taxis in New York."

"I'm not that crazy a driver. And I speak perfect English."

"I'm thinking of, oh, the time you drove me up Mount Eden for our last good-bye. And mixed up with that is a feeling of doom about Plum. She was, I mean, is, so sweet, but not innocent. You know?"

"Yes." Of course she knew. She had examined Plum. And she wanted to forget that comment about the last good-bye on top of Mount Eden. That memory stirred up too many emotions.

"It's a peculiar but very attractive mix."

Mel did not reply. She changed down gears and stopped at a red light behind a van.

"Now, Moana."

"Who's Moana?" Mel shot out.

"The masseuse. The Maori girl I told you about at the Flamingo Paradise."

Mel slipped into first gear and turned down Ayr Street.

"Well, Moana really reacted when she saw my pendant."

"The one Wiremu gave you?"

"It was as if she had seen it before, under much different circumstances."

"But you've been in the States for years."

"Exactly. So she's a relative of Wiremu. A cousin, I think."

"What about Plum?" Mel changed the subject.

"Just a feeling that some awful violence is going to happen."

"I hope not. I just can't reconcile that giant Pakeha with those blue eyes coming at me, you know, I can still see them when I close my eyes. I mean, who swapped the bodies? How did Wiremu's brother get there? Someone must have driven him. They didn't find a car of his at Clovis's house."

"Whoever swapped the bodies must've off'd Hone. It was probably that big guy."

"Who works for Terry the Turk."

"Yes."

"If that's the case, we should check in with that Inspector, er, Grimble."

"No. Don't trust him. At all. He's playing his own little game and you're just a little piece, a pawn. He'll use you, and besides, you omitted certain facts from your statement, right?"

"Right."

"If we're going to find Plum we're better off without the cops. Here, this is it. Just park over there."

As Henry eased out of the car, he leaned across the roof to stare at Mel. "Promise me you won't call him."

"Promise. But I don't know how you know that. You've never met him."

Henry shrugged his shoulders and walked down the overgrown lane to the house. The front door was open, and Henry saw the beeswax candle still burning by the empty chair where Wiremu had sat. He checked the rest of the house. It was deserted.

"I know the other address. It's up the road."

"Let's take the car."

"Why?"

"Because we'll have it," Mel explained.

"You what?" Chuck Look paced up and down the kitchen then stopped to stare at the two Wong brothers seated at the kitchen table, surrounded by apple cores. They had consumed all the chocolate brownies and the milk from the three cartons that had been in the refrigerator.

"Hey!" Ricky slammed the milk carton down on the table. He licked his lips. "We agreed we would check out these Maoris, and we did. We just got lucky. Getting her will get them mad. When they get mad they'll show us where Plum Blossom is. We'll swap. One for the other. It's that simple!" He raised his hands in a gesture of premature triumph.

"I can't believe you've gone and kidnapped a girl, brought her to your own house and locked her in the front room full of weapons. Shit! You guys were always off the deep end."

"What about her brothers, her tribe? Before you fly off the handle, why don't you go in there and talk to her. Act the big dope dealer! She didn't offer any resistance.

If you ask me, she's glad to get out of there. The guy she was with is a real asshole."

"Well, what's her name?" Chuck asked, controlling himself. Ricky turned to Martin who shrugged. Chuck looked down on his two cousins. This is what happens when you get the Wongs involved. After their mother died, they became total fuck ups. They work hard but don't use their brains.

"She won't bite you. We'll wait here, so we don't put you off." Ricky winked at Chuck.

"What about the Maori? How did you know where to go?"

"We heard at the Wok that this joker worked for Wilson, so we tracked him down and stole his girl. Okay? Is that spelt out enough for you? Why don't you go and talk to her. Act nice."

Chuck took a deep breath and stormed out of the kitchen. That spring roll he had eaten last night had upset his stomach.

Moana sat on an unopened box of nunchaku. Her chin rested on her hands. She was thinking about her first night at the Flamingo Paradise and whether she would go there tonight. If she gave half her money to Hei Hei, did that make him a pimp? She had done nothing immoral, although she would be happy never to set foot in that place again. She never wanted to see another drunken farmer or Texan again. She thought about what the nice Pakeha had said to her, about Hone Wilson and Plum Blossom. What could all that have to do with these Chinese boys taking her here?

Chuck opened the door, slowly. His caution was unjustified. Moana had not tried the door or opened the curtains. She seemed unaware of his presence as he came into her view. He coughed and she jumped. She focused her eyes on him and was surprised to see such a timid face. None of the men who had whisked her away had had their faces covered up, so was she kidnapped or what? Not for one moment did she stop to consider Hei Hei lying immobilized on his dirty carpet, bleeding from the ear. She wished she had worn panties as she pressed her thighs together.

"What's your name? I'm Chuck."

"Moana Wilson." She gave a quick smile to set the young man at ease. He was not as handsome as the driver, but his shyness made him attractive.

"Wilson?" He cursed the Wongs under his breath. The Wilsons! Who wanted to steal their marijuana! Typical! The Wongs were going to create a nasty situation.

"I'm Wiremu Wilson's niece." Moana knew the mere mention of her relative's name would have an interesting effect on her host.

"Who was the man you were with?" Chuck asked tentatively.

"Oh, him," she said, as if referring to a forgotten enemy. "He's a friend of the Wilsons. Hei Hei. A real pig. I've been with him for a few weeks, so my parents aren't too keen on me right now."

"Oh." Chuck did not know what to say next. "We're businessmen. This is our warehouse." He gestured with his hands around the room. She looked at the file cabinet, the desk, the stacks of cardboard boxes and the mutilated Bruce Lee poster with several throwing stars embedded in the wall. The irony of the gesture was lost on Moana. "What I mean is, we don't want to hold you against your will, but we would like you to stay because we've, er, got some unfinished business and it would be best if you were here. Safe. You see?" Chuck did not know if what he had said made any sense to her.

Moana got off the box and straightened her dress. Somehow she had become involved in something very odd. The Pakeha at the Flamingo, the attack on Hei Hei and now this veiled invitation to stay as their guest. All because of a woman named Plum Blossom. She picked up a fallen ninja star and threw it at Bruce Lee. It sank into his stomach.

"I'm hungry." She turned to face Chuck. "Have you got anything to eat?"

"Now we're going to have a whole bunch of bleeding Maoris coming down on us." Chuck recounted what Moana had told him. He agreed she was attractive, even though her dress was awful. "Shit. She looks like she's just come down from the country. She doesn't have a clue. And she swears she doesn't know who Plum Blossom is. So why hang on to her?"

"Because she is a Wilson, and if we let her go now she might tell her friends where we are. If we keep her here, at least we have a bargaining chip," Ricky countered.

"What if Plum is not being held by Maoris? All Bruce got was an anonymous phone call. What if they are bluffing?" Martin added.

"Shit! Don't you see what you've done?" Chuck addressed the Wongs. "If this Hei Hei finds out where you live, he'll destroy you. These Maoris are heavy. Haven't you heard of utu? It means revenge. It's part of their culture."

"Don't worry," Ricky replied. "I gave him a taste of my chucks. He won't come back. Whenever I hear the word 'culture,' I reach for my chucks." Martin laughed with him.

"Utu is central to their belief system. In the 19th century, whole tribes were fighting and eating each other all because of utu, addressing past wrongs. Shit! Now they'll come after us!"

"Relax, Chuck." Martin smiled. "No one is going to eat you. You'd taste of soya sauce."

"Don't underestimate them. They'll find out where you took her and come and get her," Chuck warned.

"I'm waiting." Martin raised his hands and smiled. He was enjoying this. Right from the time he had hit the fat Maori.

Mel hesitated before she walked down the path to the other address.

"What?" Henry murmured as Mel turned to him.

"Hear that?"

Henry knocked on the door and yelled, "Wiremu? It's Henry! Are you there?"

They heard a groan, then the door was flung open. Wiremu smiled politely, quite in contrast to the scene behind him.

"Thank god you've come, Henry! And your good friend Doctor Johnson." Wiremu had been at a loss as to how to handle Hei Hei.

Hei Hei had a rugby sock stuffed with ice stuck to his forehead. Water dribbled down his face and mixed with the blood that had oozed out of his left ear. The blood formed an ugly dark stain across the sofa.

Mel knelt down to inspect the damage. She had barely noticed him at the pub last Friday. She turned to Henry, threw him the car keys and instructed him to bring in her Gladstone bag from the trunk.

When he returned, Wiremu had fetched Mel a bowl of hot water and she was cleaning his bruised face with a cloth.

"Shouldn't we call an ambulance?" Henry asked as he saw the telephone in pieces and a motorcycle chain spread across the carpet. "Oh." He pulled a face at the blood.

"You need to get that seen to." Mel held a small stainless steel torch that shone in the remains of Hei Hei's left ear. "You took some hit. How did it happen?" She broke out a small swab from her bag and started to clean the dried blood around the outer ear.

Hei Hei stopped groaning. If he kept his eyes fixed on a spot on the ceiling, the room would not spin.

"These two Chinese jokers barged in and they took Moana."

"What?" Wiremu leapt to his feet. "Moana was here? Moana Wilson? My niece?"

Mel shot a glance at Henry who appeared shocked. Hei Hei thought for a moment before he answered.

"Yeah."

"You mean she was here? Living with you?"

Hei Hei could not tell if there was more disbelief than anger in Wiremu's question.

"You were living with my Moana? Behind my back? I mean, right under my nose?" Again there was a plaintive silence from Hei Hei. "Shit! No wonder you never let me come over. You always picked me up. You cunning Maori bastard. Did Hone know this?"

"Yeah." Hei Hei could not lie about the dead.

"Jesus fucking cow! Oh. Excuse my French." Wiremu turned to Mel who was still feeling around the mushy remains of the outer ear. Hei Hei's eyes were fixed on a spot in the ceiling. He prayed that Wiremu would not hit him.

"Who were they?" Wiremu sucked in air as he paced the room, ignoring Henry and the doctor as his eyes bored down on his friend.

"I told you, Chinese."

"Did you recognize them?"

"They had chucks, you know, like your little nephews up north."

"Is that what hit you?" Mel asked.

"Yeah."

"You're lucky to be conscious. Another inch this way and you could've been blinded." She stood up and surveyed the field dressing wrapped around Hei Hei's head.

"I can't do anymore. You'll have to go to the ER. You can make up a story how you fell out of the bath. I'll go with you and see what I can do. No promises."

"Gee, thanks, Doc." Hei Hei held the soggy rugby sock in his hands and lowered his eyes to the floor. He dared not look at Wiremu.

"Where is she? You fucking little child molester! I trusted you."

"Steady, Wiremu. She'd only been here a couple o' days. I was showing her the city. She's in trouble with her parents and I thought I was doing the right thing by having her stay here. You know? I haven't touched her. I swear. I was going to tell you, then Hone got killed. It's not what you think." He was finally caught in Wiremu's glare. The room started to spin again.

"I don't have to think," Wiremu said between his teeth.

"They're from that take-out place on Ponsonby. Opposite the Three Lamps. You know the place?"

"The Dirty Wok?" Henry chipped in.

"No. It's the Mighty Wok. I know those guys. The Wongs. Vicious lot. Teach some Maoris Kung Fu and stuff." Wiremu rubbed his chin and noticed for the first time Hei Hei's bruised and inflamed jaw. "Ha! They kicked you in the mouth too! Serves you right, fella."

He went into the bedroom to see if he could dig out any of Moana's possessions. There were some of her panties in the bathroom and an old suitcase half unpacked next to Hei Hei's unmade bed. Yes! He didn't have to think too much with Hei Hei.

"It's odd, isn't it? First Plum Blossom, now Moana," Henry mused, out loud.

"Plum Blossom?" Hei Hei tried to shake his head, but he felt as if his brain had been knocked loose.

"Plum Blossom," Mel repeated. "What about her?" She snapped her Gladstone bag shut and stood up.

"They said something about wanting a Plum Blossom back."

"Who?" Wiremu stood in the doorway.

"The slit eyes," Hei Hei moaned.

"Plum Blossom. Plum Blossom," Wiremu slowly chanted. He looked at Mel then at Henry as if they were responsible for the second abduction. "My brother is murdered, Plum Blossom is stolen away. Now my little niece is gone. Terry the Turk must be behind Plum missing, but Moana?"

"Perhaps these Chinese think you've got Plum, or you're working for this Terry," Mel offered.

"I don't see how these Chinks would connect them up. I have to pay a visit to Terry's house. I know where he lives."

"Oh. We did get called in by a cop called Grimble over the fire," Mel began. She quickly informed Wiremu of what she and Clovis had told the inspector.

"Shit. I'm still not safe. I reckon they'll be expecting me at the tangi. I can't even say good-bye to my brother. Give me the keys to the Morrie." If Hei Hei had deceived him about Moana, what else had he lied about?

Wiremu lost sight of Mel's BMW as she sped to Auckland Hospital. As his car made its slow ascent up Bassett Road, an unmarked police van came up the hill and parked opposite the driveway to his house.

• • •

Hei Hei called Terry after he slipped out of his cubicle to a phone booth on the same floor. Mel and Henry had left him in the curtained room in the Emergency Room after Mel had talked to one of the doctors in charge. Hei Hei used his good ear to listen to the cheerful message on Terry's answering machine.

"You've got his brother coming over to see you this afternoon. He's looking for Plum Blossom, and he's looking for his niece Moana who was taken away this morning by two Chinese thugs from the Mighty Wok. He's really angry and will stop at nothing. Watch out."

Hei Hei hung up and hobbled back to the cubicle.

The Morris Minor backfired as he switched off the engine. The widow Wadman who lived opposite Mr. Turner peeked through her lace curtains and muttered to her poodle: "My god, Ruffles! It's a Maori!" She watched Wiremu kick the car. Ruffles barked at the Maori.

With the car finally silent, Wiremu pressed the buzzer by the intercom in the wall. There was no reply. He tried again. Nothing. Wiremu could not climb over the iron gate, so he walked along the wall until he came to a large oak tree that overhung the property from the road. He jumped up to grab a branch with both hands. He swung his feet up to the branch and pulled himself over the wall, missing the jagged pieces of glass stuck on top. He fell onto a Norfolk pine seedling that broke in two. At least it was not a native tree, he consoled himself as he stood up and wiped the pine needles from his trousers.

Wiremu breathed in the fresh damp grass of the cut lawn. He noted that each window had thin metal security strips across them. Wiremu thought someone could have seen him go over the wall. His car hardly fit in. An old lady could be calling the police right now and giving them his description. He jogged to the back door and patio.

There was an outside chance Plum could be here. He was angry with Hei Hei for what he had done to Moana, and he was annoyed with himself for bringing Plum and Clovis into his life. If he could find Plum, then that might lead him to Moana.

He knelt at the back of the house and noticed two long narrow windows set just above the concrete. There was no sign of any detection device. He stood up and kicked them in, breaking the silence as the glass hit the basement floor.

Plum Blossom sat on her cot and rocked back and forth. Her knees were under her chin and her arms were wrapped around her legs. She jumped when she heard the very faint cracking of glass. A wild hope flashed through her mind that the Wong brothers had come to rescue her. Then there was silence. Plum could hear her own heart beat. She could not bear the tension anymore. She screamed at the top of her lungs.

"Let me out! Let me out!" And gasping for breath, "I'm in here! Help! I'm here!" She ran to the door and started to pound it with her little fists as she screamed again. For a few seconds she dared to think someone would set her free. Her ears rang from her screams and she hit her forehead and her fists against the door.

Wiremu did not know if his ears were playing tricks on him, but he thought he heard a tiny muted scream, then another followed by a dull pounding. He could not see the front gate. Wiremu sensed that he had moments before the police would arrive. He sprinted across the lawn to the back wall, jumped up to grasp the top with his hands and pulled himself over, falling into a heap of rotting leaves. He checked he had no cuts, there was no glass on top of the wall. He ambled down a garden path that led to a driveway between a wooden house and an old brick garage that was covered in vines.

He could hear police shouting as they ran around Terry's house' and there was a dog barking. A big dog. He walked to the garage, opened a side door and spotted an old black bicycle. He checked the tires.

Wiremu turned the bicycle around, wheeled it out of the garage and down the driveway. He took a sharp right at the street to avoid any police cars. His knees buckled outward because the seat was too low, but Wiremu pedaled as if he was on his morning bike ride. He promised himself he would return this rusty bicycle to its owner. It went just as fast as the Morris Minor, downhill, only quieter.

They could have the Morris Minor. It was registered in Hei Hei's name anyway, and that blood-caked vicious bastard deserved to be picked up after he got back from the hospital. With Hei Hei out of the way, the rendezvous would go smoothly.

Plum Blossom sat by the door next to the crushed polystyrene cup. She thought she heard muffled voices and a dog barking, but could not trust her own senses. She was too exhausted to call out for help. Her fists were bruised and her throat was sore from her screaming. She put her face in her hands and finally gave way to tears.

Wiremu stood the bicycle by a gate at the back of Mel's house. He walked through the neighbor's garden and banged on Mel's back door. He assumed there would be a police car outside her front gate. He tried the door after a short interval. It was locked. As he would have to wait for them to return, he stepped into the garden and plucked a yellow grapefruit from the tree. He sat down on the steps to peel it. With the cool bitter juice on his lips, Wiremu ate for the first time in over twenty-four hours. He held the empty peel in his hands and listened to the song of a blackbird.

• • •

Hei Hei sat in a small cubicle in the emergency room. The pain in his ear was now tolerable. The bleeding had stopped, and he could hear with his right ear well enough to listen to the registrar talk to another doctor about how they should file a police report over his injury. Mel and Henry had left him to fend for himself. All he needed now were a bunch of cops to storm in and ask him awkward questions. Anything he said would go into that wretched Pakeha computer.

First he needed a beer, then he had to find Moana. He needed more than one beer, he needed many beers; that would fix his head and lubricate his creative juices for ideas on how to handle those Chinese boys. And he had to avoid Wiremu.

He put his shirt back on, peeked through the curtain and, seeing the way was clear, strode out of the hospital, his chest puffed up, his belly tucked in and a large white bandage wrapped around his head. He ignored a police car that raced up the ambulance driveway to the Emergency Room at the opposite end of the building.

Terry rushed to his house with John as soon as the police called him. A large longhaired Maori male had climbed over his wall. Although there were hundreds of Maoris that fit that description in Auckland, Terry could narrow the field down to one suspect, Wiremu Wilson.

When Terry stepped out of his car, there were three police vehicles parked in his driveway and a dog squatting in the middle of the grass. The handler, in uniform, held the leash and looked the other way. That's all he needed, dog turds on his immaculate lawn. At the back of his house, Inspector Grimble squatted by two ground-level windows that had been smashed.

"You seem to have an intruder." The inspector stood up. He turned to face Mr. Turner then Mr. Eustace.

"I'm sure you scared him off doing your job, Inspector." Terry smiled back. How had the cops broken into his property? Only his electronically tuned box could open the gate from the outside. He hoped one of the cops had gone over the top then manually opened it before overriding the electrical system.

"Why would a large curly topped Maori want to break into your nice peaceful home?" Grimble kept his eyes locked on both characters.

"Probably after the family silverware." Terry shrugged his shoulders. John maintained his sneer. The plainclothes detective next to Grimble snickered, then saw John's cold blue eyes.

The inspector raised his eyebrows then bent down again to look through the low windows.

Terry stood there wishing the cops would disappear off his property, from the whole bleeding Island of Aotearoa. God bless 'em.

"Let's go in and see if he's taken anything," Grimble suggested, like a good sport.

Terry did not hesitate. It was part of the game. If he denied the inspector entry and threw him off his grounds, he knew the cop bastard would come back with or without a warrant and search the place from top to bottom. After all, if Wiremu Wilson was sniffing around for something special, Grimble would love to find out about it too. And what of Plum Blossom? Had she heard the breaking of glass? What was she doing now? Terry knew the cell was virtually soundproof. He had locked John in there once.

"John, I think I left a porno magazine under the bed, could you check?" Terry locked the door on John who went berserk. John had tried to break down the door. Terry had not even heard a whimper upstairs or outside.

"Yes. You're welcome, Inspector. I don't believe we've had the pleasure of giving you a tour. My wife collects antiques, you know."

"She's out, I take it."

"Yes." Terry smiled a little too hard. He was not going to tell him she had been sent to Sydney with her brother to negotiate the final details of shipping a container load of sinsemilla hidden in Victorian furniture.

"You really must show me the basement. I want to see if we can get any prints from inside the window." The inspector sounded concerned.

Terry played along. He knew the inspector was desperate for any clue as to what he was up to.

"I'm considering excavating under my house. You know, increase the market value. How much did this job cost?"

"Oh, too much. You know how contractors are. They always take so much longer than they estimate and finish sticking you." Terry smiled back. The lying shit! He already had a two-level house with room for two cars underneath for his miserable little Honda and his wife's seven-year-old Morris. But how could he contradict the inspector? He had considered blowing it up last year.

Terry led the inspector down the thickly carpeted steps to the basement, followed by John, who always caught his head on the beam at the bottom of the stairs and muttered, "Fuck it!"

"You must have been on really bad terms with your contractor, or did you do it to cut costs?" Grimble asked as Terry led him through the basement.

"What?" Terry scrunched up his eyebrows. Then it clicked. He's spotted it. He's got a bleedin' tape measure in his head.

"The basement is smaller than upstairs. Usually basements follow the outside wall plan. Yours doesn't. Curious."

Terry stood relaxed, hands by his side, smiling back at the smart cop. The bastard contractor has cheated me, he cursed.

Plum Blossom awoke and peeled herself off the floor. Her hands were so sore they throbbed. She had dreamt of Clovis breaking through the window, coming to rescue her. In the dream she saw where she was imprisoned, an abandoned warehouse in Ellerslie, in an underground cell.

Plum tried to remember more details of the warehouse and wondered if this was an example of her being psychic, of astral traveling. Maybe she could travel out of her body, see Clovis and lead him back to where she lay. She often flew in her dreams. Perhaps if she went to sleep again she would fly out of her cell, to freedom.

She stood up and swayed as the blood rushed to her head. Stretching her arms out, she yawned loudly and burped, then looked around the cell. It was exactly the same. Plum decided she had to examine minutely every surface of the room, to search for some clue as to her whereabouts.

Plum could not beat her fists on the door, who would hear her anyway? Between the wood paneled wall and the door was a matching wood panel. She tapped the doorsill. Solid. No gap between the door and panel. No. A small gap, but padded inside. Plum bent down and found her plastic knife. She attempted to dig into the padding but nothing would come loose.

Then she noticed there was no doorknob and no keyhole. She returned to tapping around the door, listening to any change in the sound.

Terry wanted to get upstairs as quickly as possible. He had John down there with him, and that seemed a stupid idea now. What if the inspector's sidekick was upstairs nosing around in his study? Not that Terry had anything incriminating lying around. Still, you never know what one seemingly innocent observation could lead to.

Sergeant Cadd tried to pull open a drawer. It was stuck so he gave it a tug. The drawer flew out of the bureau onto the floor with a crash. He hurriedly picked it up and slid it back into its tight slot. Turning around he listened for any movement from the basement, then Cadd gently shut the lid of the bureau and tiptoed to the door of the study. He tripped over a small book that he had not seen fly out of the drawer. He picked it up and noted it was an old textbook on acids. Cadd heard footsteps and the door of the basement swing open. He could not find a place to hide the book so he slipped it inside his jacket.

The loud crash made Terry jump.

"Perhaps we really have a thief upstairs," he snarled at the inspector and ran up the stairs followed by John. At the top of the stairs he turned to the inspector.

"I think we need police protection."

Grimble had wanted to stay in the basement, examine it more.

Plum Blossom heard a dull thud. She could not locate where it came from. She could no longer bear the isolation. She let out an explosive scream. She banged her head against the door.

Terry the Turk at the top of the stairs yelled into his house with his high tenor voice:

"Who's there? Am I really being robbed now?"

The inspector did not appreciate the irony as he followed John into the hallway. Terry closed the basement door behind the inspector and marched into the living room to face Sergeant Cadd. The sergeant stood in the center of the Persian rug, hands behind his back, rolling on his heels, looking at the plaster cornices around the ceiling, like butter would not melt in his mouth. The bureau was shut.

Chapter Eight

"Have any trouble with Tony?" Matthew asked Clovis in the cramped room backstage that smelt of stale beer and cigarettes.

"You mean that big Samoan?"

"Yeah." Matthew grinned.

Tony was the four-hundred-pound Rarotongan bouncer. He stood at the bottom of the steps leading up to the second floor lounge, the Gluepot, where the music stage was. He was security and Matthew's friend. Matthew made sure Tony got 5 percent of the gate, and Matthew always drew a big crowd.

"They just searched my violin case as if I was carrying a machine gun," Clovis joked, relieved that Matthew was not going to vent in front of the other members of the group.

"They're really nervous tonight, for some reason." Matthew winked at Clovis as if to reassure him he was among friends.

"Oh. I should introduce you. Clovis and I go way back. You know Rodger, on keyboards." Clovis shook Rodger's hand. In the Cat's Pajamas, Rodger had a full-length beard, hair to his waist and a paisley waistcoat that Clovis swore he slept in. Rodger now sported a crew cut, a dark suit and white shirt with a narrow black tie.

"You dig the outfit? Rodger is the weirdest one here. Looks like he's a Mormon. This is Sheila. Every good group deserves a girl bassist."

Sheila raised her tuning machine to Matthew. She wore a teased platinum blonde beehive. The tight black leather skirt was too short and showed the tops of her black nylon stockings. Her black sequined top and black eye mascara completed her look.

"Love your outfit," Clovis replied.

"Yeah, it's my new beehive. Very patriotic." She pouted.

The others hooted.

"This is Billy Whitehorn, our lead guitarist. Billy, you remember Clovis?"

"Yeah. The Ying Tong Song."

Matthew and Billy erupted into the first bars of the song.

"You should go over a few licks with Clovis so you can do fifths and octaves and stuff, you know," Matthew continued. "And this is Rua. You guys know each other, right? See, we've got everyone, white boys, a girl and a Maori." Matthew raised his hands in the air.

Clovis and Rua hugged. He was a three-hundred-pound six-foot Maori with eighteen-inch biceps, who could beat any drumhead into submission.

Matthew left Billy and Clovis to practice guitar and violin runs together. He went downstairs to talk to the pub's manager and check on the gate. Matthew had friends at the cash register, and he took precautions not to get screwed out of his 80 percent take from the $5 cover charge. A running tally would not hurt.

Clovis unwrapped his violin from its silk scarf, tuned it quickly to Billy's electronic "A" and uncoiled the wires to his amplification system as he explained how it worked to Billy.

"A friend in Wellington made it for me. It's a contact mike on the bridge, see, plus a pick up modified from a Gibson Les Paul here."

"Far out. It must be an angel of god, like mine." Billy's eyes bulged.

"Which doesn't touch the bridge or alter the acoustic sound, though with this weight it's a little muted," Clovis continued, not sure if he had heard correctly. "I get two signals coming through this pair of wires which I use singly, split and put through different power sources and change their sounds again, or I can put them together so I get a straight reproduction. I get real eerie effects and some wild stereo. Also with a delay function through a synthesizer, I can play against or with myself."

"You play with yourself?" Sheila asked.

Clovis didn't know how to reply to her. So he smiled and connected three small metal boxes with short wires he took out of his side pocket. Billy looked on, his mouth wide open.

"This goes straight in here, the master box. I can split them into these two or over the PA system or a slave unit or whatever. Are you using your own equipment?"

"You're kidding. Of course. But we're using their PA as well. Hey. You know. We should really have our own mixing board out there, but like, Matthew prefers to do it himself. He's got a mini right in front of his mike on a stand. He keeps control that way. Kind of like Moses on the mountain with condoms in his back pocket. Know what I mean?"

"Yeah." Clovis nodded although he did not have clue what Billy meant. He did know the same old Matthew was going to go berserk at him after the show and take his share of the money to help pay for the Studebaker. Clovis could see it coming. No wonder Matthew was so nice. Billy showed Clovis some of the riffs and licks he would use and they quickly ran through these together.

"Shit! There's a big crowd out there. Let's get going." Matthew rubbed his hands and roared with no trace of irony. "Rock and Roll!"

Almost a parody, Clovis mused, almost.

Hei Hei had been drinking beer all afternoon downstairs in the public bar of the Three Lamps. His kidneys ached and he had pissed blood, thick red clots of it. His ears bothered him, even though the dull throbbing had stopped. What would it be like if he went upstairs to listen to his favorite local band, Particle Board? He downed his last beer and hauled himself up the crowded staircase to the lounge together with three of his close mates, Rere, Mokau and Freddy. He had forgotten about his large white head bandage until Freddy started to call him a sheik.

"It's a Sikh! Dummy!! A sheik is a rich Arab! Besides, this isn't a turban! You Maoris are a bunch of racists!"

Hei Hei found some seats for Rere, Mokau and Freddy by the windows and a few Pakehas moved away without being asked. He looked around the lounge. There would not be any of Wiremu's people; they would be at the marae.

Clovis stepped out onto the narrow stage and squinted at the audience. He knelt down, set his boxes in a row, adjusted the dials, then ran two black cords to two different amplifiers. He tested the sound levels, toyed with the reverberation controls on one amplifier, then played a quick lick over all four strings that led to a high "A" that changed to a harmonic. The note hung in the air and quivered as he twiddled the knobs on the floor boxes. That note sent a charge through the audience. Clovis and the rest of the band could feel the excitement.

Hei Hei put his left hand over his left ear and grimaced. He sent Rere to get more beer.

The Gluepot had not changed. The red walls were darker, there was no real stage lighting, just a bunch of colored spots aimed at the stage. Clovis could make out thick velvet curtains that covered the windows on the right. The long bar on the far left was jammed with young men waving their empty jugs at two bartenders. Framed prints of race horses lined the back walls, an echo of another era when older men would smoke unfiltered cigarettes, discourse on the day's racing form and the occasional dance with their wives.

Clovis did not see Henry, Mel and Wiremu enter when the house lights dimmed and Particle Board swung into their opening number. Despite his size, no one recognized Wiremu. Mel had cut his hair to short tight curls. Clean-shaven and dressed in Henry's light grey woolen sweater, Wiremu could pass for a missionary from the Islands. Mel had added a pair of black-framed glasses to complete the conservative look.

Wiremu would have laughed at this change, but he was weighed down with grief. He was not at the tangi, sitting by his brother's coffin on the Mangere marae. That was where he would be able to unload his sorrow, sing a waiata and spend one last night with his brother's spirit. Hone would have wanted the tangihanga at Mangere rather than up north. At the marae he had helped launch Te Ropu Matakite (Those with Foresight), the Land March.

The police would be outside the marae, waiting for him. They would not expect him to be listening to a local band in a Ponsonby pub. This time he did not have the shotgun up his trousers. He wanted information about Moana and Plum Blossom and the Chinese gang he would have to face.

Sheila unzipped her black leather dress and threw it over her hundred-watt bass amp. Her long legs, in black nylon stockings, were held up by a black and red frilly garter belt. She kept the beat with her bass. She rubbed her Fender bass guitar between the creamy parts of her thighs and stroked the neck as if it were a giant penis. Her thighs were caught in the white spotlight she stepped into. Her low bass line walked across the top of the spellbound audience. The dance floor was jammed tight with sweating bodies. No one could dance, only sway against each other and wave their hands up in the air. Men in the audience stood on their chairs and stretched their necks to get an eyeful of this blond bass player in black panties.

Sheila built up the tension and speed of the bass line as the other members of the group waited in silence for the last phrase that would signal their full volume entrance. Matthew smiled; he had lost his bar count as he stared at Sheila's small rounded buns. Best player on two feet, he swore. Pity about the cardinal rule he set himself, the only rule he had kept; never screw female members of your band. Boy, was she hot tonight. Maybe he should fire her. Nah. Then it arrived. The last four bars. The last four beats in the final bar slurred to a slow false end.

Clovis on his electric violin, Billy on his black Gibson Les Paul, Rodger at his Roland synthesizer and Rua using his double snare drums, bass pedal and four cymbals hurtled into a grand chord that hung in the air then exploded at breakneck speed. Billy and Clovis kept in perfect tune, an octave apart soaring through the riff that became a repeated melody over Rua's crisp drumming and Sheila's firm bass.

The crowd roared their approval. Sheila came to the edge of the stage and executed a high kick at the audience, teasing the men with a quick peek at the insides of her thighs. The audience erupted in a burst of roars, whistles and screams.

Billy slipped into a fast riff to leave Clovis open for his spot. Clovis looked over at him and Billy nodded back. He was surprised at how good Billy played. Despite an acid scrambled brain, he could still make his guitar sing.

Matthew was beside the drummer beating a cowbell 1-2-3-4. His mini mixer up front was unattended and turned up full. So this must be my instrumental, Clovis surmised as he changed the riff and hit a switch on one of his boxes. His violin became a cross between an alto saxophone in tone and Jimi Hendrix's Stratocaster.

Clovis Tibet closed his eyes, danced over his fingerboard and sang with his bow. He accented the first and third then the second and the fourth beats as he whirled around the riff and ran up and down the violin, chorus after chorus.

Clovis sustained a high "C" at the edge of his E string, changing the tone with his foot controls. Billy broke out of his supporting chords and held the same note on his guitar, bending it a full half tone up then down, so that Clovis too imitated these bent microtones. They started to change notes, mimicking each other.

The dissonance between the two stringed instruments, as if they were animals crying to each other, was too intense for Hei Hei. His ears wanted to explode, as he sat in a corner surrounded by his mates. He spotted a tall Chinese man edging his way through the crowd near the stairs. Before anyone could restrain him, he leapt up and hurled a full beer jug across the room at the tall figure.

The jug missed the young man and hit a Samoan woman in the back of the neck and drenched her large pink dress in beer foam. She shrieked and jumped up. Her eyes caught the Chinese young man and she swung her right fist into his chin. Too shocked to react, he took the blow and collapsed.

Hei Hei roared. "Atta boy! Sock the Chink!"

Sheila jumped up and down on the stage with her hypnotic bass riff to Billy's soaring guitar solo. The entire dance floor was jumping in unison with her.

"Shit! That's Hei Hei!" Wiremu spoke in Mel's ear as he caught a glimpse of the flying beer jug.

Mel and Henry turned from the stage. They watched from their corner seats as Hei Hei yelled at a nearby group.

An unseen hand let fly another jug of beer aimed at the Samoan table. The Samoan's boyfriend was drenched. This giant in a purple shirt picked up the entire table, glasses, ashtrays and plastic beer mugs and hurled it in the general direction of the unknown assailant.

The band was so involved in the music and the audience's response that they did not notice the beginning of the riot, except Matthew. Matthew was banging on his cowbell and he saw everything. Oh Jesus! he mumbled. There go the takings! The manager will deduct the damages from the gate, blame the band for stirring up violence, and then he'd say we did not fulfill our contract by playing the set hours. How the fuck could we? If this were a movie we would break into "God Defend New Zealand" and the entire crowd would stand up with their hands on their hearts and belt out the national anthem. But this was real life. All he could do was beat the shit out of his cowbell, one, two, three, four, one, two, three, fuck!

Ricky Wong crawled to a safe table then got to his feet. His face was creased in pain. He had been enjoying the music whilst keeping an eye on a group of Maoris. But he could not make out anyone who fitted Wiremu Wilson's description in the lounge. He had not seen Hei Hei, only felt the beer jug whiz past. What if that Maori was somewhere in this chaos? He ducked again as something large sailed past. He tried to get to the stairs but dozens of people already had the same idea.

The music stopped. Clovis cradled his violin, picked up his boxes and ran to the back room. Billy with his Les Paul and Sheila with her leather dress and bass guitar followed. Rodger disappeared behind them. Rua stood with his arms folded in front of his drum kit holding his drumsticks like knives. No one was going to put a hole in his drums. Matthew stood next to him, clutching his cowbell. He could not understand how this had happened.

Ricky managed to get to the stairs behind a group of screaming Pakeha girls, one of whom clutched her right eye as blood poured down her black satin dress. Tony stood at the bottom of the stairs and blocked a group of young Maori men from going up whilst letting the frightened crowd out.

Once past Tony, Ricky headed straight for the Hungry Wok. He wanted to talk to Moana. She had not told them everything. He wanted answers.

Hei Hei had recognized the Chinese man who had taken Moana. He left his three mates to deal with the Samoans nearby as he worked his way through the crowd. He followed the object of his revenge down the stairs. Hei Hei ducked into the doorway of an unlit shop as three police cars followed by a large black police bus squealed to a halt outside the Three Lamps. He watched his target cross the road and enter the takeaway.

Wiremu ushered Mel and Henry in front of him down the stairs. They squeezed past Tony as a stream of eager blue uniforms rushed into the pub with their drawn batons.

Hei Hei walked to a doorway opposite the takeaway shop. He could see two men behind the counter and vats of boiling oil. Hei Hei reckoned the shop would empty out soon as word spread about the riot and the curious onlookers converged on the ring of police vehicles.

The downstairs bar filled up with the rock audience who ordered more drinks to relieve themselves of the pandemonium upstairs. Wiremu wanted to wait for the first wave of police to rush upstairs before they made their discrete exit.

"Weren't we doing this last week?" Henry asked as they followed Wiremu.

Hei Hei walked one block away from the Three Lamps and down a side street. On the left was a wooden fence and a gate to a ramshackle house. Just inside the gate on concrete steps were two empty glass milk bottles. He scooped one bottle up and slid it into his leather jacket. He crossed the street to a large dumpster at the back of a discount furniture store and, shuffling with his feet, found a few polystyrene peanuts that he picked up and squeezed into the milk bottle. He continued his walk down the street until he came to a familiar car. His mates were still upstairs smashing heads whilst he opened their trunk. The handle came off and the lid sprung open. Hei Hei felt around the spare tire. He eventually found a long rubber tube, half an inch in diameter.

He walked around to the gas cap, unscrewed it and eased the tube down the hole. Blowing air out of his lungs, Hei Hei bent over and sucked as hard as he could on the rubber opening. After all the beer he had drunk, his ribs did not hurt so much. The cool liquid hit his mouth as he squeezed the tube shut and stuck the tube into the bottle. He half filled the bottle and thanked his friends for not having an empty gas tank. He screwed the cap back on, threw the hose back in the trunk and took out a greasy rag to wipe his mouth and hands. He winced as the rag caught on his swollen chin, although the fumes seemed to help the throbbing in his head. He closed the trunk and turned to the sidewalk as the headlights of a slow-moving police car turned into the street from Ponsonby Road and hit his eyes. He turned into the darkness with the Maori cocktail tucked into his jacket. The rag was now partly stuffed into the mouth of the bottle; the peanuts had turned to jelly in the gasoline.

A large crowd had gathered behind the police cordon as Hei Hei stepped to one side of the Hungry Wok. He peeked around the corner and saw there were two customers at the counter. Behind him, flashing blue lights bounced off the shop windows. He could smell the pungent smell of the gasoline seeping through the rag hidden in his jacket.

Terry looked at his Rolex. It was time for Plum's dinner. He boiled two eggs, put two pieces of toast with butter on a paper plate and poured hot water over a tea bag in a polystyrene cup. He took a small glassine packet out of a tin from the back of a kitchen cabinet and stirred this white powder into the cup.

He carried Plum's dinner down the basement steps, carefully undid the secret lock to the other basement in the closet and, shutting it again, knocked on Plum's door.

"Dinner time," Terry half-sung in his high-pitched voice.

With the tray on the ground, he unlocked the door and peered in. Plum was seated on the bed, her knees under her chin. She was frightened.

"I brought you some dinner. You know I'm not a good cook, but this will go down well."

Plum Blossom was not impressed by such friendliness. Her throat was so dry that she grabbed the tea as soon as Terry placed the tray in front of her. She poured the tea down her throat without tasting it.

"I'll get you some more later, after you've eaten your eggs." Terry was genuinely concerned. He had not given her enough liquids. He should have provided her with a plastic water bottle like bicyclists carried.

"Thanks," Plum let out.

Terry knew he would have to do all the talking, show a little nervousness, a little vulnerability. He took a deep breath and began.

"I know what happened, happened, Plum, but I must trust you now with some deep confidences. Probably what you're going to hear will shock you, but you have to trust me just as I'm trusting you with these facts." There was no response from her. She peeled her first egg. Who was he kidding? Who was she going to tell?

"Your three cousins in Pukekohe are growing marijuana. Well, that's okay. The trouble is the Maoris want it. They're bringing down a big shipment themselves from up north. Now it turns out these Maoris know about the greenhouses in Pukekohe. You know, the ones behind Bruce's house. They've been out there and plan to take it all. Of course, they're not going to turn up with knives and axes and whatnot. But they do want the stuff, and they want it bad."

He waited for a response, but Plum chewed her egg.

"They know you and your relationship to Bruce's family. They also know Wiremu Wilson was staying with you. What Wiremu has got to do with all this, I don't know. But he's mixed up in it somehow.

"Anyway, they were going to kidnap you and hold up your life for the harvested dope. It was that simple.

That's why I had Big John keep an eye on you. He wanted to warn you, but he got jumped on instead. Then some Maoris came over to your house and tried to kill him. He put up a terrific fight, you know how Big John can get, and he managed to escape."

Plum had finished the egg. She gave Terry a blank look.

"So I brought you here. I know it was against your will, and I know I appear inconsiderate, but you see, I had no choice. Plum, I still love you. I care for you a great deal, and it would kill me if anything happened to you. You can't deny the past. What we once had."

Plum slowly peeled her second egg.

"Plum, you can't be out there. No one can protect you like I can. You think the police would? What a joke! Those Maoris would find you. They control all the dope in this town and anyone else watch out! I've already let the Looks know what's happening. Other than that, I just have to sit tight and protect you."

Plum sneered.

"Plum. You have to trust me. You know my methods are a bit unorthodox, but you know they work. Right?"

"Bullshit," Plum whispered, her throat still sore. The eggs had not helped.

"What? I didn't hear you, Plum." When Terry raised his high-pitched voice a tone higher, he sounded meek.

"Bullshit!" she rasped.

"Just remember the last time you were with me, I protected you from your own family. They wanted to run you in as a prostitute. I supported you, I…"

"Who else knows I'm here?" she croaked.

"No one. Why? Should I tell someone?" Terry was concerned.

"Oh you." Plum gazed at the cold white toast. She lost her appetite, but she needed her food if only to sustain her rage. She had never won an argument with him, even though he always made it appear he was giving in to her. "I sh'd never've listened to you when I first met you, and I certainly don't trust you now. You're using me just like you use everyone else."

"Plum, with you, it's different. I thought we had something special. I've shown you in umpteen ways how much I care for you, even risking my family life and all the years of love and devotion I've received from my wife. You know that."

"My arse." She bit into the toast.

"You know, I wouldn't bring this up but it was very painful when I said good-bye to you at the airport, and I did pay for your ticket, right?" He saw her drop the toast and lie down on her cot, her eyes slowly closing. She continued to chew, then she stretched out and put her arms under her head and fell asleep.

Terry watched her slow breathing. Her pale brown body seemed so fragile and precious under her clothing.

He knelt down beside her and peeled back her right eyelid. He ran his left hand down her legs to her thin ankles. Perfect. He took from his pocket a length of soft nylon rope and gently tied her hands behind her back. He then rolled her over onto her stomach, made sure her hair was away from her mouth and she could breathe, then stepped back to admire his handiwork.

He bent over her and ran both his hands up the insides of her legs till they reached her panties. He could feel the heat coming from her. Parting her legs, he raised her skirt over her back, he massaged her buttocks before running a finger down the crack to the softest part of her body, her inner thighs just where they met her pubic hairs. The feel of her flesh through her panties gave him goose bumps. Terry bent over and kissed both buttocks. He ran his mouth down her crack to her dark moist mound. He expected to inhale her own peculiar sweet smell of lust, but instead he was assaulted with the smell of dried urine. Of course, Plum had not had a chance to wash. How could he forget? She usually smelt so sweet, so fresh.

Terry pulled her panties off. He gently parted her buttocks again and gazed at the tight brown hole that had given him so much pleasure.

In those intimate moments, Terry had found a new joy in knowing Plum Blossom. A rediscovery of what sex could be like with a young woman. He had indoctrinated her into the realm of anal sex, taught her how to move, to grip him with her strong tight muscles. He hungered for this unique experience again.

That Plum should enjoy this act and be grateful to him, this, Terry assumed to be true. All these memories had aroused him again, as did her mute, open availability. He slid his left index finger down between her buttocks and played with her perineum and the tight opening. He could not control himself. He had to do it, go where no man but he had gone.

Terry the Turk bounded up the steps to find a jar of Vaseline in his bathroom.

Ricky had spotted Hei Hei in the middle of the riot as the Maori made his way to the stairs at the back of the lounge. In the confusion outside, he had lost sight of the small fat man with a white turban. He ran across the road to the shop.

"I've seen him, let's go!" he yelled to Chuck who was behind the counter with Martin. There was no time for questions. Three people were at the counter. One, a tall man with short blond hair and blue eyes, turned away from Ricky and walked out of the shop with his two spring rolls.

"We'll be back for the rush," Ricky shouted over his shoulder as he took off his apron. He followed Chuck out of the shop leaving Martin on his own. A large crowd had gathered around the police cars and vans.

John Eustace stood two doors away and watched Ricky and Chuck scan the crowd. He did not know who they were looking for, but he was intrigued by the riot at the Three Lamps. There were now traffic police at each end of the block on Ponsonby Road, sealing off all cars. All the flashing blue lights added to the confusion.

Ricky and Chuck spotted their man with the white head bandage across the street. John Eustace finished the rolls and licked his greasy fingers. He crossed the road and headed towards the police cordon to get a better view of the two men. All three watched the Maori with the white head bandage approach the Hungry Wok. Between them were groups of drunk and distressed men and women and police shouting instructions to each other.

Hei Hei took the bottle out of his jacket. He lit the very top of the rag with his lighter. He counted, one Pakeha, two Pakeha, three Pakeha. The flames shot out a foot, there was so much oil in the rag.

He stepped back and, with his throwing arm extended, threw the burning bottle high into the shop then turned and walked away without looking back.

The bottle flew in an arc over the two men waiting and bounced on the counter, before smashing in the rear wall over the two vats of hot oil. Martin raised his head, as he held a strainer with the spring rolls, to see the gasoline spread over the vats. It was like a slow-motion film. The last image Martin would see was the remains of the rag as it fell in shreds into one of the vats. He had no time to leap over the counter or shield his face from the flames that shot out from the vats.

The jelly from the broken bottle was on his hair and hands. There was an explosion and a blinding white flash. He was saturated in burning oil. His one scream could not have been heard above the roar of flames and a second larger explosion that blew his remains out of the shop into the street. The two young men were incinerated where they stood.

Hei Hei ducked around the next corner when he heard the second louder boom followed by the breaking of glass. Then came screams, and the whole sky above him lit up like a giant bonfire. He rubbed his hands as he approached a late model red Holden and tried the door. It was unlocked. He took a knife out of his pocket and quickly hot-wired the car. He backed out of the parking space and drove down the hill in the opposite direction to the commotion. His body no longer ached.

Wiremu turned his head suddenly to the big red-colored windows. He felt the shock wave first in his guts. He swung around and grabbed Mel and Henry by the shoulders. Before they could ask what was happening, the shock wave shattered the red windows. Drunken patrons were showered with tiny particles of glass that exploded across the bar. An intense white flash followed that bounced off the mirrored surfaces and then the boom came, a deafening sound that kept coming, like thunder right overhead. After, there was complete silence for a long second. Then screams from outside, followed by shouts and cries for help in the bar. The impact of the explosion had been so strong that windows up and down the street had been shattered.

Mel, Wiremu and Henry staggered out of the bar in shock. Wiremu brushed pieces of glass out of his short hair and looked across the road. The entire two-storey wooden building that once housed the Hungry Wok was engulfed in a massive wall of flame. The fire was the color of Wiremu's eyes. This was how his brother had died. Death by fire. Wiremu felt the heat on his face, oblivious to the bodies running past him covered with bloody pieces of glass, yelling for help, over the wailing of sirens.

This is it, Wiremu thought, his mind clear amidst the confusion around him. After all the events of the last week, now, someone has firebombed the Chinese takeout. Mel had gone back inside the pub to assist an old man who had been thrown to the floor. He was too drunk to understand what had happened.

"What's going on?" Henry asked Wiremu.

"That was the Wongs," Wiremu muttered.

John Eustace, farther from the impact of the blast, thought he had seen everything, and he followed Hei Hei as best he could by pushing through the crowd.

Ricky and Chuck were oblivious to the injured bystanders. They fought their way to the next corner but could not see Hei Hei and the white bandages.

"Martin! Martin! What about Martin!" Ricky was screaming, but Chuck kept a tight grip on him as they reached the first corner. He had to find that Maori. They could feel the heat from the fire. The police were trying to clear the street for the fire trucks and ambulances. The fire was spreading to the adjacent shops, and flames leapt up to the roof directly above what used to be the Hungry Wok.

At the corner, Chuck bent down and tried to see through a car window farther down the street. In the dark he could barely recognize the big white bandage. He shouted to Ricky to keep an eye on the car while he got their car parked less than a block away.

Chuck raced to Ricky without switching on the head-lights. He swung open the door for Ricky to dive in and took off down the hill. Chuck swerved around the next corner in the direction Ricky saw Hei Hei's car turn.

John Eustace saw the two Chinese drive away in their white Holden. His car was parked on the other side of Ponsonby Road. He walked two blocks away from the conflagration to a phone box and called Terry.

Wiremu caught sight of John Eustace first, and then Mel recognized him. Her body went stiff.

"That's the man who attacked me," she whispered, her voice lost in the wails of sirens and the roar of the fires.

"Yeah. That's him, all right. Big John," Wiremu whispered behind his glasses. He did not want to ask Mel why she had stopped treating the injured. He knew what she wanted to do.

"Where? Who?" Henry could not understand what was going on. There was too much happening around him. Smoke, noise and crowds of people pushing past made everything confusing. Policemen with bullhorns were ordering everybody to evacuate the street. Mel gave him her car keys and told him to meet her two blocks away on Ponsonby Road. The car was accessible without being caught in the roadblock, and she wanted to keep the big figure in her sights.

Terry the Turk picked up the phone on the first ring.

"Our little brownie just firebombed the Hungry Wok," the gravelly voice said.

Terry checked the small back meter attached to his phone. The needle did not move. No one else was listening in on this conversation.

"Holy shit. So there really is a Maori Chinese war." He paused to catch his breath. "You sure it was him?"

"Sure." John turned around to marvel at the blazing skyline, the red and blue strobe lights of ambulances, fire trucks and rescue vehicles. The entire block of wooden shops was on fire. It was beautiful. The streetlights were off. He stood in darkness so he could see the red flames leaping up to reach the black sky.

"Better come back quick. We've work to do."

Hei Hei weaved in and out of the back roads of Ponsonby on his way up to Karangehape Road. He took his time, not wanting to speed or attract attention in his hot car, which he thought he might seriously convert, it was that much faster than the Morrie. Where had that oaf Wilson taken his car? He hadn't come back with it. There were probably police cars all over Ponsonby searching for the Chinese takeout bomber, if they knew it was firebombed. The cops would take days to work out what had happened. "Police suspect arson although the investigation is continuing." Hei Hei could hear the cautious statement on tomorrow's TV news. Although he did stick out like, like a Maori with a head bandage.

He checked his mirror and saw a car behind him. He had just turned another corner. No car could be taking the same meandering course as him. He swung around the next corner and watched to see if the car followed; it did. He accelerated, took the next corner without braking and turned into the first open driveway with his lights off. He pulled on the hand brake and slid down in the driver's seat to watch through his rear mirror as the white Holden went past. Hei Hei undid his head bandage and threw it out the window. He backed out and followed the car from a safe distance, not switching on his lights. I'll teach these little fuckers how to tail, he muttered to himself.

When Chuck reached Karangehape Road, he looked over to Ricky.

"Fuck the cunning bastard. Where is he?" he yelled as he beat the steering wheel. Ricky insisted they continue to Grafton Bridge in the hope of sighting the car.

"The bugger's disappeared!" Ricky screamed. That he had lost his brother in a fireball was slowly beginning to sink in. He knew there would have been no hope in rescuing Martin so he had pursued the man whom he held responsible for the fire.

"Let's cut this detective crap and go back to the house." Chuck spoke softly as they waited at the lights at Grafton Bridge.

Wiremu walked with Mel away from the inferno and stood in the shadows to see John come out of the phone booth.

"Do you think he did it?"

"I don't know. But I want to find out." Wiremu's eyes adjusted to the darkness. "You stay here, and when Henry comes, pick me up and we'll tail him." Wiremu bounded after John, keeping in the shadows.

John Eustace climbed into a new black Ford he had taken off the Ellerslie lot. He had fake plates on and the odometer was disconnected. He took off towards Epsom as fast as he could.

Wiremu swung into the back of Mel's car and pointed in the direction to where John's car had disappeared.

"What about Clovis?" Henry asked.

"Clovis is all right. Now drive!" Wiremu shouted.

Henry drove as fast as he could, but after three red lights they could find no trace of the black Ford.

"I bet he's gone to see his boss. I know where he lives, keep going."

Mel remained quiet. This was her second fire in a week, and with Henry's liberal use of her brakes, she felt sick.

Clovis sat in the small back room behind the stage. He cradled his violin case between his knees. Plum was missing, and he had just witnessed his second pub riot. This town was like the Wild West.

"God fuck it, Sheila! If you had'nt'a taken off your bleedin' dress there wouldn't've been a riot!" Matthew muttered to the whole band.

"That's not true," thundered Rua. "Some big Samoan hit a Chinese joker in the head. It had nothing to do with Sheila."

"Anyway, it cost us a gig. Now he'll never pay us. I have to get my car out of a garage in bleeding fucking Pukekohe somewhere and pay off the roadie."

"I'll go and see Tony. It sounds quiet out there now." Rua stood up.

"Atta boy! Watch out for those cops. They don't like big Maori boys. Ah? Like to lock 'em up. Er?" Matthew muttered in his best Maori imitation. He was not getting out of that little room till it was absolutely safe.

Hei Hei parked his car halfway up Grafton Road. He watched the Chinese get out of their car and quickly walk up the steps of a wooden house.

The effect of all the beer he had drunk began to wear off. The pains in his chest surfaced, and his left ear started to throb. He wanted a quick, brutal confrontation with the Chinamen and to spirit Moana away to safety. If he had his Morrie, he knew he had a shotgun under the tire. Damn that good for nothing Maori for taking his car! Bleeding Maoris! Always borrowing things and never returning them. No respect for the individual's rights. No sense of the European civilization and the refined homo sapiens Pakeha. I ask you. What a stupid people!

Hei Hei had never walked away from a tough situation, and he was not going to start now. He eased the car down to where the two Chinamen had parked, left the car running and checked the trunk. He took out a tire iron.

"Do you need me for anything else, sir?" Sergeant Cadd poked his head into Inspector Bernie Grimble's office. The inspector had his feet up on the desk as he read through the textbook on acid.

"Yes. Come in. Sit down."

The textbook had come back from fingerprints. The only clear prints had been Turner's. What was interesting to the inspector was that the book had fallen open on the chapter on corrosive acids and metals.

"Now Turner has a huge car lot. Why would he be interested in corrosive acids? And why would he keep such a book in the bureau? Hidden in a drawer. Not in his library where every other book in his house is."

"Perhaps he wants to melt down registration numbers on engine blocks and restamp them with new ones. You know, for converting them and insurance."

"Nice try, Cadd, but acid is too impractical, too messy. No. I want to go back to his house. Don't know what I'm looking for, but we'll check the place out, then go to his lot."

The phone rang. Grimble received a briefing on what was happening on Ponsonby Road. He slowly replaced the receiver and addressed Cadd.

"Now I really want to check out Turner's house again."

"He's dead. Blown up. One minute we were in the shop behind the counter, the next we were thrown back by the blast. I still can't believe it. I mean …" Ricky fought back tears.

"We should be back there. But the shop's gone. Martin's gone, and we saw the Maori fella. So we tried to follow him but lost the bastard." They were seated around the kitchen table with Moana. She had been drinking tea and playing solitaire when they burst in.

"Knowing Hei Hei, he probably followed you here. He's a cunning bugger," Moana spoke. "He wants utu. He'll hunt you all down and try to get me. And I don't ever want to see him again."

"Let him come. We have enough stuff here to knock him back to the Tang dynasty," Ricky boasted. He winked at Moana.

"Tung," Chuck corrected as he smiled at Moana. "Tang is a powdered orange drink."

As soon as Terry heard John gun the Ford through the open electric gates, he ran outside to wave John around the back. John eased the car up to the back door without going on the grass.

"Come on," was all Terry said as he beckoned John down to the basement.

In the cell, Terry whispered to John, "She's drugged and tied up. Pick her up and put her in the trunk." He had already tidied up the cell. He now double-checked his housework. There was no trace of an inhabitant. He had wiped the entire room clean of prints and disinfected all surfaces. Not one piece of Plum was left, not one smear of Vaseline.

John zigzagged through Mount Eden and turned right onto Great South Road.

"I've got a feeling that we should put Plum in a safer isolated place. We've only a day or so left before this is all sewn up. Er, John?"

John stretched his shoulders. He wondered what Terry had done to Plum and whether it was before or after he had drugged her. He hoped he would get his turn.

Hei Hei sat in the driver's seat again and searched through the glove compartment. He found a rolled joint, sniffed it and let out a low whistle. Bad boy. Whoever left this here was asking for it to be confiscated. He took out his lighter and lit up. After the third toke, his mind was clear, so clear it was frying. He disconnected the wires and the car engine died. In the silence, he could visualize every little detail of his plan with his heightened sense of perception.

Bruce Look lay on his side of the bed. His wife was fast asleep next to him, ignorant of his nightmare. Every time he shut his eyes he saw the new Volvo dissolving in black and green fumes of acid. He had told his wife the car was in the garage for a checkup.

The phone rang next to the bed. Bruce stood up to answer it. He wanted to be ready for that Maori voice. It was Chuck. Bruce listened in silence as Chuck recounted what had happened in Ponsonby.

Martin was dead. The Hungry Wok was blown up. The Wongs had kidnapped Moana Wilson, who was related to Wiremu Wilson. Was this the Wilson who had called him? Bruce could not make sense of all the events. Perhaps Tony could piece everything together.

"I'll let Tony know tomorrow. It's too late to call him now. Call me if you hear anymore. I'll be here." Bruce placed the receiver back on the hook and looked over to his wife, who did not stir. He felt numb.

He found a blanket in the closet and went to lie on the sofa. His wife had insisted that the air-conditioning be turned down to 70, and he felt chilled to the bone. They had to come up with a plan.

"It's okay! I was there this morning. In fact, I came right over the wall." Wiremu directed Henry to the unofficial back entrance, where he had borrowed the bike.

"I'm not being a party to breaking and entering," Mel repeated.

"Don't worry. I'm on my own. Just stay here. If I'm not back in ten minutes, go to Newmarket Road and call the cops. Say you've spotted me going up Terry's street. Act alarmed then hang up. You can turn the lights off and neck. Eh?"

There were no lights on in any house.

"And you?" Mel asked.

"I don't know. I'm making this up as I go along. I don't want to be caught by Terry and his henchman. Not if they're armed."

"Are you?"

"Nah." Wiremu slipped out of the car and disappeared down a driveway.

"Well, I think we should take Wiremu up on his suggestion."

"I'd give anything to see Wiremu climb over a wall," Mel whispered, ignoring Henry's comment. She wound down her window and listened. "I only hope he finds Plum." She turned to face Henry, her brow creased. "I just want this to be over. When we came back from New York, I thought we'd live happily ever after."

"This is not some American movie."

"For one thing, it's longer. This has been going on for a week. Seven days of bloody tension and suspense. Ever since we followed Wiremu through that damn pub window. Why did we do it?"

Henry had no answer to such a simple question. He took hold of her hand and leaned over to kiss her.

Hei Hei crouched at the bottom of the steps and listened. There was no movement in the house. No lights on. Nothing. He had finished the joint and felt totally aware of his surroundings; the smell of the blocked drain to his left, two dogs barking at each other up the valley, a speeding car backfiring down Grafton Road, a hedgehog sniffing out a slug near the clothesline.

The back door creaked open and a tall figure slowly walked out into the garden, stopped and urinated over a bush. Hei Hei slid back into the shadows. He could not identify the figure. He hesitated for a moment, then the figure turned around and stomped up the steps and shut the door. He cursed himself that he did not have enough time to hit the bugger over the head. Hei Hei waited for the footsteps in the house to stop.

Hei Hei lost track of time; the weed he smoked must have been stronger than he thought. The house was silent. They had to be asleep. All he had to do was tiptoe in, find Moana, take her out the back door and knock anyone who came near him over the head with this iron. It was a good plan. He crept up the steps and tried the door handle. It was unlocked.

Wiremu knelt at the bottom of the stairs that led to the porch and the back door. The house was dark and no car was parked in the driveway. He listened for anything that did not fit in. There were cicadas rubbing their wings near him, some restless birds up in a palm tree and a small dog yapping in the distance. He breathed slowly and deeply, the scent of a gardenia bush, sweet and rich, was nearby.

He heard a car come up the driveway. Two doors opened and shut. There were footsteps up to the front door and, after much jangling of keys, the door opened. He rose to his feet and saw the light of a torch skimming the walls. No house lights came on. He crawled to the small window he had broken that looked down into the basement and saw the two intruders next to the farthest wall. One shone his torch on the other's face.

Wiremu watched Grimble and the other man disappear into a closet. Hadn't he read a book about this once, in Para, by a joker called Lewis who wrote about lions and witches and yes, a wardrobe?

Henry checked his watch. "Ten minutes."

"What?" Mel had her head against his shoulder.

"He's been gone ten minutes."

"Can you see where this will end?"

"No. Not at all. Can you?"

"No. That's what's so disconcerting. When I treat a patient, I discern all the symptoms, signs, do tests, get a diagnosis... everything's analyzed and I can tell what's going to happen. There are probabilities, statistics... a lot of things are indefinite, I mean, we can't see into the future, but there's some stability, some vision. A core of understanding. With this, it's like... like..."

"Looking into darkness."

"Yes, exactly. Like nothing."

Mel shut her eyes and rested on Henry's shoulder. He checked his rear mirror. He heard a dog bark, then another deeper bark. Henry switched on the ignition. Mel turned around to see Wiremu running towards them with a small poodle yapping at his heels.

Hei Hei leaned against the wall in the kitchen with his tire iron over his shoulder, at the ready. His eyes had adjusted to the dark, and he listened for any sounds in the house.

He walked to the first door. If anyone were going to swing a nunchaku at him, he would block it with his tire iron. The floorboards were noisy, noisier that the kitchen door. The hinges were like witches wailing at a full moon. He squatted in the hallway and waited. He did not know if it was paranoia, extra sensory perception or too much weed and beer, but someone was in the front room. He could feel their presence. He wanted to kick in the door and beat the living daylights out of them. But the thought occurred to him that Moana might be in there.

Hei Hei reached for the doorknob and slowly pushed the door open. He peered into the room, but it was pitch-black. If there was no one in the room he would have to climb the stairs, probably very creaky stairs. He waited, then as he edged past the door he leapt up ready to strike and he heard a whooshing noise. He lunged with the tire iron, but when he did not connect, he rose up and slashed the iron again in the direction of his invisible assailant. The iron caught in a chain and he came nose to nose with the holder of the nunchaku. Hei Hei tried to head-butt the attacker and missed. He received a whack on the uninjured side of his head. Then he brought his knee up to where he sensed his attacker's balls were, but he did not know if he made contact because he was punched and kicked again.

He lost his bearings, then a bright light shone into his face. He lashed out with the tire iron at the source of light but was hit again first on his head then on his left elbow. He tried to strike out again as he lurched from the room to the front door. He felt something in his back, tore the door open and headed to the car. His head was groggy from all the hits and his left arm was numb, but he could not start the engine. He slipped the brake off and cruised past the house he had come from and saw a tall figure in the doorway. Every light was on in the house as he looked back. He struggled with both hands to hot-wire the car again as it picked up speed down the hill.

Ricky shut the door and turned to Moana.

"You were great with the torch. Perfect timing."

Moana stepped closer to him. "You were amazing with the chucks." She was so close to Ricky he could smell her hair. "You're my protector." She put her arms around him and rested her head on his chest.

Ricky lifted her chin and kissed her.

Chapter Nine

Saturday

Clovis woke up late with a hangover. The events of Friday night came back to him like a bad dream. His soaring violin solo, the riot, the explosion outside, the whole block burning down, and they had not been paid. Matthew had been correct. Damn! And the manager threatened to charge them for the damage. He realized he was in Mel's living room, on the sofa. There was a knock on the door.

"A Matthew's on the phone! Can you talk to him?" Mel asked.

Clovis grunted a yes and got up. He was surprised to see he was still wearing last night's clothes, and the room began to spin as he walked to the door.

"Yeah?" Clovis rested his head against the kitchen wall and shut his eyes. Why was the kitchen spinning as well?

"Clovis Tibet. I need you to come with me to pick up the Stude tomorrow. Be over my place by three at the latest. Okay?"

"Sunday?"

"Yes, Sunday. Today's Saturday. And it is followed, always, by Sunday, which will be tomorrow. It's guaranteed. Remember you left my prize possession on the

Motorway. It's now fixed. I need someone to go with me so they can drive the other car back. As long as they don't break down again. Understand?"

"Yeah. But, but Plum is still missing, I might be tied up."

"Look. You can go out and see her grandfather again. Be at my place three sharp. Got it?"

"Yeah." Clovis let the receiver fall into the cradle. He turned very slowly, counterclockwise, to face Henry and Mel. He repeated Matthew's instructions to his audience.

"Here's some coffee. Special brew." Mel put a full mug on the table. Clovis eased himself into the chair.

"You really knocked back a lot of whisky." Henry sat back, arms behind his head.

"Where's Wiremu?" Clovis asked as they both stared at him.

"Went to return a bicycle he borrowed," Henry spoke up.

"Do I hate this drive. It's boring." John Eustace stretched out his big frame in the driver's seat.

"It'll be quicker coming back. And you'll have some satisfaction. Eh?" Terry watched John drive. "I'm so glad we moved her. After last night."

"Do you think they got inside?"

"Yeah. The door wasn't shut the same. I keep the basement locks in a certain way. I could swear he was down there. The little shit."

"You could dust the place. File a complaint."

"Nah. No time for that. Besides, he can enter if he thinks there's drugs. He didn't find anything, so we're safe."

John noticed that it was always "we" if they were in trouble and "I" if they had done something great.

"And I had this strange feeling in the house, I felt, violated. You know?"

John wanted to say "like Plum," but thought better of it. "What about the alarm?"

"Seemed all right. Shit. They're professionals. They're the police, goddammit! But Grimble thinks I'm involved in Plum's disappearance. That's why he came; he's not Drugs."

"But Plum hasn't been murdered."

"You're very observant. He's connected that burnt Maori with Plum and assumes some big deal is going down. He probably thinks I'm masterminding the whole thing. Although, even I wouldn't dream of bombing the Hungry Wok. Ouch! That was bad. Are you certain our little Hei Hei did it?"

"Sure as I'm next to you."

"Beautiful. Hei Hei's days are almost over."

"His girl didn't check in again last night. There was no reply to the phone number she gave us."

"Did you sneak back to the Flamingo last night, John?" Terry spoke as if he were addressing a naughty schoolboy.

"Couldn't help it. Not after carrying Plum into the warehouse."

"Who'd you have?"

"Laurie."

"The school girl?"

"She dropped out."

"How's she doing?"

"She's opening up." John paused and let out a sigh.

"Careful with her. She's earning two hundred a night."

"Only a hundred and sixty. Last night."

"You sure?"

"Of course. I keep tabs. Remember. It's my job."

"Just go easy on Laurie. Don't fuck her up. Look what happened to Juicy Lucy. Now there was a girl could earn five hundred a night. No sweat. She had great teeth."

"Good morning, sir!" Cadd stood in Grimble's doorway.

"Come in. Get a good night's sleep?" It had been his last order to his sergeant.

"Yessir," he lied. Cadd had spent half the night arguing with his girlfriend. She was upset that he had entered a private dwelling without a search warrant. He was upset that he had told her. Lately he had been confiding in her. He left out the bit about hauling the murdered Maori into the house and then finding the body burnt to a crisp. But he needed to get this off his chest. Now he regretted what he had started. She could not handle the stories. He should have taken Grimble's advice a long time ago, when the inspector had addressed the newly promoted detectives: "Never take your work home with you. Talk to other cops. They're your only friends. It's a brotherhood. No one else can understand the pressures, the strain, the responsibilities."

"Good. You're going to need it. We've a long weekend ahead. By the way, you were pretty good with that alarm."

"Thank you, sir. I located it last time we were there."

"Before you found the book?"

"Yes, sir."

The phone rang and Grimble picked it up. He mumbled into the receiver then hung up, not taking his eyes off the sergeant.

"That piece of plastic spoon we found under the, er, bed, has a partial of Plum Blossom's thumb."

"But how can we admit that as …"

Grimble held up his hands.

"Don't worry. That's taken care of. The report'll be dated Monday. And I'm going to get a warrant to tear apart every place he owns, piece by piece." He swung around in his chair, pulled out a file from a cabinet next to his desk and laid it on top of the other files and reports.

"Get ten copies of this. It's a list of every property he has interest in. We're going to find Miss Plum Blossom in one of these. And she'll probably tell us, if she's still alive, who killed Hone Wilson."

The phone rang again as he sent Cadd out of his office.

"Wally McShane here!" the voice at the other end barked. "Thought you'd like to know we've been getting lots of rumors about something big, for Sunday."

"Sources?"

"Usual. Mainly Maoris on bail trying to swing a deal. Plus a low-grade dealer we're nurturing."

Grimble did not want to know how McShane interpreted the word "nurturing."

"There's no pot on the streets."

"You're right, Grimble. That is, for people who still deign to smoke god's own weed."

"You're very patriotic this morning."

"No. Pissed off at all this cocaine. I've got a terrible feeling about it."

"Keep me posted, will you? I mean anything. It might be linked to this homicide case."

"You mean that coconut Wilson. He was a DB man." McShane referred to the beer brewed by Dominion Breweries.

"But his brother isn't. Wiremu Wilson's also wanted for that shotgun incident."

"Do you think he had anything to do with that fire last night?"

"Could be. I've got a team watching the tangi, and he hasn't shown up."

"That's odd."

"Yes. A Maori so immersed in his Maoritanga that he can't attend his own brother's tangi. I ask you."

"How does all this tie in?"

"That's what we've got to find out." Grimble was not going to tell McShane about the search warrants until the last possible moment. He did not want the drug squad cowboys crashing through windows while his men went through the open doors.

Plum woke with a start. She saw a polystyrene cup on the floor. She could smell the coffee. A croissant on a piece of paper was next to the cup. She had a headache and felt nauseous. She sat up on her camp bed and felt wet between her thighs. It was too soon for her period. She tried to stand up but was overcome by dizziness. She was not in her cell. She had been moved. Probably drugged as well, for she did not remember anything. She stuck her finger up her dress and under her panties and felt the stickiness. She held her finger up to her eyes. No blood. Vaseline and that familiar smell from the Flamingo Paradise that she swore the walls were covered with. Plum closed her eyes and wiped her hand on the side of the bed.

When she stood up, she vomited. There was nothing in her stomach. In a hot sweat, Plum dry retched over her coffee and croissant. How she wanted to spit out every part of him that was still inside her.

She swore she would do anything to annihilate Terry Turner, even if it meant losing her life.

• • •

Hei Hei's apartment was deserted. There was blood on the sofa and the telephone lay in pieces on the carpet. There was a terrible smell coming from the kitchen. Wiremu went to his house and called Hokianga.

Rangi was cleaning a spark plug from the 1968 Bedford truck parked in the barn. When he heard the phone ring, he carefully placed the spark plug and a piece of emery paper on an oily rag on the driver's seat and ran to the house.

"It's me. Is everything set?"

"Yeah, why aren't you at the tangi?"

"It's too hot."

"Oh. I'm sorry about Hone. I mean, I, well, you know how I felt about him. He was an example to all of us, and..."

"Okay. I understand. Is it all packed?"

"You bet." Rangi had supervised the entire process in his barn.

Hundreds of uprooted marijuana plants had been hung up to dry in the rafters last year after the police had come to raid Northland. Wiremu had not lost as much of the crop as he had suspected. They had decided to stockpile and hide half their harvest and store it for the inevitable drought next summer.

Rangi and his crew had packed the dried and cured leaves and buds into quarter-pound plastic bags that were carefully weighed and sealed.

They planned to sell each bag for $300 to gangs and dealers and the hippie network of shorthaired '60s' kids who were now lawyers and accountants and architects. Twelve hundred dollars a pound was a bargain at this time of year. It was also the best of dope, strong, sweet and hallucinatory enough to demand the higher price. The dealers would love selling it.

There were 120 bags in a box. Thirty pounds meant $36,000 a box. There were 120 boxes in the truck; 3600 pounds equaled $4,320,000. A staggering amount for a truckload of green leafy material taken from public lands. There was no capital investment with this crop, only sweat and secrecy.

Wiremu confirmed that everything had been packed according to his specifications and that Rangi had double-checked all the bags. A ten percent error would cost almost half a million dollars.

"Now listen carefully," Wiremu continued. "Meet me at five o'clock. You know the Helensville turnoff on Titirangi Road?"

"Yeah." Rangi swatted a fly that landed on his trousers.

"Okay. Before you get to Titirangi Road, about a half-mile up, there's a little track on the left. It's not marked and it looks like it goes nowhere. But it does. It'll be real dry there, so drive up till you come to a fallen log. Cut the engine and honk twice. Only twice. You got it?"

"Yeah. Of course." He swatted another fly. Wiremu made him repeat the instructions.

"What truck did you load?" Wiremu asked.

"The Bedford."

"What? What happened to the Toyota?"

"They went down to the tangi in it. Don't worry. The Bedford'll be jake. I'm fixing it."

Wiremu did not know how to react. Here they were with over four million dollars in merchandise and they were using an old truck that might not make the trip. How could you justify three and a half tons of dope on the back of a truck to a traffic cop who has stopped you because you're in a ditch and can't start your engine? He had no control of the situation up there. All he could do was hope and pray Rangi knew what he was doing. If

Hone were alive, he would have been up there making sure everything went according to plan.

"Don't let me down. Five o'clock. No later. No sooner." Wiremu hung up. He did not tell Rangi anything about Hei Hei. He had changed the rendezvous and the distribution plans, and Rangi had decided to use the Bedford instead of the Toyota. What if Hei Hei had snitched to the cops about a Toyota truck loaded with dope? Wiremu's mind wandered off on the possibilities of Rangi breaking down in Dargaville and trying to bribe the local cop with a bag of grass.

At the rendezvous, Wiremu would take several boxes to a cave nearby and conceal them with sacks. Other cartons would be repacked into large plastic garbage bags and hidden farther up the road in locations he had scouted out with his brother two weeks ago. After the initial deliveries that night, any additional sales would involve cash up front and a map to guide the buyer to the merchandise. For an extra fee a guide could be provided. But Hei Hei would no longer be the guide.

Then he would be off to see Alan Crispfeldt, Esquire, with the cash. Bags and bags of cash. To invest in short-term high-interest loans. Up to 25 percent for six weeks! Before the land deals could be worked out.

Every toke a Pakeha inhaled was another sod of earth back to Maori. Into the hands of the Ngapuhi they smoked. This was revisionist history. Maori karma with a vengeance. And there was no Paraquat or 2,4,5-T sprayed over this stuff. It was organically grown on Her Majesty's lands. Royal weed!

"Shit! The little buggers! They haven't packed it up yet." Terry gave the binoculars to John as they stood next to their car on a rut-filled road at the back of Pukekohe.

John adjusted the focal length and scanned the four greenhouses of the Look brothers.

"No. Not in that one."

"Not in any of them!"

"They had everything hung up and cured the last time I poked around."

"We'll shock them into action."

"With Plum?"

"No. She's the bait. See over there. No white Volvo. One Land Rover. A motorbike. No Honda and no Ford."

"Er?"

Terry got back in the car and sat in the driver's seat. John hurried in as Terry fired up the engine and backed up.

"Cars usually follow their owners. Bruce's wife drives the Ford and Tony Look has the Honda. Tony was home this morning when I phoned. And Bruce has sent the wife and kids packing because he expects violence. Which is correct. But he's got the wrong place and the wrong time." Terry wrestled the car through the ruts and swerved onto another dirt road.

"Are we going to play Maoris?

"No need," he smiled. "No prisoners."

John grinned. He had heard the expression before.

Bruce stood in the center of the greenhouse. He took a deep breath of the harvested crop before them. Chuck ran his hands over a tray of buds that were cured.

"Is Tony coming over?" Chuck asked.

"Later," he sighed. "He's going to mow his lawn, then clean his car. He has this routine he won't change, even now."

"I don't think he's as concerned as we are."

"Yes, he is."

"He wants to hold out. Plum doesn't mean anything to him. Another number. He's thinking like a Pakeha. No sense of family. And he's an accountant. A cost accountant! Like that fucking Prime Minister. You know?" Chuck stood up and went red in the face.

"What do you think we should do?"

"In principle, we shouldn't gamble with Plum's life. We should give them what they want. And a lot more."

"How?"

"Martin's gone. That Maori raided the Wongs. We're all in danger now. Not just Plum. We can't trust anyone outside. Agreed?"

"Yes."

"We can deliver a lot more than this." Chuck grabbed a handful of dried buds. He crushed them in his fist and they turned to powder. "Is this worth a life?"

"I never said it was. But why should we give in to these people, be they Maori or whatever."

"Exactly." Chuck waited again to get Bruce's full attention. He wiped his hands.

"What are you thinking?"

"Well, it isn't legal."

"Is this?"

"After that incident with that Maori last night, we stayed up till dawn thinking of all our options. And…"

"Come on."

"Ricky has contacts, and through swapping some seeds, he managed to get some C4 explosive and a couple of radio controlled detonators."

"Do you realize what you're saying?"

"Yeah. We've thought this through. We could do it without jeopardizing innocent lives. I mean, Ricky worked it out." Chuck explained how Ricky was going to arrive later with everything they needed.

• • •

Tony Look knelt by his lawn mower in his garage. He had the new rotary two-stroke on its side and was trying to loosen up the clumps of grass that were around the blade. He was careful not to catch his fingers on the sharp metal. He had disconnected the spark plug so the motor would not accidentally turn and cut his fingers off. Once he had swept the drive and the inside of the garage, that damn grass seemed to blow everywhere, he would wash and wax his car. Water was not beading on the paint, so he wanted to apply a better wax compound.

His wife and children had gone out for the day, leaving him in peace. He needed this time every week to gather his thoughts and tender his newly laid concrete paths and driveway and trim the best lawn on the street, in fact, the only lawn on the street. The other houses were being built or had been finished but were unoccupied.

At least he could not be blamed for bringing down the tone of the neighborhood, as first on his street. He was not considered a Pakeha, he was still Chinese, an outsider. He had overheard comments about "how hard those Chinese work, you've got to give them credit," but he could do nothing about such attitudes other than mow his lawn and be more respectable than the others. How respectable could he be with four greenhouses loaded with sinsemilla, which were the object of a blackmail attempt by a Maori gang who had abducted a cousin of theirs?

He scraped harder with his screwdriver inside the underbelly of the lawn mower.

Tony thought about the phone call he received that morning. A high-pitched man's voice had asked who he was, and when Tony had identified himself, the voice had inquired if his wife was home. When Tony had answered no, the voice had hung up. Was that a burglar or one of his wife's friends? His wife did not have any male friends.

Tony heard something behind him and leapt in the air clutching his screwdriver. The tall figure had shut the garage door and advanced towards the frightened gardener. Tony saw a smaller man to the side of him and thought it strange that he wore black gloves and a nylon jacket in this heat.

John Eustace walked up to Tony and grabbed his right hand, pulling him off balance. He kicked him in the left knee, and Tony dropped the screwdriver and fell to the floor. John held the right wrist and tightened his grip.

"Listen. Why aren't you packing up your pot? Those Maoris mean business. They'll kill Plum."

Tony Look was silent. He tried to say something but was paralyzed with fear. John acknowledged Terry's discrete nod by tightening his grip.

"Speak up. We want to help you. Let him go, will you?" Terry acted annoyed towards John. He eyed the frightened kneeling accountant with concern. Tony Look held his right wrist and turned to stare at his short assailant.

"That's better." Terry sounded encouraging, as if addressing a naughty child.

Tony took a deep breath. "Where is Plum?"

"That's what we'd like to know. She is a friend of mine, and I'm concerned about her safety. I believe some Maoris have her."

The tall man with the cold blue eyes hovered over him.

"And please, who are you?" Tony stood up and brushed some dirt off his trousers whilst keeping his eyes on both men.

"I said we're friends, and we've heard from these Maoris that you're supposed to give them your harvest for Plum Blossom."

Tony glared back but did not reply.

"And we also heard you're not going to give up your crop and that the Maoris were going to rape then kill, very slowly, very, very slowly, your little cousin. Or is she your niece? Whatever." Terry paused for a reaction. There was none. "Then they're going to take your crop anyway. And the saddest part is, you'll be helpless against them. Outnumbered, out armed and out thought!"

"That's not true!" Tony shot back.

John stepped up to the lawn mower, kicked it over onto its wheels and pulled the cord. It would not start. He examined it then connected the spark plug. He started the motor. Tony inched away, keeping an eye on the silent man.

"So, you have a plan? Er? How will you get Plum back?" Terry's voice was raised several tones to make himself heard above the noise of the lawn mower.

Tony's eyes darted around the garage as he tried to find a way out of this. He could not imagine what was about to happen to him as Terry motioned John to come within earshot.

He darted for the door that led into his house, but John leapt on him and pushed him to the concrete floor. Tony gasped for air as the big man sat on his back. Terry grabbed a coil of thick yellow nylon cord that hung on the wall and threw it to John.

"Hang him up there." Terry pointed to an exposed beam in the center of the garage. John bound Tony's feet tightly together and slung the rope through the beam. Tony clawed at the concrete floor, but before he knew what had happened, he was swinging from the beam, his hands loose. John tied the other end of the cord to a nail and walked over to the lawn mower.

Blood rushed to Tony's head. Upside down, he tried to grab his legs and the cord with his hands, but he could not reach. He hung his head down and focused his eyes on the upside down figure revving the mower.

Terry stuffed an oily rag into Tony's mouth, relishing the panic in the victim's eyes. John smiled as he moved the mower closer to the suspended Tony.

Terry waved John to back off, and he knelt down to whisper in Tony's ear.

"What are you going to do with the pot?" He looked at Tony for some time then removed the oily rag from Tony's mouth.

Tony spat in Terry's face. Terry stuffed the rag back in his mouth and stood up. He walked back to the garage door. He found a box of oversized black plastic garbage bags and took out two. He pierced the bottom of the bag and put it over his head, making holes for his arms. He threw one to John who followed his example.

In his executioner's garb, John revved up the mower and grinned at his suspended victim. He lifted up the lawn mower so it was at right angles to Tony who put his arms around his head. Tony could see the blade rotating at a high speed inches from his nose. Tony tried to protect himself from the advancing lawn mower that spat dirt and hot exhaust fumes at his face. He instinctively tried to push the mower away, but he caught his left hand in the advancing blade.

Splinters of bone and blood splashed across John's black plastic apron. Tony tried to scream as loud as he could but he choked on the oily rag. He swung his body away from the blade and attempted to pull himself upright using the hand he could still feel.

John pushed the lawn mower into Tony's swinging body. Pieces of clothing and tissue splattered across the garage. Every frantic move Tony made meant that the blade would cut deeper and deeper into his body. John pressed the blade again and again into the helpless flesh. Terry stepped back and watched in silent fascination as John worked.

When the rag fell out of his mouth, Tony's mouth moved up and down, but he was unable to cry out. Blood poured out of the exposed gashes and tears to form pools under his suspended body. His eyes were open but were blinded by the blood dripping down his face into his hair. Pieces of his arms that remained attached to his shoulders twitched.

The lawn mower jammed on something and the engine seized. John stepped back to admire his work. Then he noticed the mower had stopped and he dropped it. He could not take his eyes off the mutilated body dangling in front of him.

There was silence in the garage punctuated by the drips of blood. It was moments like these that John felt a rare feeling come over him. A life had been snatched away and he had caused this. There was such a power and finality to his actions. He smiled sweetly at his boss. John tore off his plastic apron and left it on the floor.

"Come on, let's get outta here," Terry muttered as he stood next to the garage door. The smell hit him. A mixture of blood, feces and god knows what else, that was inside the Chinaman. The sight and smell disgusted him. Chop suey Tony. He would never be able to eat chop suey again. How many fledgling drug dealers had been chopped up in their own home? There's always a first time, he mused as he pulled off his garbage bag, turned it inside out and threw it to John. "Put the other one in this and we'll dispose of them later."

"Do you think they'll get the message?" John asked as Terry drove back north on the Motorway.

"They'll deliver everything to us now. I'll phone 'em tonight. They'll be in a panic. Tell me that garbage bag isn't leaking all over the car?"

"No. I put it inside a fresh one."

"Good. He won't be needing it."

Terry would have the bags, gloves and clothes burnt back at the Ellerslie lot. The plates would be changed on the car and the car would be repainted by Monday.

"I hate these new suburbs. They look like death." Terry sighed.

John turned to Terry back at the lot.

"You know, I was thinking. We could have lit the rag in his mouth and poured petrol around him. If he dropped the rag he'd've gone up in flames, and if he had kept it in his mouth, he'd've burnt his face. It would have been less messy."

"Jesus, John. You're getting creative. You've had too much fire this week. Remember the house in Ponsonby and last night's fire. Some smart cop might link all this together. No, we did a fantastic job on him. The first lawn mower murder. Right out of a horror movie. Good enough for the Guinness Book of Records! We should'a taken Polaroids!"

"Okay, boys! What's for lunch?" Hei Hei burst through the front door, but he startled no one. The three men who lived in the house were upstairs fast asleep. He walked into the kitchen and took a beer out of the refrigerator. He sat down at the table by the telephone and dialed a number in Hokianga. When the phone started to ring, he bit off the bottle top. He was able to take a full swig before Rangi picked up.

"Hey, Rangi mate. How ya goin'?"

"Hei Hei! G'day mate," Rangi shouted back. He cradled the receiver on his left shoulder and wiped the grease off his hands with a rag. Rangi idolized Hei Hei.

"You heard from Wiremu, right?"

"Yeah. He called earlier."

"He's in real trouble and his brother dead and all, it's real tragic."

"Yeah. I know. He's changed the rendezvous. I'm leaving early tomorrow morning."

"So he told me." Hei Hei gambled that Wiremu had not told Rangi about Moana and their little quarrel. If he had, Rangi would have been halfway to Auckland by now to rescue her. "Do you think you'll find it okay?" Hei Hei took another swig of beer.

"Easy. What about you?"

"I don't know, there's lots of turns up there, I could get lost. And I can't reach Wiremu again 'cos he's in hiding."

"I said it's easy. If you miss the turn off, you'll hit Titirangi Road about a half mile later. Just go back and it'll be on the right, instead of the left."

"Okay. But what about the time? Is everything loaded and ready?" Hei Hei had been with Wiremu scouting out secret drop off points.

"Don't worry, Hei Hei, it's going to be all right. I'm leaving at dawn. I've plenty of time. I'll be there at five. Wiremu insists I be on time."

"You're a good man, Rangi. Stay cool and don't speed."

"I can't, I'm driving the Bedford."

"See you there." Hei Hei hung up. You dumb fuck Maori, telling me the rendezvous and time like that. And he's driving the old truck. All that money in a piece of shit that could break down in the middle of nowhere. "Excuse me, Officer, but could you give me a tow, I've got tons of grass in the back and I've to reach this place by five otherwise Wiremu will kill me." Hei Hei could hear Rangi's voice in his head as he emptied the beer down his throat. He let out a belch guaranteed to waken his friends upstairs.

• • •

Chuck Look tried to observe the speed limit on the Motorway, but he constantly had to ease back on the throttle as he climbed to over a 100. The machine hummed between his legs as he weaved between cars on the way to Tony's exit, keeping an eye out for speed traps.

"Welcome to Exclusive Mahana" the painted sign declared at the entrance to the new development. Chuck parked his Kawasaki in Tony's driveway. The lawn had been mown, but his car was still dirty. He called out but there was a strange silence. He looked up and down the street. He did not see a soul. The lawn was immaculate. What a strange brother he had. Growing grass! Real legal grass!

Chuck took off his helmet and called Tony's name again. All he could hear was a peculiar sound. The garage door was not completely closed so he lifted it up. Light flooded in and a strange odor hit his nostrils. The smell was like cow dung, only stronger. He called out Tony's name, twice. There was no answer, only the buzzing.

He noticed an odd shape hanging from the center rafter. As he stepped nearer, he saw the noise was coming from hundreds of bluebottles and other flies clustered over this shape. The lawn mower was on its side with the blade faced away from him. Flies were crawling over the floor of the garage underneath the shape. The floor was glistening with the frenzied insects.

Chuck cautiously stepped towards the sound. He felt nauseous as he bent down and stuck his finger in the dark glistening pool. He held his finger up and sniffed it. A fly landed on his finger to lick the blood. Every hair on his head stood up as he stepped back and screamed. The scream echoed through the garage. The flies were swarming over his dead brother.

He knocked the lawn mower over and noticed something caught in the blade. He bent down and recognized part of Tony's right hand that had been severed at the wrist.

Chuck rushed inside to the toilet and knelt by the bowl. He retched so hard he felt his stomach lining coming out of his mouth. His splashed his face with water and tried to get the buzzing sound out of his ears and the stench out of his nose. He could not. He ran to Tony's king-size bed and dialed Bruce. Martin blown up in the city was bad enough, but the murder of his own brother was the end. He controlled his shock as he tried to talk to Bruce. He wanted to spare Bruce the details. He did not want anyone else to see or hear what he had.

Bruce was surprised at how calmly he took the news. He drove over there as fast as he could in the Land Rover. Chuck was still in the bedroom, crying. He was shocked at the sight in the garage. He cut the body down and stuffed it into a large black plastic bag. He dislodged the remains of Tony's hand from the mower and placed that in the bag. He emptied a can of fly spray into the bag then over the dried blood on the floor. He sealed the bag and lifted it onto the back of the Land Rover. He then used the hose to wash the lawn mower and the garage floor. The blood that had congealed on the floor finally dissolved in the jet of water and ran down the driveway in a pink stream to the street. Soon there was no trace of Tony left, only the wet concrete floor of his garage. Bruce watched as half-dead flies drowned in the flow of water.

The phone rang and Bruce got up to answer.

"Hey! China boy!" A deep Maori-like voice grunted over the phone. "You're a hard joker to catch. I hope you'se doing what you'se supposed to be doin'."

"Who is this?" Bruce shot back.

"Now, now, my little yellow friend." The voice went a tone or two higher. "You don't want to end up like your brother, er? Chop suey! Ah!"

"Where is Plum? I want to talk to her!"

"She's safe. Listen. I'm calling you'se guys at five, tomorrow afternoon. Have all the dope in a truck. Every last bud. We know it's ready to pack up. We'll call and tell you where to go. We take the truck and you'll get Plum. It'll be that simple. No funny stuff. And if you'se have the cops there, Plum will have a fate worse than your brother, and you'se go away forever for growing that stuff. Ha! Got it? I call at five!"

Bruce tried to yell back, but the phone went dead. He turned to Chuck, the receiver still in his hand.

"Five o'clock. Tomorrow."

Bruce looked at Chuck. They had buried their brother near the glasshouses in a shallow grave, unsure what to do with him.

Hei Hei fit sideways into the phone booth in the lobby of the Masonic Arms Hotel. He told Terry he could have as much pot as he could buy outright after tomorrow, and that Wiremu was no longer chief. Hei Hei hinted at the time and location of the drop-off point.

Terry hung up and thought for a moment before he dialed a number that connected directly to Wally McShane's office. In his Maori accent, Terry told McShane about the drug rendezvous in Titirangi tomorrow. He dropped Wiremu Wilson's and Hei Hei's names.

Terry hung up and grinned at John.

"One phone call. That's all it took. The cops are going to bust those Maoris and seize all their pot and probably shoot each other to death whilst we are peacefully picking up our stuff down south. Couldn't be neater."

"What about Plum?"

"I'm going to visit her now. Give her dinner. You off to Laurie?"

"Yeah. It's Saturday night. Even bad guys like to have fun on Saturday night."

Sergeant Cadd stood in front of the inspector's desk. Grimble had his hands clasped together under his chin, deep in thought. In front of him was the initial arson report from the Hungry Wok fire. The sergeant had missed his dinner and had called Donna to tell her he would not be able to go with her to the movies. Saturday night was movie night. He had wanted to see *French Connection 2*, Donna wanted a comedy, any comedy. He told her he would be working all night, the rest of the weekend.

"Well, Cadd, what do you think about that?"

"I don't know, sir. I can't see the connections."

The phone rang and Grimble grabbed it. Wally McShane barked his name so loud even Cadd could hear him. McShane had a big drug bust planned for Sunday in Titirangi. He was ecstatic. Wilson was supposed to be there, to meet a big shipment coming down from up north. McShane had the information from several sources and he was going up there in force. Would Grimble like to come along for the ride? Naturally Grimble accepted. He hung up and gritted his teeth at Cadd.

Grimble called the commissioner. He wanted a search warrant for Turner for tomorrow. He could not wait another day. After the Titirangi bust, anything could happen. There was no answer from Commissioner Thompson. He would try later.

• • •

The space was different, a yellow light shone on her from a high ceiling. She sat on an old sofa. She tried to stand up but fell back onto the sofa again. She wanted a long hot bath, fresh clothes and to see Clovis. She remembered what Terry had told her and did not believe one word. She managed to stand up.

The door was locked from the outside. The windows were barred. There could be daylight outside and she would not know. She returned to the sofa. A light went on somewhere in the bigger space that surrounded her and she heard footsteps. She recognized them and cringed.

A bolt slid back and a key turned. The door opened, and Terry walked in carrying a large brown bag.

"Hello, Plum." He smiled as if visiting an old friend on Saturday night. "Brought you your favorite, Hawaiian burgers and coke, plus some carob cake for afters. Thought you'd be hungry." He turned to lock the door on the inside with a big black key.

"Why are you doing this to me?" The words came out blurred. She wanted to attack him with her fists, kick the little man in the balls, but she fell back onto the sofa.

"Don't be upset, Plum. I mean you no harm. How could I hurt you after everything?"

She turned her head and tried to vomit. But nothing came out but a thin line of spittle that hung in midair.

"You need some food in you. Tomorrow I'm going to take you to your friends once we've straightened everything out and you're safe again."

"You mean..." The words did not come out of her mouth.

"Then you'll realize I really have protected you from a vicious gang war between the Maoris and the Chinese. It's been gruesome. You're lucky you've been under my protection. God knows what would have happened to you out there. Even the police couldn't've helped you."

Plum ate the pineapple first, then the warm hamburger. Terry chewed his burger, seated on a chair opposite her. He kept an eye on her as she concentrated on her food. All day he could not stop dreaming about her; her two round buttocks, the soft skin between her legs. How her hair hung over her shoulders. How sexy she was, even when unconscious.

Once she had finished the fixed drink, he would turn her over on the sofa and enjoy her again. But this time he would not need to tie her up. It would be a perfect Saturday night.

Chapter Ten

Sunday

"We've come this far." Henry looked in the rearview mirror as he drove. "So we have an idea about what you are up to, but don't want to know. All we care about is Plum."

"I know. Same with me. After this is all over, you must come up and stay with me in Hokianga. It's great up there."

"Wiremu, I'd love to, but I can't mention anything about moving up north, otherwise, Mel will hit me!"

"You'll like it up there." Wiremu sat in the back with his left leg stretched out on the seat as far as it would go. He wanted to arrive early. Mel had come up with a story that if the police stopped them, they were on a Sunday drive up to Piha. They had picked up a scholarly looking Maori on the way.

Rangi had started at dawn and arrived at Dargaville by lunchtime. He bought a meat pie. The local cop had parked next to him and seemed oblivious to the truck and its hidden cargo. The meat pies were as bad as Rangi remembered. He watched the cop drive off before he started up the Bedford. He stopped in Helensville for a chocolate milkshake. He had plenty of time to get to the rendezvous. He planned to be in Auckland later in the evening to hang out with friends, drink a few beers and swap stories about trucks and dope.

Inspector Bernie Grimble came up to Inspector Wallace McShane after the briefing.

"It's a good plan," Grimble said, clutching McShane's hand in a viselike grip. "If everything goes well."

"We've enough men, so, if anything goes wrong, we'll be able to handle it."

There were a total of eighteen men in camouflage jackets and trousers who filed out of the room. The two inspectors, also dressed in army issue green pants and shirts, followed the squad to the garage. Grimble took an unmarked car, a new Ford Falcon. Cadd, dressed in a matching uniform, got in beside him. Under their jackets they wore shoulder holsters with Smith & Wesson Model 10 revolvers.

"Nervous?" Grimble switched on the air-conditioning. He could see Cadd sweating.

"No, sir. Excited. Never been on such a big bust."

"Stay behind me. You're more likely to be shot by them than by a Maori."

"If we get Wiremu, he'll be able to give us answers to Plum Blossom and Terry Turner. When we come back tonight we can pick up Turner and sew everything up."

"Maybe." Grimble did not like such confidence coming from his sergeant. The commissioner had agreed to the raids on Turner's properties and had recommended a judge who had signed the warrant.

Cadd monitored the police radio as they were informed about the search at the Flamingo Paradise.

Uniformed officers were about to enter Turner's house and the Ellerslie car lot.

"Tell them to keep men posted at each site until we return. Why couldn't they do them all simultaneously?" Grimble muttered as he followed the other cars and van up New North Road to Titirangi.

"Go on a little farther. See this bend? Go around it." Wiremu scanned up and down the road and could see no other traffic.

"I'd feel happier if we knew where Hei Hei was." Henry slowed down. Wiremu had tried to phone both Hei Hei and Rangi early that morning. Neither had answered.

"Not yet, another hundred yards." Wiremu kept looking through the rear window. "I haven't been able to contact him. But I wouldn't put it past him to come up here with his own men. I've had the feeling lately that he was branching out on his own, even though he said he was lining up new dealers. Hei Hei's a cunning bugger."

Henry stopped and turned to face Wiremu. "I'll honk twice if I see anything odd. Just don't expose yourself if it gets nasty. Call us afterwards, okay?"

"Don't worry about me. You've been great. Great friends. I'll remember this." Wiremu paused. "I really mean it about swapping dope for Plum. Once I secure it, I'll contact him."

"Be careful," Mel let out as Wiremu gently closed the door and disappeared into the dense bush.

As Henry pulled away he saw two cars at the bend about two hundred yards behind. "They look official. Maybe four men to a car." He glanced at Mel as he drove.

"I don't like them. Let's head back and toot the horn." She kept her eyes on the two cars in the distance through her side mirror.

Henry turned the next corner, skidded to a halt and turned around. They saw, parked ahead of them, three Holden sedans, a Ford Falcon and a large unmarked black van with three aerials coming out of the roof.

"Shit! They're soldiers!" Mel spat out. She slid down under the dashboard.

Henry slowed down as he passed the parked vehicles. The lead car had turned around so that the driver could talk to the driver in the next car with their windows down. They blocked Henry's side of the road, so he tooted his horn twice. They gave him a dirty look as Henry eased onto the shoulder of the narrow road and crawled past them.

"Let's hope he hears that," Mel muttered, still under the dashboard.

"What are you doing? They're out of sight now."

"Someone might recognize me."

"Do you think they were soldiers?"

"Cops. Some special unit. Wiremu is going to be in a lot of trouble."

Henry came back to the Titirangi Road intersection and turned left.

"Does Wiremu mean what he said about the swap?" Henry asked as Mel sat upright and rearranged her hair.

"That might be academic at this point. I wonder, though. Is that what Turner has masterminded all along? And we've been the suckers falling into this?" Mel kept glancing back. "What are you doing?"

Henry pulled into a row of shops in Titirangi Township.

"Want an ice cream?"

"I can't believe you're thinking of ice cream at a time like this."

"We've done all we've promised."

"Turn around, go back there." Mel pointed to the road next to the one they had come from at the intersection.

"What are you up to?"

"Just go up there."

Henry drove up the new road. "The bush is probably crawling with cops. They'll have guns. I mean, it's a bad scene. You're not, oh no." He slowed down. Another car, a young couple in a convertible, overtook them.

"I've gone this far for Wiremu. If he is our key to Plum, I want to see he comes to no harm."

"But what if you get caught? You admitted yourself you have your suspicions about him."

"I'm an innocent party. Go and get an ice cream and wait for me back here in say, half an hour. I went to pee in the bush and got lost. Okay?" She looked at her watch. "I'll be back by six."

"That's a big pee."

Henry came to a stop. "No. I'm not going to let you go. Do you think after all these years, we've finally got together and I'm going to lose you because you want to play Wonder Woman? Forget it!" He grabbed her firmly by the wrists. She twisted out of his grip so that she held him tightly.

"Don't worry. I'll be very careful." She leaned over to kiss him quickly, keeping a grip on his wrists. "That's the nicest thing you've ever said to me. And who's Wonder Woman?" She slipped out of the car before Henry could answer and disappeared into the bush.

Wiremu had managed to climb a small ridge when he heard the BMW's two horn blasts. It was too soon. Something had gone wrong. He could turn back and stop Rangi farther up the road, but if the Drug Squad or the Armed Offenders Squad or every bloody cop in Auckland was crawling through the bush, what difference did it make? He had no radio or getaway car, so he decided to stay put. He did not want to be caught in a truck with three tons of grass. He would spend the rest of his life in Para and join his half-brother again, Rawiri. He wished he had Rawiri by his side now.

Wiremu maneuvered through the undergrowth and vines until he came to a spot where he could see the opening with the fallen log and the track that was wide enough for one truck. He spotted six men in camouflage gear bearing M16s jog down the track. Definitely narcs, he could tell by their attitude and their mustaches. Every plainclothes cop went to the same bad barber. Not like his Mel special. He automatically ran his right hand through his short hair to check its length.

Wiremu watched them take up positions behind the five-finger and pinewood trees. They moved without noise. The bush was so thick it was possible for someone to walk past them less than a foot away and not be seen. He remained motionless. He noted the positions of the six and relaxed. He had some time before Rangi drove into the trap.

Henry leaned against the BMW and finished his ice cream outside the shop. He had already counted ten more cars take the turn to Helensville. He lost count after half an hour, then he spotted a red Holden full of young Maori men. The car went so fast he could not identify the driver.

• • •

Hei Hei's car bounced up the track to the fallen log. He turned off the engine by disconnecting the wires under the steering wheel. Rere and Mokau, two giants with black hair down to their shoulders, got out and stretched. Freddy, as small as Hei Hei, but fatter, surveyed the bush and grunted. They wore jeans, boots and leather jackets, despite the heat.

Hei Hei exited and breathed in the fresh air. The three Maoris stepped over the log and into the small clearing, where they lay down in the tall grass.

"Just as well you fire bombed that wok place." Rere coughed. "Otherwise we would've been locked up. They sure panicked when all the windows blew in. Never seen so many cops run away!"

"Yeah. And we were really teaching those Samoans a lesson," Freddy added.

"Should've bought some beer. This is hot work." Hei Hei laughed as he stepped over the log and joined his mates. He scanned the surrounding bush and noted that the clearing was in a densely wooded hollow. He had come here a few weeks ago with Wiremu when they had scouted out possible locations. This one was ideal for an ambush, which was why they had not chosen it.

There seemed to be nobody else in the bush. There was no sign of any cars parked off the road, and his instincts told him that when Wiremu arrived, he would be able to deal with Wiremu and Rangi very quickly, before they unloaded the truck. Hei Hei knew that Wiremu would come up here alone because he did not trust anyone. No other Maoris who had worked with Wiremu had been contacted. Wiremu was too hot.

Hei Hei flopped down in the grass and looked up at the blue sky. A perfect late summer afternoon. The cicadas rubbed their wings together to form a peaceful backdrop. Being in the bush always brought out the poet in him. He started to think of a new poem about the Piwakawaka as he saw a pied fantail flitter over his head. Its song made him smile.

Wally McShane had the van hidden behind a clump of trees near the turnoff they had targeted as the rendezvous point. From the tinted rear window they could just make out the gap in the bush where the track was. He communicated to his men on a radio frequency reserved for the Drug Squad. The tail car with two of his men headed towards Helensville. They were to spot the vehicle with the dope then turn around and follow it back, out of sight. Grimble and Cadd had parked their car farther down the track and now sat next to all the communication equipment in the back of the van. The van housed cabinets for armaments, first aid gear and seats for 12 men in full gear.

Cadd and Grimble sweated. It was over 90 degrees in the van.

Grimble watched the red Holden turn up the track and whistled. He expected another truck or a van, or maybe several vans and cars, but why only one car full of Maoris?

"Recognize anyone?" McShane asked Grimble.

"Couldn't see too clearly from here. Was that Wilson?"

"That would be him," McShane growled.

"Then again, he could be there already."

McShane had ordered his two sharpshooters into position opposite the concealed track. He had two cars hidden, off the road, on either side of the track, in case he had to block or pursue anyone. He had three extra men in the van, one to operate the communications systems, one to administer first aid, and Sergeant Adams.

He had placed two more outside on his side of the road, ready to back up the six in the clearing. With everyone hidden there was no need for roadblocks or an overt presence. McShane had planned a quick, efficient strike and arrest. He hoped no one was listening in on his radio band other than the boys back at Cook Street.

The men crouched in the bush and listened with their earphones as McShane talked to the tail car. Each officer was equipped with a tiny plastic mouthpiece that extended from their earphone to a miniature radio concealed in their back. This was their first full-scale operation with the new hands-free communication system. They wore 9mm Browning pistols, spare magazines and assault knives on their belts and held M16s or their own preferred rifle with scope. McShane had handpicked the men for this squad and they represented his most experienced officers.

Cadd fingered the revolver he wore on a shoulder holster. He felt like a real cop, just like the heroes he saw in the cinema. He had used the Model 10 many times on the range, and he had watched Grimble qualify with his. Cadd wondered if he could use it on a live target, what it would feel like to aim at another human being and squeeze the trigger?

"Unit One, keep those four in your sights but don't move. We expect more soon," McShane spoke into his microphone.

The leader, Saunders, confirmed the order and that the four Maoris were laid out in the grass, relaxed. They had no visible weapons. The policemen could hear the cicadas that were picked up and amplified through the radio.

The tail car called in that they had passed an old Bedford truck with a sealed canopy. One young Maori male at the wheel. McShane instructed them to turn back and follow out of sight, then wait behind the last bend before the track. Cadd and Grimble listened to the driver give his commentary on the truck that was now a quarter of a mile ahead of him.

Rangi gawked at the older Ford sedan as it passed him. It did not look like an undercover car. But the two big Pakehas and one with a mustache, well, they had to be cops. Easy does it, he thought. He kept his eyes open for any other sign of the police as he crunched down into second gear and looked for the turn off. He found what was the track, but he went past it, eyeing the surrounding bush. He slowly drove to the Titirangi Road intersection and pulled over at the shoulder. He looked around for anything unusual and tried to gather his thoughts.

"He's gone past the turn off. Permission to pursue." The radio in the van crackled.

"No! Drive off the road and stay hidden and wait for instructions," McShane retorted. He turned to Grimble as if seeking confirmation.

"Could he have seen the car?" Grimble offered.

"All units stay in position," McShane spoke. "He might have been spooked. If he doesn't come back soon, we'll go after him. A truck like that can't go far." McShane hunched his shoulders and waited. The three detectives stared through the rear window towards the road, willing the truck to come back.

McShane had to have the Maoris caught red-handed with the narcotics in the truck, that is, if the truck contained marijuana. To pick them off separately made for a weak or no case. The truck had to come back.

• • •

Rangi knew he had to make a decision. Something he was not good at. If they were cops, they could have been heading elsewhere. He had not seen anything in his side-view mirrors nor had he spotted any other activity on the road. If he drove into Auckland, what would Wiremu think? That he had stolen all the pot? Or that he was going to another rendezvous? He wiped his face with his hands. He wanted to get rid of this load and drive into Auckland empty. If he rode into the city with a load of pot, he would be killed. Some gang member would knock him off. The load was too valuable.

Rangi dropped down to first gear as he came to the opening again. He stopped the Bedford. He waited with the engine idling. He looked up and down the road. Then he stared into the bush.

McShane and Grimble could see the truck from their rear window. They looked back at it in silence, not daring to move or speak.

Finally, Rangi made a loud grating noise as he tried to find first gear again. If this was an ambush, to hell with it! Rangi thought. He had done his job. He could not get told off for following orders, could he? He was just the driver.

"He's about to turn in. Keep your positions," McShane uttered into the microphone. He could not mask his excitement. He gave the thumbs-up to Grimble who smiled back. They watched as the truck pulled into the track and wondered how the hell the Maori driver could not see them. They were so close.

Rangi could see nothing but trees. It was so dark in there. It was black, not green. He drove as far as he could to the fallen log. Branches hit the sides. He pulled up the brake and switched the motor off. Then he noticed a new red Holden in front of him. Shit! The fuzz! He was petrified. His instincts had been right. He should have kept going. It was too late now. He listened to the engine die and the water gurgle in the radiator. Then there was silence.

He remembered to hit his horn twice. He kept turning his head as he sat in the cabin with his arms folded.

No cops jumped out from behind the trees to surround him. Who would not have heard the noisy old Bedford? Wiremu, please appear and relieve me of my agony, he prayed.

Hei Hei was almost asleep when he heard the truck approach. He poked his head above the grass and saw Rangi behind the wheel. Hei Hei looked back at the surrounding bush and waited for someone else to make a move. He saw that Rangi looked nervous.

"G'day, mate." Hei Hei stood up and waved to Rangi. Rere, Mokau and Freddy rose out of the long grass together.

Rangi sighed with relief, pleased to see a familiar face. He climbed down from the cabin and scanned the bush again. He did not want to voice his fears for he hated to be laughed at.

"Seems real quiet here. Where's Wiremu?" Rangi tried to act as casual as possible. He jumped onto the log and his eyes scanned the trees and undergrowth. It did not feel right, but he could not tell if it was his paranoia or something more definable. He did not mention the plainclothes cops he spotted farther up the road.

Wiremu watched where he thought the six cops were hidden and assumed they were observing the Maoris in the clearing. Although he could only spot four; the truck obscured the other two. Outnumbered and outgunned, (what had changed?), he was not going to act first.

"Don't know. Thought he'd be here." Hei Hei shrugged and looked around. Show yourself. Wiremu, and see what happens, he said to himself. He turned and headed to the back of the truck, the others followed him.

Wiremu watched as he saw four of the hidden cops begin to crawl towards the Maoris. He could make out their white earpieces, just like the Secret Service agents that guarded the President of the United States. That meant there were more cops somewhere. The entire bush could be swarming with them. They could be spying on him. He scanned the bush slowly and tried to catch a flash of gunmetal or an odd movement. When he turned back, he had difficulty in spotting the four who had advanced in their camouflage gear. Then he saw how near they were to the fallen tree and his truck full of dope. They were going to arrest Hei Hei and seize all the grass. Over three tons of it! He had to do something. Two of the cops were almost up to the fallen tree.

He cupped his hands and yelled as loud as he could.

"E Hei Hei, he aha to koha ma ku?!!"

("Hei Hei, what is your gift to me?!") It was the sentence Potatau called out to Te Rauparaha when Potatau was surrounded by Te Rauparaha's men and was about to be massacred.

Wiremu's words echoed through the clearing.

Hei Hei could not tell where Wiremu's voice came from, but he immediately understood. He squeezed out of the back of the truck with a sealed plastic bag of marijuana in one hand. He stuffed it into his pocket and reached inside his jacket for his sawed-off shotgun. The other three followed, bringing up their shotguns.

Hei Hei had underestimated Wiremu. The bastard had surrounded him and was going to try to blast him out of the bush. Rangi, who was beside the truck, leapt up into the cabin and stuck his head under the steering wheel. He wanted no part of any violence.

Every policeman in the bush heard the call to arms, and they wondered how many more Maoris were out there.

The echoing cry unnerved them as they crouched, holding their rifles.

"What is it?" McShane barked.

"A Maori war cry. There's more of them out here. We can't see them," one of the hidden men whispered as he watched his Maori targets behind the fallen tree.

"It's an ambush." Saunders came over the radio.

Wiremu saw two cops peer out from their hiding places and look around. He could see the whites of their eyes and sensed their fear.

"It's Wiremu! We're fucking surrounded. We'll have to fight our way out." Hei Hei aimed his shotgun at the bush hoping to see a target. The other three had their shotguns at the ready as they spread out from the back of the truck and ran to the fallen tree.

"Ena whakamaku ki enei whakamaku!" he yelled back at the trees. ("Your popguns against ours!")

The Piwakawaka reappeared to hover near Hei Hei's wild hair as he lifted his head above the fallen tree to catch the first cop at point-blank range. The cop was about to bring up his rifle when Hei Hei emptied one barrel into his face. The cop's head splattered over the grass behind him. The explosion temporarily deafened every policeman with earpieces.

"Fuck," Hei Hei grunted. "Cops."

The policemen in the van did not know what to make of the roar that came over the radio.

"They've got Saunders," a voice crackled.

"Everyone move in now! Take them out." McShane gave the order he had dreaded. They had planned a simple ambush, a surprise arrest with a lot of manpower and no shooting. Saunders was to get close and yell out the standard line about being surrounded by police and drop your weapons and stick your hands in the air, but the Maori war cries had upset everything. Bloody fucking Maoris. Playing by their own rules. McShane didn't even know what the fuck they had yelled out. There could be a whole tribe of them up in the bush armed to the teeth. Please, god, don't let anyone listen in on my channel.

Wiremu could make out two camouflaged cops ease into better firing positions.

The next policeman got into a crouched stance in the grass and trained his rifle on Hei Hei's chest as he fired. Hei Hei turned at the last second and caught the bullet in his left shoulder. He staggered and watched as Rere, spotting the flash, turned to fire both barrels at Hei Hei's attacker. The policeman fell over backwards screaming.

To Hei Hei, who had endured more pain in the last day than he had in his entire life, an extra bullet going through his left shoulder did not make much of a difference. He stuffed his shotgun into his jacket and clambered over the tree using his right arm. When he got to the man who writhed on the ground in agony, Hei Hei tore the 9mm pistol from the cop's holster, aimed the barrel at the man's head and squeezed the trigger. Nothing happened. He flipped the safety and pressed again. The pistol jumped in his hand as he fired twice. The screaming stopped and the policeman lay motionless on the ground.

Hei Hei ducked down as he turned and aimed the pistol at his next attacker, who, half-hidden in the bush, had popped up and fired at him. Hei Hei kept squeezing the trigger until he could see the body fall over and jerk in the grass as the bullets hit it. Hei Hei collapsed next to the dead policeman with his legs splayed behind him. He used the cop as a shield. He let drop the empty magazine and replaced it with one from the dead man's belt. The other three Maoris kept under cover, not knowing where the other policemen were hidden or how many there were.

"Anderson's been hit. Three are around the truck with shotguns. The fourth is lying next to Saunders on the other side of the log." The voice crackled over the radio. They had all heard the pistol and rifle shots.

McShane turned to Grimble and Cadd as they anticipated his order. They eased their way to the van side door. Adams remained hunched over the speaker to the radio.

"Take the two outside. Get up behind the truck but stay under cover," McShane yelled at Grimble. "Karl, take the kit up there and see if you can get to the wounded." He turned to the radio operator, "Radio in a medi-vac now."

The two detectives ran across the road with their revolvers drawn. The other policemen in camouflage gear followed. Three carried rifles, the fourth a large first aid kit.

Mokau was at the rear of the truck when he aimed at the two men dressed in camouflage gear he could see running up the track. He fired one barrel at each of them. He clipped the first in the leg, who collapsed whilst the other dived for cover and opened fire from the ground. Mokau rolled over and under the truck to reload. A stream of bullets raked the ground around him and burst the tire nearest him, but he remained unhurt. He crawled to the side of the deflated tire, his shotgun held in both hands in front of him.

Freddy knelt down by the fallen tree and spied one of the policemen who had taken up a position where the track opened up. He raised himself so he was kneeling in the long grass with his rifle aimed at Rere. Freddy fired at the man and missed. The short barrel was not accurate over twenty feet. The policeman rolled over and sprayed the top of the fallen tree with bullets. Freddy ducked and broke open his barrel to reload. The gunfire stopped and he peeked over the top to see the man he had missed crawling to a rock for cover.

Hei Hei, on his belly behind the body, spotted the man and came to his knees with his pistol in one hand. He emptied the magazine into the torso of the crawling policeman as Freddy leaped up from cover and spotted another with a rifle behind a tree. He fired both barrels at the tree and the blast blinded the marksman. The cop fell over, his earpiece and microphone smashed by pellets. His face was covered in blood. He could not see. He lay in the undergrowth, silent, lest he be executed like Anderson.

Hei Hei picked up the M16 next to the cop he had shot and put the stock to his good shoulder. He looked down the sights, scanning the bush for any movement. He saw a glimpse of metal behind a bush and he let fire with the M16. The shots went wild, but the figure ran towards a more substantial tree. Rere aimed at the man and squeezed both triggers. Hei Hei adjusted his aim and sprayed the tree. Between the two of them they managed to hit the man's knees before he reached cover.

Wiremu watched Rere and Hei Hei mow down the last policeman he had counted in the bush.

Mokau crawled backwards to the front of the truck. He could not get under the engine, so he rolled over and ran back to the Holden hunched over. The sharpshooter hidden in the bush hit Mokau in the back, breaking his spine in half. Mokau died as he hit the ground.

Mel heard shots fired as she came over the ridge. On another occasion she would have enjoyed walking through the bush. But she worried that Wiremu had been the cause of the gunfire as she came to a gap in the trees and made out a clearing in the distance. She could see the truck and the red Holden and what she took to be little puffs of smoke. The shots echoed through the valley so that it sounded like a battle. She kept to the shadows as she picked a path down the hill.

Hei Hei's shoulder stung. He managed to turn his head and yelled at Rere and Freddy.

"Where's Mokau? Get these guns." He stumbled back to the other man he had shot and pulled out the pistol and the magazines for the M16. Rere ran over and snatched the other rifle. Hei Hei pointed to the side of the clearing nearest them. Rere and Freddy ran to his left, into the bush. Hei Hei went back to the fallen tree. He took his shotgun out from his jacket; he reloaded it and placed it with the pistol on top of the fallen tree. He eased his eyes over the trunk and aimed the M16 down the track. Let the Pakeha come. I'm going to die how I lived. They'll never capture my fucking spirit, he cursed under his breath.

The sharpshooter, who had been clipped in the legs by Mokau's blast, could see Hei Hei's head over the fallen tree. He waved the four advancing policemen back. Grimble and Cadd went to one side of the track whilst the other two disappeared into the undergrowth on the other side. The two detectives hit the dirt when they heard the M16 fire at them. Branches and leaves crashed down on their heads.

Wiremu stepped out from his hidden vantage point and edged downhill so that he could come up behind Rere. First he was betrayed by Hei Hei who had come to kill him and steal the truck, then Hei Hei must have been snitched on, for the police were out in force. He had to be careful lest he be shot. He was a Maori and a target even though he had not fired a shot, yet. He took out his shotgun so he could either use it or throw it away.

Sergeant Adams was the oldest and most experienced in the squad. McShane had been reluctant to use him, but now he had no choice. He had his men in the three cars listening to their radios. His assistant had already radioed in on another channel for a medical helicopter and as many St. John's ambulances as possible. The Armed Offenders Squad was being assembled, and the nearest police stations in Henderson and Titirangi had been alerted and were rushing up there. By the time anyone arrived, it would all be over.

He had instructed Adams that there would be no survivors. Every last Maori had to be shot. To endure the police inquiry would be one nightmare, but to be dragged through a trial? There could be no witnesses.

Adams crept along the edge of the path opposite the side Grimble and Cadd had taken. He saw the trees above them raked with gunfire and noted the line of fire. He kept under cover and in the shadows. The surviving policemen had radioed in their positions. Adams heard through the radio that the two Maoris, armed with captured M16s, had run up the adjacent ridge with two policemen following them. The other Maori was behind the fallen tree.

Once he had managed to get to higher ground, Adams moved under a five-finger bush and found he had a perfect side view of Hei Hei. He got the Maori into his sights and squeezed off a burst. Hei Hei's body moved back and forth as it was ripped by the bullets. He fell to the ground, facedown. Adams radioed in his hit and ran across the clearing to where the other two Maoris had disappeared. He kept in contact with the two pursuers as he raced through the undergrowth to meet them. As he climbed over the next ridge, he saw a small gully that was ideal for an ambush.

Grimble and Cadd, without radio headsets, followed the two marksmen across the clearing. Adams directed them to steer the remaining Maoris back into the gully he had selected.

Rere and Freddy hid behind a thick totara tree, back to back. They caught their breath and waited to hear their pursuers come crashing through the undergrowth. They planned to poke their guns out from behind the tree and cut them down and then escape across the next ridge. Freddy knew if they kept in that direction, heading into the setting sun, they would come across a road. They could follow this back to Titirangi and hitch a ride to Auckland. He did not think about roadblocks, just about Hei Hei. How could Hei Hei die? They had heard an M16. He must be alive.

They heard a crashing sound, and when it got nearer, they nodded to each other and swung their weapons around the trunk. But the two cops sprayed the tree with a rapid burst. Rere and Freddy swung back behind cover. They had seen that the two cops were far apart, and that if they made a run for it they could get mown down in the cross fire.

Adams heard the gunfire and was informed of the position of the two Maoris. He changed his plan and sprinted through the bush and up the adjoining ridge to get in position behind them. On this side of the ridge there was less vegetation and he made good speed. He was well ahead of Grimble, Cadd and the other two who were crashing through the thick bush, searching for the fifth Maori.

The two Maoris stuck their guns out again to draw fire, quickly withdrew them then swung around again to fire back. Their shots went wild though they did see where the two cops were hiding. Rere reloaded his shotgun. Freddy set the M16 to automatic. He whispered to Rere that he would fire a couple of bursts and that Rere should run to the next tree on his right. He would follow, once Rere let blast with his shotgun. "Don't shoot me, now, you fat Maori bastard," Freddy finished. Rere had too much adrenaline in his blood to joke.

Adams came into position over the ridge as he saw Freddy fire back at the two policemen pinned down. He aimed at Rere as the larger Maori ran to the next tree. The bullets ripped Rere's stomach open as he fell. Freddy turned to where the shots came from and tried to fire back, but he was hit in the chest three times. He slid down the tree trunk. His chin rested on his shoulder as blood dribbled out of his mouth.

Adams radioed in the two hits and alerted everyone that there was still one Maori not accounted for. He bypassed the two policemen who had been pinned down and double tracked over the ridge again. His instincts told him the other Maori was somewhere close by, hiding.

Wiremu heard the M16s below him. His shotgun at the ready, he quietly pushed his way through the dense side of the hill away from the clearing and to where he thought the firing had come from.

Mel felt she was surrounded by gunfire. She expected to see armed policemen appear at any moment in front of her, so she climbed a tree on the side of the ridge to see what was happening. If anyone came near her, she could stay up there, immobile, for a long time. Nobody would look up a tree expecting to see a woman. Balanced on a wide branch, she leaned forward and saw the top of Wiremu's head appear through a five-finger bush to one side of her.

. . .

Grimble, Cadd and the other two had fanned out across the ridge and were sweeping the area with their weapons. Their eyes followed their front sights as they scanned for the missing Maori. The two policemen kept in radio contact with Adams on the other side of the ridge and with McShane in the van. They went from tree to tree, not knowing when they would draw fire.

Grimble, on the right flank, spotted a bush rustle ahead of him. He walked with a crouch, careful not to crack any dry twigs or trip over the vines in the undergrowth. With his revolver in a two-handed grip, he recognized his prized Maori despite the short haircut. He was right behind Wiremu Wilson.

Wiremu sensed someone was behind him and slowly turned, bringing up his shotgun to fire. Grimble could not believe his luck as he aimed at the Maori. He was about to squeeze the trigger when he was hit on the right shoulder. He lost his balance and fell to the ground flat on his face. The revolver dropped from his hand. Wiremu froze his right index finger, in shock.

Mel had dropped onto Inspector Grimble, knocking him out. She slipped off his shoulder with her left foot and rolled over on the dirt to quickly regain her balance. Wiremu saw Mel give a powerful front snap to the fallen policeman's head. She turned to him and waved her hand back. They sprinted up the ridge and over into the next valley. Expecting to feel gunfire rip into their backs, they ran down the hill as fast as they could. Mel pointed in the direction she thought Henry would be waiting for her as she kept ahead of Wiremu. They did not say a word.

. . .

Hei Hei opened his eyes. He was facedown in the grass. He knew he had been hit. He could taste blood in his mouth. He could not feel any part of his body. All he could think of was that he had to get to the truck and drive away. If he made it back to the city, he would survive. He tried to lift himself up but fell back. Now he felt a sharp stabbing pain in his chest and back. His shirt was wet, but he did not look down. He got up on his right elbow and dragged himself to his feet using the log for support.

There was a policeman with his back turned towards Hei Hei, attending to the injured marksman farther down the track. Hei Hei fell over the trunk onto his back. He gritted his teeth and managed to stand up without screaming. He grabbed at the red Holden and slid his feet towards the Bedford truck, leaving dark red smear marks along the side of the car. His boots made squelching sounds. When he got to the cabin, he tried to pull himself up the step by grabbing the door handle. He failed. He kept trying to reach up with his right hand. He finally managed to swing into the cabin and collapsed into the driver's seat. As he reached for the ignition, he caught sight of a shape hidden under the dashboard.

"Fuck! Hei Hei, you're gonna get us all killed!" Rangi whispered as he eased his head out. "Shut up," Hei Hei croaked as he started up the motor and forced the gear stick into reverse.

The truck lurched forward as Hei Hei realized he was in first. He fought the stick with his left hand to pull it into reverse, although he thought he was going to lose his arm in the process. His sight went blank and he gasped for breath. He tried to focus on the side mirror as the truck went backwards heading straight to the fallen marksman and his attendant.

The policeman with the first aid kit had secured tourniquets to both of the fallen policeman's legs. There was little he could do about removing the pellets imbedded in his fellow officer's thighs. He looked up to see the truck backing into them. He screamed into his mouthpiece that someone was moving the truck as he dragged the half-conscious marksman into the bush.

"Hey, Rangi! Look in your mirror! Guide me out!"

Rangi had no choice but to lift up his head and peek out the side window. "To your right. To your right!"

The truck's front wheels ran over the marksman's feet before Hei Hei could straighten up. He picked up speed down the track as he saw the opening to the road.

McShane immediately ordered the cars to block the opening. Two cars formed an inverted V, whilst the third blocked the road. The two policemen leapt out and squatted behind their vehicles, their M16s aimed at the Bedford.

Hei Hei could barely steer with one flat tire and his left arm was getting weaker. He did not hear Rangi shout. His ears hurt from all the gunfire. He felt the truck crash into the cars as a bullet shattered his side window.

The rear bumper of the Bedford swiped the side of one car then dug into the other, pushing both back into the road. The tires were shot out by the intense fusillade of bullets, but Hei Hei kept his foot on the accelerator as the wheels continued to dig into the road. Rangi screamed above the gunfire that he should give up, but Hei Hei was too close to death to surrender.

The three policemen moved back to the road's shoulder and continued firing in short bursts at the cabin as it came into their sights. The windshield shattered and Hei Hei was blinded by glass as he vainly felt for the gear stick. His left hand would not work, and he had to force his right hand across his body as he ground into second gear. He hit the accelerator with all the energy he had left. A stream of bullets ripped through the metal door and into Hei Hei's side. The truck lurched forward, veered off the road and slammed into a tree. The rear wheels were still moving as the nearest policeman waved to the others and ran to the front of the truck. He duck-walked up to the driver's side, slid up to the smashed window and poked his rifle inside. He raked the cabin with a prolonged burst. He stepped back, swung open the door and his partner emptied his magazine into the body slumped over the steering wheel. Hei Hei, riddled with dozens of bullets, was finally dead. There was a low moan from under the front seat, and without identifying the source, the first policeman emptied the remainder of his magazine into the curled up body at point-blank range. The moaning ceased.

"We have the fifth one. He was hiding in the cabin," the policeman radioed in as he stood on the steps of the Bedford.

McShane called the others back and set about preparing the landing site for the helicopter.

Wiremu and Mel heard the last volleys of gunfire then silence. They stopped and bent over, hands on their knees to catch their breath.

"That's it. They got Hei Hei. They must've had an army," Wiremu gasped. "We better hurry before they set up roadblocks." He broke open the shotgun, took out the shells and threw them away. He smashed the barrel against a rock and slipped the broken parts into a stream they forded. He then scattered the shells that were in his pockets.

Mel found the next ridge and the tall totara tree she had used as a marker. They jogged through the bush for another ten minutes before they sighted the road below them. Around the next corner they saw Henry leaning over a map spread on the hood. He looked lost.

She appeared by the driver's door and held her finger to her lips as Henry opened his mouth. She slipped into the car and started it as Henry threw himself in and closed his door. She spun the car around.

Mel's face was scratched and pieces of bush were stuck in her hair. She was panting, and her face was covered in sweat. She slowed down at the next corner and Wiremu crawled in. He lay across the back seat as Mel worked through the gears. Winding down the road to Titirangi, three ambulances screamed past her followed by a procession of police cars with flashing blue lights.

They rode back in silence.

Bruce Look collapsed in his armchair. He shut his eyes and tried to block out the world with his sinsemilla stained hands.

Chuck went to the kitchen to brew a fresh pot of coffee. They had not slept the night before. When Ricky Wong had arrived with Moana late afternoon, they had immediately set to work in the glasshouses. They had stuffed all the dried and cured leaves and buds into bags they had already prepared. They had not cared about weights or properly closing the bags. They just wanted to get the job done.

Chuck had collected several bags of buds for his personal supply. Moana had stuffed her pockets with buds. Later in the kitchen, she had emptied the contents into small plastic bags she carefully sealed.

"All I want is to get rid of it and get Plum back." Chuck came back with a full pot of coffee.

Ricky came through the back door and rubbed his hands. "It's set. Five pounds of C4, over the fuel tank."

"I'm not driving," Chuck shot out.

"It's okay. I will. It's perfectly safe." Ricky tried to smile to instill confidence in the others and impress Moana. Moana was not amused. Even her relatives did not fool around with explosives.

"No. I drive. It's my responsibility." Bruce removed his hands from his face. His eyes fell on Moana who sat cross-legged on the carpet. He could not help wondering if she wore panties under her short floral dress that was stained with blotches of dark green. He caught a glimpse of hair as she shifted her knees. He had kept his wife away till later tonight. She was staying with relatives in Onehunga along with Tony's wife and children. He promised he would explain everything to them tonight.

"Chuck, let's go outside and look at it." Bruce stood up.

They squatted by the truck and tried to see the plastic explosive and the detonator. They could not make out the package.

"I know this sounds crazy, but tell me what you think. Let's dig up Tony's body and put it in the back of the truck."

"What are you saying?" Chuck was surprised.

Bruce seized his brother by the shoulders. "He's dead. We can't have his body here forever. I can't tell his wife what happened to him. Can you?"

"We blow up our own brother?"

"She's already suspicious that I wouldn't let her speak to him the last time I called. That's unlike Tony."

"What about the remains?"

"There'll be none. He'll be over the fuel tank."

"It'll be like killing him, again."

"The Maoris will be blamed for his death. We can say he was taken hostage and put in the back. Or we can just tell our family what happened and not say anything to the police. How will they know it's our brother?"

"It's macabre."

Bruce let go of Chuck's shoulders. "Let's go and dig him up."

Chuck and Bruce were back in the living room by ten to five to wait for the phone call.

"You don't have to use this." Ricky held the small radio device in his hand. It was an aluminum cased box, the size of a small transistor radio, with an extendable aerial. It had one red light and a red button that would activate the radio controlled detonators set in the C4 package. Now that he had set the detonators, the reality of what he had done began to sink in. What if his bomb did not explode? What if his bomb killed innocent people?

"No, we'll use it. The question is when." Bruce had removed the license plates from the truck and screwed on an old pair he had found at the Markets. He had smeared the plates with dirt. They were untraceable. The registration number on the engine block had been ground off and there were no papers in the cabin to link the truck to his family. That is, if there was a cabin left, afterwards.

"On the Motorway," Chuck suggested. "I could ride ahead on my bike so I wouldn't lose them. You'd be farther back in the Land Rover. It would look like a crash."

"Tons of sinsemilla going up in flames. That'll be an awesome sight." Ricky stretched out on the carpet.

The phone rang. Bruce checked his watch. It was eight minutes past five. He let it ring five times before he picked up the receiver. All eyes were on him.

"Collision Corner," the Maori voice spat out. "You know, parallel to the Motorway. Five thirty. It'll take you twenty minutes to get there. Don't be late, as Plum is impatient to see you."

"Let me talk to Plum. How is she?" Bruce shot back.

"That truck better be full, 'cuz we'll be taking it."

Bruce heard the click then listened to dead air then the dial tone. He set the receiver down. It sounded like the same person, but there was something different about the quality of the voice. The tone was a little too high for what he thought would be a Maori.

He informed them of the time and place. "It's about a mile from the Motorway. It's hardly used now. I'll drive the truck. Ricky will take my Land Rover. Chuck, you ride behind on your bike. Keep out of sight. After the swap, you follow the truck and we'll be behind you."

"The side mirrors are fixed so they can't see behind them," Chuck repeated.

"But they'll have at least another vehicle. Maybe more?"

"What about Moana?" Ricky asked.

"She should stay behind." Bruce did not like the idea of her being at Collision Corner, and he did not like the idea of her at his house alone. At least she had been a great worker in the glasshouses, with or without underwear.

"Moana can keep out of sight in the Land Rover, and she might be able to recognize them."

Ricky looked across at Moana.

"I'm not missing out on this," Moana stated.

Terry Turner and John Eustace parked their car, a nondescript Ford from his Ellerslie lot, on a slight rise half a mile south of Collision Corner. It was the only vantage point where they could see the intersection and the road where the truck would be coming from. They stood by the Ford and scanned the horizon with their binoculars. They wore sports jackets in the February heat. Terry had his black and white houndstooth and John his extra large blue blazer.

"There's some dust," John croaked. His throat was still sore.

"That's probably their newest. We'll wait for them to stop. There's a Land Rover behind them. See anything else?"

"No. Guess they're not going to walk back."

"They better not be armed."

It was his one fear. That the Chinese would see it was only two of them and shoot them, with or without Plum. He doubted it. Still, some people could be pushed to do outrageous things. He had thought of using Plum as a shield, bringing her out in front of him before John inspected their truck. But what if something went wrong and they did shoot at him? He did not want Plum to be harmed. Besides, she looked disgusting. Maybe they would not want her back? And he could keep her. Wishful thinking is dangerous, he frowned.

"If they try to be aggressive, we'll cut them to pieces."

John patted his jacket.

"How's Plum doing?" John asked as he kept his binoculars trained on the truck and Land Rover as they approached the intersection.

"About as well as anyone would be on a day like this." Terry went to the back of the car, unlocked the trunk and lifted it up. She had worked her blindfold loose. Her hands were still tied behind her back and her feet were bound with the same rope, hog-tied, so she could not move. She opened one eye to blink at the bright light. Terry was relieved she had not vomited.

"One short walk and you'll be free. Plum, you'll be safe as I promised. I never break my promises. You know I've always protected you."

He had explained to her that morning, after she had finally woken up, that if she ever went to the police, she and her entire family would be killed. But how could she contemplate that? Her cousins had grown a huge amount of marijuana.

"If it wasn't for your greedy cousins, you wouldn't be in this position now, Plum. It's really the fault of your own family."

Terry leaned over her. She wanted to talk. He loosened the gag. Plum had worked up as much saliva as she could from her parched throat, and she spat at Terry. He jumped at her unexpected action and hit his head on the top of the trunk. He took a step back and slammed the trunk shut as hard as he could. "Ungrateful bitch!" he muttered. He looked down at his trousers and saw that her saliva lay on his crotch. He wiped it off with a handkerchief.

Bruce climbed down from the truck he had parked a hundred feet from Collision Corner. Before the Motorway was built, the corner was notorious. You could not see the corner until you were on top of it, and motorists refused to stop at the intersection. Dozens of people had been killed there in spectacular crashes.

Bruce watched a Ford sedan come to a halt on the other side of the intersection. He held the ignition key in his right fist. Chuck kept out of sight behind a small rise farther back. Ricky was in the Land Rover, parked twenty feet from the truck. Even Moana, who was in the back seat, had a good view of the Ford. There was no other traffic on the road.

"Shit. They're not Maoris," Moana whispered from behind the front seat. "That's Terry the Turk and his henchman, Big John."

"Do you know them?" He did not take his eyes off the small fat Pakeha and the big man in the blue blazer.

"Everyone does," Moana continued. "He's the biggest crook in Auckland. He controls everything."

"And we're about to give him all that pot."

Terry walked right up to Bruce. John was to one side, one eye on the truck and the Land Rover behind. He unbuttoned his blazer.

"Who are you?" Bruce asked.

"We're the collectors. Is it all in there?" Terry pointed to the truck.

"Everything. Where's Plum?"

"All four glasshouses?" Terry's eyes bore into Bruce's.

"Yes," Bruce spat out. "Where's Plum?"

Bruce started to sweat. What if these two killed him and took the truck? What if Plum was already dead? He squeezed the truck key in his fist.

"She's in the car. You'll get her once the goods are inspected." Terry motioned to John who walked to the back of the truck, not letting his eyes off the Land Rover.

Terry remained close to Bruce, enjoying the fear of his victim. Bruce looked as if he had not slept in days. A man who would not go to the police. A man Terry could call on later for a favor, a veiled threat or just good old extortion. Terry wanted this man to remember this moment.

John untied and lifted the canvas flap at the back of the truck and peeked inside. He turned back to see Terry and then over at the Land Rover. He did not recognize the man in the Land Rover. John swung his legs up onto the tailboard and threw up the flap then waded through the center of the truck between the packed garbage bags. He felt several of the bags then selected one at random. It took some time for his eyes to adjust to the darkness. The smell and heat inside was intense. He opened the bag wide, sniffed and reached inside. The closeness in the truck intensified the rush of powerful resin that assaulted John's nostrils. He inhaled and felt an instant high. He plunged his hand farther into the garbage bag and brought out a handful of small bags full of dried buds.

He repeated this process three times until he came to a wall of bags.

He eased himself down from the truck, stood to one side and squinted to let his eyes adjust to the harsh sunlight. He could have sworn he saw a second person in the Land Rover, but when he opened his eyes he saw the one young male staring at him.

John walked back to the cabin, hauled himself up on the foot rest to peer in, then he climbed down and got on his knees to examine underneath the engine. He took his time. He was going to drive the truck. He would much rather have gotten someone else to do the job, but Terry had insisted.

He walked back to Terry and stared at the man who stood to attention face to face with his boss.

"Feel high just sniffing the stuff."

"Well?"

"Looks all there. Dry. Cured. Packed."

"Where is Plum? I want to see her."

"Where's the key?" John held out his thick paw. There were buds stuck to his fingers.

Bruce held up his closed fist.

"Go back and get her," Terry ordered John as he handed him the keys to the Ford.

John walked back to the car with one eye on the Land Rover. He wiped his elbows and hands free of buds and bits of leaves. He opened the trunk and gazed at the tied up Plum with her hair over her face and her gag removed. He bent over her and removed the hair from her face. She turned her head and tried to bite his hand but missed. He withdrew his hand and placed it on her bare leg. He could feel her tense up as he ran his hand up her thigh. She kept her knees locked tight as she gritted her teeth. He moved his hand up the back of her thighs to her buttocks and pushed them apart. She hissed at him but could only move slightly to the left or right. John slid his index finger down her crack to her anus and pushed it in as hard as he could till he could feel his knuckles pressing against her flesh. She screamed in pain as he moved his finger back and forth inside her.

"Come back and work for me. You'll like it," John croaked as he worked his finger in deeper. Then he slowly eased his finger out. He held it up in the air to inspect it then wiped his finger in her hair. "Dirty bitch."

John untied the bindings to her feet and hauled her out of the trunk. She spat at him and almost fell over before he caught her and dragged her to the truck.

By the time she had staggered into Terry and faced Bruce, she had an idea of what was going on. There was a truck in front of her.

Terry put his hand out for the key to the truck whilst John held Plum with both hands around her elbows. Bruce was shocked to see the condition of his cousin. Her dress was stained and her hair and face were filthy. She was barefooted and there appeared to be dried blood down her legs. Bruce let the key drop into Terry's outstretched palm.

"Start her up, and then you get Plum." Terry stepped back to take Plum by the elbows as John climbed into the cabin and turned over the motor. Terry went to sniff her hair, to get one last reminder of their time together, but he quickly recoiled and held her in front of him at arm's length.

John turned the motor. Nothing happened. He tried again and the motor turned over but did not fire. The truck came to life on the third attempt.

Bruce moved back, and looked across at the Land Rover. He had an uncanny feeling that they were all going to be shot. Both men were probably armed. They had killed Tony yesterday, so why not the rest of the family today?

A cloud of black fumes shot out of the exhaust as John revved the engine. Terry pushed Plum away from him and to the side, not towards the Chinaman. He quickly walked back to the car. Bruce instinctively stepped forwards and held out his hands to catch her and hug her even though he had never held her in his life.

"Don't forget your promise, Plum," Terry yelled at her as he eased into the Ford.

Bruce held the shaking Plum in his arms as he watched the car back to the side of the road to let the truck go past. The Ford followed the truck as they headed towards the Motorway.

The Land Rover started up and drew along side them. Moana opened the door and Plum climbed into the back as best she could with her arms tied behind her back. Bruce took over the driving from Ricky. Moana untied the knots around Plum's wrists.

Plum stared at Bruce and Ricky, then the Maori girl she had not seen before.

"You don't look so bad, Plum. This is Moana. She's been helping us." Ricky had half turned in his seat to examine Plum as Bruce accelerated to Collision Corner and turned onto the Motorway. A black motorcycle overtook them. Chuck had his black visor down as he disappeared to catch up with the truck.

Plum rubbed her wrists back to life.

"What happened to you, Plum?" Moana asked.

• • •

Matthew sat behind the steering wheel of his red and white 1956 Studebaker and grinned. Clovis Tibet leaned over the open side window and peered in at Matthew.

"Feels good to be in my baby," Matthew sang.

"You know I feel bad about the car breaking down and all that."

"Don't worry, man. Plum'll turn up probably sooner than later, and we'll do another gig or two and you'll pay me back this bill here." Matthew held up the garage's invoice to Clovis's face.

"But not at the Gluepot."

"Not at the Three Lamps," Matthew echoed. The car was at the back of a large service station next to the short access road to the northbound side of the Motorway. There were three pairs of pumps under a large metal awning and four garage doors to one side for repairs. Inside the glassed-in office was the pump attendant, a refrigerator and freezer for drinks and ice creams and two candy vending machines.

"You got any money on you?" Matthew held up the keys to Billy's '65 Chevy Impala SS. The car had a noisy muffler and threadbare tires, but Billy loved it almost as much as his Les Paul guitar.

"Yes, a little, why?"

"Well, fill 'er up and return it to Billy. He needs it tonight." Matthew threw the keys at Clovis and, before he backed out from between two parked cars, he yelled at his violinist, "And don't break down again!"

Matthew eased between the pumps and headed towards the Motorway.

Clovis walked over to the Chevy, started it up and backed around to the pumps. He was very careful with the loose clutch. He got behind a van that was full of small children and a yapping poodle. He waited for his turn at the leaded regular pump.

• • •

John steered the old truck on the far left northbound lane of the Motorway. Terry should be right behind him, but John could not see him because the side mirror was stuck. He did not want to pull over and fix it. When he got the motor up to 50 miles per hour, he suspected the fuel gauge did not work. He tapped the gauge but it remained on a quarter full. He planned to pull over at the next gas station that was ahead. He did not want to run out of gas on the Motorway. When he came to the service station, he slowed down and pulled over.

The service station was doing a brisk business on Sunday afternoon. Three cars were ahead of John as he drove up to the canopy. He jumped out and checked that the top of the truck would clear the canopy. It would not. John stood with his hands on his hips.

"Why did you stop?" Terry had pulled up next to him.

"The gauge is broken."

"Fill her up quick. Then let's get outta here." Terry looked around nervously. John had to turn the truck around then back it up to the nearest pump on the other side of the canopy, as Terry directed him.

When Chuck saw the truck pull into the gas station with the Ford right behind it, he panicked. He came to a skidding stop on the shoulder of the Motorway. He tried to spot the Land Rover because he knew this would be the time Ricky would decide to push the button. Chuck had lost sight of the Land Rover a couple of miles back, in his effort to keep the truck in view. If they were out of sight of the truck, they might get anxious and push the button, regardless. The plan had been to wait for the right time, even if that meant blowing up the truck somewhere in Auckland.

"Don't worry," Ricky explained to Plum Blossom. She had regained her senses and understood what was going on. "This has a range of over three miles. Just because they're out of sight doesn't mean this won't work." He held the radio-controlled device in his right hand for Plum to see. She leaned over the front seat, fascinated. Moana sat upright and wondered where the bad smell was coming from, her or Plum.

"I can't see Chuck," Bruce complained. He kept checking his rearview mirror. A traffic cop was behind them on a Honda 750 motorcycle. To Bruce, it appeared the cop was hovering in his mirror.

Ricky extended the aerial to its full length.

"We can't do it if we can't see them. There're innocent people out there," Bruce pleaded. He looked to the horizon and the busy Motorway and the traffic policeman on their tail. "Shit." He whistled. "I think he's going to stop us."

"Don't be stupid. We're not even speeding." Ricky tried not to turn around as he held the radio device in both hands. If they all stared at the cop, he would pull them over.

"If we wait any longer we might be out of range. We might lose them forever. Then what? What if they find it? What would they do to you, Bruce? Your family?" Ricky asked.

"Do it. Just do it," Plum muttered. She stared at the device Ricky held in his hand. Her voice was hoarse and tense. "If you knew what he did to me, you'd destroy him." Her voice choked and she fought back tears.

• • •

Clovis had put $5 worth of gas in the Chevy. He gave the money to the attendant, turned around and noticed a tall lanky man in his thirties smiling at him. Clovis recognized the grin but not the face.

"Hey, partner! Fancy meeting you here." The thin man hailed Clovis like an old friend.

Clovis's expression changed to mild surprise.

"Hot diggity! That place you recommended was too much. Got a little Maori girl. She was as tight as a young ewe, if you know what I mean."

"No. I don't." It was the man from Suicide City in the Mercedes who had picked him up the last time he was out here.

"Anyway, I hadda rush back. My dad was a little crock. Too much piss. But he's okay now and I'm back for another taste of the wicked city. Can't wait!"

"Take care," Clovis muttered, unable to remember the man's name. He heard the Mercedes pull away from the adjacent pump.

He opened the door to the Chevy and caught sight of a large man in a blue blazer staring at his car. The man stood next to an old truck.

Clovis knocked his knees against the steering wheel. He adjusted his rearview mirror and saw a smaller man who stood next to the giant. Clovis started the engine, revved up the motor and slipped into first. He let the clutch out too fast and stalled. He started the engine again and eased out from the pump, riding the clutch and making a whining noise with the transmission. A family of five in a Toyota pulled into his space. Two children were screaming in the back for ice creams.

Another car pulled up ahead of him, temporarily blocking his way out. There was a large Samoan family squashed into an oversized American car that had most of its markings and paint removed. He held onto the hand brake as the car backed out to give him room to leave. He thought of Wiremu and what could have happened to him that afternoon. He squeezed the steering wheel and released the hand brake as he edged past the big car.

Chuck spun his back wheel around and aimed his Kawasaki at the oncoming traffic. He could not see the Land Rover and could not imagine what had held them up. He let out the throttle and charged down the shoulder of the road zooming past cars going against him who honked their horns. He climbed to 50, 60, 70 miles per hour. Where were they?

He spotted them as the traffic cop on the Honda switched on his siren and flashing light. Chuck tried to wave one arm to attract Bruce's attention. He could see people struggling in the Land Rover. As he attempted to brake, an oncoming car clipped his front wheel and he lost control of the bike.

Clovis Tibet stopped at the edge of the service station and looked back at the oncoming cars. He waited for a reasonable gap in the traffic in the inside lane. He was unsure of the Chevy's acceleration and he had no desire to be rammed and then have to inform Billy and Matthew what had happened. He let the clutch out when he saw a gap and stalled. He pulled on the hand brake and tried to start the engine again. It would not turn.

John Eustace climbed back into the cabin satisfied that the fuel tank was full. He could not find a spanner to fix the side mirror, but that did not bother him. He wanted to get moving. He saw Terry walking back to his car with an ice cream cone, smiling like a little kid.

Now there is cool, John mused. The man has millions of dollars of dope in an old truck stopped for gas on the Motorway and he gets an ice cream.

"If you won't, I will!" Plum Blossom screamed.

"We can't do it out of sight. Look at all these cars," Bruce yelled back.

Ricky sat in the front seat and held the device in his hands like an ice cream that was about to melt. The aerial pointed forwards.

"Shall I or shan't I?" He asked. To him it was still a game. He did not know if the detonator would work. It could have become detached with all the jolting of the truck. He turned back to face Moana.

Moana's eyes widened and she shouted, "Look out!"

Bruce saw the motorcycle coming towards them down the inside of their lane. Then he recognized the bike. The siren behind them went off. Bruce saw a car ahead of them clip the motorcycle and send it out of control. He slammed on his brakes to avoid running over his own brother.

When the Land Rover braked, Plum leaned forward and grabbed the device out of Ricky's hand.

Ricky screamed, "No! No!"

Bruce thought Ricky was screaming at the bike as he saw Chuck lose his balance and skid across the road towards them. The traffic cop was to the right of Bruce so he could not swerve the Land Rover out of the way. The cop could not see the biker lose control.

Ricky grabbed Plum by the wrists and tried to tear the device from her. The aerial poked Ricky in the eye. Moana hit the back of Bruce's seat as he braked hard and went into a controlled skid. Plum broke free with one hand and pushed the red button with her thumb.

"Die! Die! Motherfuckers!"

Bruce heard Plum screaming as Chuck and the bike came sliding towards the Land Rover as he grappled with the steering. He tried to estimate where the wheels were going and where Chuck's head was moving as he felt a clunk as they finally came to a stop. The traffic cop came to a halt farther down the road, narrowly missing the bike as it spun on its side. Cars rammed into each other, as they could not brake in time. Both lanes were blocked with multiple collisions.

They heard one explosion, followed by more explosions, until there was only a thundering roar.

Plum dropped the box and fell out of the Land Rover. Her head had smashed against the front seat and there was a gash on her forehead, but she was oblivious to the pain. She ran sobbing in the direction of the explosions.

"You motherfuckers! You motherfuckers!" she yelled. "Burn in hell!"

John Eustace had switched on the ignition when he felt something like a huge hand lift him from his seat and throw him against the windshield. It happened so fast he had no time to think. His forehead smashed through the windshield and his hands became detached as they traveled through the broken glass. Pieces of his spinal cord and rib cage flew up into the air for hundreds of feet.

The first explosion ignited the fuel tank that was outside the cabin and adjacent to the driver's seat. The force was enough to engulf the entire canopy in flames. The fuel pump next to the burning truck was knocked over by the blast and threw up a geyser of gasoline that quickly flooded the concrete concourse.

The second explosion occurred as Terry Turner, realizing the truck had been bombed, tried to run away from his car. He held his ice cream cone outstretched in one hand as the river of flaming gasoline ran past his shoes and ignited his trousers. He tried to stamp out the flames and waved his arms frantically, spilling the ice cream over his houndstooth jacket. His shoes melted into the concrete and he could not move. The flames came up to his knees and the flesh from his calves and feet started to fall off. He screamed in pain before he fell over and was drowned in the fire, his entire body consumed in black angry flames. Then the bullets next to his chest cooked off.

The next eruption blew out the remaining pumps. The canopy collapsed over the Samoan family trapped in their melting car. The young couple with the children and poodle, were incinerated in their metal coffin. The wall of flames spread out from the concourse to the Chevy as Clovis tried to restart the engine. The back tires exploded and the paint ignited as Clovis tried to push the door open. The metal expanded and jammed the door. He lifted his knees up and kicked the door with both feet. The door fell off and he leapt out to sprint across the road and away from the burning river of gasoline.

He threw himself into the ditch between the north and southbound lanes as the next blast sent shock waves over him. Billy's car blew up as Clovis turned his head to see the firestorm reach up into the sky.

The underground fuel tanks exploded, tearing the ground up and hurtling the remains of the trapped cars and fuel pumps into the air. The gasoline charged with oxygen and intense heat rose up into an inferno that could be seen and heard for miles. Clovis struggled to breathe as he half crawled and half ran away from the conflagration. He did not know what direction he headed in, but he ran as fast as he could. The fire sucked in the surrounding air creating a fierce wind that seemed to draw him back.

Plum did not stop running until she came to within sight of the burning service station. She could smell the gasoline and fire. She imagined she saw Terry and John in the flames, burnt to an agonizing death. No one could have survived the inferno. She half walked, half hobbled down the middle of the empty road gasping for breath. Traffic on the southbound side of the Motorway had come to a halt, out of range of the paint-searing furnace Plum walked towards.

She felt the heat against her face. She looked up to see a huge black column of smoke. She saw a tall bearded figure running towards her. She thought his beard and hair was on fire. Then she recognized him. She ran as fast as she could towards him, crying his name that was drowned out by the roar of the firestorm.

As Clovis ran away from the heat, he thought his clothes would ignite. Then he saw a lone figure in front of him, a small barefooted woman in a short dress with a pageboy haircut.

Bruce leapt out of the Land Rover. He had no time to catch Plum as she ran away. He saw she had dropped the device in the back seat after she had pressed the button. Chuck was pinned under the front of the Land Rover, his legs and chest stuck under the front drive shaft. Bruce knelt down beside him and eased off the helmet. Chuck looked up to him, his eyes were dazed and blood came out of his mouth as he spoke.

"Service station," he uttered. He closed his eyes and tried to breathe. He opened them again when Moana knelt beside him and touched his forehead.

"Please, god, don't let this man die," she prayed.

Chuck tried to smile. "I won't. I can't move."

Ricky had already taken the jack out from the back and was securing it underneath the Land Rover. The traffic cop radioed in for help, though the dispatcher had trouble believing his request for every fire truck in South Auckland.

Mel stopped her car on a side street at the top of Ridge Road at Wiremu's request.

"It's okay." He turned to Mel and Henry. "I know a car back here I can borrow. I'm going up north to say good-bye to Hone. Then I'm lying low. So don't worry about me. I'll survive." He leaned forward and gave Henry and Mel an awkward hug.

"You saved my life back there. One day I will repay you. You two go get married and take a nice long honeymoon." He forced a laugh and hit them both on the back. "Look at that!"

They saw a huge tower of black smoke rising into the sky.

"I only hope you find Plum soon. Give my love to her and Clovis." He slammed the door and hopped over a fence and disappeared.

Mel and Henry sat in the car motionless, gazing out at the black smoke. Mel reached out and held his hand.

"I wonder if that is connected to us?"

Henry frowned as Mel gazed into the distance.

"Did you hear what he said? Go get married."

Mel turned on the radio. Maybe there was something about the fire. Procol Harum was playing "Too Much Between Us."

They sat holding hands as the black cloud grew thicker and higher.

• • •

Inspector Grimble had an ice pack on his neck. Cadd knelt beside him in the grass as armed policemen ran back and forth. More ambulances arrived. The three dead Maoris lay spread out where they had fallen, and Hei Hei and Rangi were still entombed in the Bedford. They awaited the photographer and the forensic team.

"No fucking Wiremu Wilson. A dead Hei Hei who would have squealed his head off and half the drug squad shot up. Christ!" he muttered. "I could've sworn I saw him in front of me in the bush. I could've sworn. I can't remember a thing."

McShane stuck his head out of the communications van.

"Bernie! It's for you. The commissioner! I've never heard him so angry."

Inspector Grimble dragged himself out of the back seat and tried to straighten up. He had the worst migraine of his life. He lifted his neck back to see if there were any clouds, and in the distance farther south, he saw a huge column of black smoke climbing into the sky.

Plum and Clovis fell into each other's arms. He picked her up and swung her around and around, unable to say or understand anything. She was alive! Tears filled his eyes. She buried her head in his singed beard and held on as tightly as she could. She kept repeating, "Clovis. Clovis," as he held her tight. "Don't ever leave me again."

• • •

Shanghai Sam stood up and arched his back. He had spent all Sunday afternoon weeding and hoeing between the parsley plants. He caught sight of a huge spiral of smoke, like a pillar of death to the northeast. He had heard a series of booms earlier but had thought nothing of them. There was no wind and the air and insects were still.

Sam wiped his brow. He felt sad that he was estranged from his young family. They no longer visited him or showed him respect. He was the forgotten grandfather, not the patriarch he would have been in the old days. Everything had changed. How he regretted the coming of this modern age. There were no more traditions.

He stared at the black column and wished that all the enemies of his family were climbing up to hell in that thick smoke. He stood and watched it for a long time, until it reached through the ceiling of the blue sky to the heavens.

THE END

Notes

PAGE 8 **Operation Weedout:** There was a concerted effort in the 1970s to destroy marijuana plants grown on Crown Land (public lands). Huey helicopters used in the Vietnam War, from the US Army, moved large quantities of harvested marijuana plants to central collection points where they were incinerated. Flowering plants spread marijuana seeds across Northland. Opossums and other mammals could be seen lying in the bush, stoned, gazing at the clouds.

PAGE 8 **Maori:** a native of New Zealand. The loose translation into English of the word Maori is "ordinary people." There is no plural of Maori in the Maori language, so there is no such word as Maoris. However, as this story is set in the 1970s when awareness of the Maori language was beginning to be revived, I have used both the singular and plural, depending on context.

PAGE 9 **Pakeha:** a European settler, Caucasian or white person.

PAGE 10 **The kauri forest that Wiremu visited:** Before the 1800s, Northland was one vast kauri forest. By the turn of the next century, the Pakehas, who had sailed to New Zealand, had razed the kauri forests, stripped the land of the giant trees and seized huge tracts of

Maori land. Land that belonged to Wiremu's tribe, the Ngapuhi.

The kauri trees stood like gods, over one hundred feet high and sixty feet wide, with no branches for the first forty feet. Kauris had provided the strongest, hardest timber in the world, free from knots or other imperfections. These giants had been seedlings before the fall of the Roman Empire.

PAGE 10   **Maori gangs:** Despite the rise of well-organized Maori gangs in the 1970s who dominated the illegal drug trade, there was little political will in Wellington to tackle such groups. The commissioner's plan to take on Wiremu Wilson instead makes sense in light of such a political climate. Besides, the gangs in the 1970s were better trained, armed and more violent than the police.

PAGE 11 **Hone Heke:** Hone Heke was a famous Maori warrior from the mid-19th century who had outwitted Pakeha settlers and provoked some of the sillier and more tragic episodes in what Pakeha historians called "The Maori Wars." Hone Heke had chopped down the British Union Jack at Kororareka three times, the symbol of British rule, the flag that so many Englishmen had died for. The repeated dismantling of the symbolic flagstaff by Hone Heke led to an outbreak of hostilities between Maori and Pakeha and what became known as the Flagstaff War. Many lives were lost and the town was destroyed, which in turn precipitated the arrival of enlisted British Army soldiers in New Zealand. These hardened, bitter soldiers did all they could to destroy the faith of Maori in European civilization.

PAGE 11 **The Treaty of Waitangi:** Now recognized as the founding document of New Zealand, the treaty was signed by over five hundred Maoris in the 1840s and by Queen Victoria's representative, the Governor General. Hone Heke and Te Rauparaha both signed the treaty. The document is still the subject of much debate. The passage of the 1975 Treaty of Waitangi was in part influenced by the Maori Land March.

PAGE 15 **Anal scarification:** Dr. Johnson's lecture on Dr. Kegel's exercises.

Dr Johnson had given Plum Blossom a thorough examination at the Women's Clinic. She noted that Plum had intense anal scarification. She had casually asked Plum if she ever had anal sex. Plum said no. Mel gave her a lecture on genital hygiene. If a man entered her in the rear he could not go anywhere else. Fecal matter in the vagina, she told Plum, was a bacterial disaster. Even a minuscule amount can give you a very dangerous vaginal infection that can take hold before you are aware of it.

"It's not for me to tell you what to do with your sex life, Plum," Mel had finished her lecture to a blushing Plum. "But let me tell you how to tighten your love muscle. It's called the pubococcygeus or PC for short. When you squat down, spread your legs and urinate, that's the muscle that stops the flow. Here, I'll give you some exercises to do that will give you more control." Mel went on to describe the Kegel exercises, a series of isometric contractions devised by a Californian doctor in the late 1940s. Dr Kegel's research was the result of helping women after childbirth to cope with urinary stress and incontinence, without resorting to vaginal surgery. One of the side effects of his exercises was the fact that some of these women started to have fantastic multi-orgasmic sex. The same muscle that controls the flow of urine also goes into rapid spasmodic contractions that make up a vaginal orgasm.

Mel instructed Plum on how to practice Kegel's flicks, holds, gradual holds and bear downs.

"Flicks are contractions done rapidly. Holds are when you squeeze your PC as tight as possible for up to ten seconds. This is ideal when watching a movie or just sitting down. Gradual holds are more advanced and call for a gradual squeezing of the PC until after ten seconds you cannot squeeze it any tighter. Bear downs are best not practiced at the movies. They entail bearing down for ten seconds as though squeezing out a bowel movement, which you don't do, of course. All four exercises should be repeated in sets of five. After a few weeks you can build up to sets of twenty or more, twice a day.

"In a couple of weeks you'll notice a difference. So will your lover," Mel had finished.

PAGE 21 **Hone's Political Science Thesis:** Hone had majored in New Zealand History at Victoria University in Wellington and was working on his doctoral thesis, "The Influence of New Zealand Law as enforced on Maori, 1945-1975, as evidenced in the Pakeha social structures and Pakeha justice." He planned to complete his history the following year. He had assembled a series of case studies full of damning statistics and lurid testimony. Rewritten for publication, it was going to become, he hoped, a popular history of Pakeha injustices to Maori. Hone did not want his older brother to be included in his research as another casualty.

PAGE 22 **Armed Offenders Squad:** Formed in 1964, this was a specialist unit of trained police officers carrying firearms and wearing protective clothing. In the 1970s, most police officers only carried a baton.

PAGE 29 **Clovis's whole wheat bread recipe:**
Clovis did demonstrate to Wiremu his secret whole wheat bread recipe.

"First, you get a large ceramic mixing bowl like this and warm it up with hot water." Clovis adopted the air of a television cook. He held up a medium-size stainless steel bowl and with a flourish, swirled water around in it. Wiremu appreciated the theatricality.

"Then you fill it to so (about sixteen ounces), but I never measure. It's all intuition. You have to feel good about yourself, about life and about bread. All cooking is love. Pure and simple. If there is no love, you can't cook. If you are filled with love, then maybe you can cook. See, it all comes naturally, flows. Now dissolve two tablespoons of honey in the water. Notice the water is not too hot or too cold. It's just the right temperature for the yeast to grow and feed off the sugars in the honey."

Clovis took a small packet of yeast and crumbled it into the bowl. He stirred the contents with the spoon he used for the honey and the mixture went cloudy.

"Now we put a cloth over this and leave it in a warm dark place like inside a gas oven that isn't on or a linen cupboard." Clovis put a clean dishcloth over the bowl and put it in the oven. The pilot light and the February heat would keep the yeast at a warm temperature.

"You can use potato water or anything that's got sugars in it, but I prefer honey because it's hygroscopic, so after the bread is baked, it keeps moist. And Manuka honey gives such a rich flavor to the bread."

Clovis half filled the large ceramic mixing bowl with whole-wheat flour. He sprinkled in some salt and left a hole in the middle of the mixture for the yeast to be poured in, in about an hour, maybe forty-five minutes.

Clovis took the stainless steel bowl out of the oven after thirty-five minutes. There was a rich brown skin on top. He poured the mixture into the ceramic bowl of flour, stirring it with a big wooden spoon. The mixture was wet and sloppy. He unfolded it onto a wooden board that had been dusted with flour for kneading.

"Kneading bread is like making love to a woman," Clovis began.

Plum rolled her eyes. Here we go again.

"Pictures can't tell you how to do it. It's technique and sensitivity and soul. The bread responds to your touch. You can only go so far before putting it in the oven to rise."

Clovis sprinkled more flour over the ball of dough and kneaded it till it was the required consistency; not too wet, not too dry, not overworked nor under kneaded. He rolled the dough out and broke it into two pieces before placing them in the well-oiled baking tins Wiremu had prepared. The dough filled the length of the tins but only came halfway up. He placed the covered tins in the unlit oven again, to rise. In forty-five minutes he would light the oven and bake the bread. The two tins would by then be almost overflowing with the risen dough.

PAGE 30 **Mount Eden:** Mount Eden Prison is situated in the Auckland suburb of Mount Eden, close to where Dr. Mel Johnson lives. It is a forbidding stonewalled prison built in the 19th century and still exists despite a massive fire caused by a riot in 1965.

PAGE 32 **The so-called treaty, the Springboks tour and the Land March:** Wiremu refers to the Treaty of Waitangi that was being challenged and rethought in the early 1970s. Prime Minister Norman Kirk cancelled the Springboks tour of 1971 after the police predicted mass civil unrest and violence if the apartheid all-white South African rugby team played the All Blacks in New Zealand. The Maori Land March took place in 1975 where over 5,000 Maori marched on Parliament and presented a petition signed by 60,000 people calling for the end of the sale of Maori land.

PAGE 33 **Mana:** a Maori concept that denotes deep spiritual power and bearing. Male and female Maori leaders and tohungas had mana, as did warriors.

PAGE 34 **Maori language:** Maori (the word is now commonly spelled as Māori) is an official language of New Zealand. From the mid-1970s through the 1980s there was a strong movement to teach Maori in schools. Maori is now taught in schools as a second language and there are radio and TV broadcasts in Maori.

PAGE 35 **Makutu:** Makutu is generally believed to refer to occult powers or behaviors and conditions that cannot be explained by traditional European culture and science. Makutu can also mean witchcraft or sorcery, including the dark arts used to kill people. We are hindered by our western definitions and concepts in understanding what makutu means.

PAGE 37 **Ngapuhi:** The tribe or iwi based in Northland. Wiremu, Hone, Hei Hei and Moana are Ngapuhi.

PAGE 37 **Tohunga:** loosely described as a Maori wizard or shaman or wise man, tohungas can be seen as gifted spiritual leaders who could communicate between known and unknown worlds and possess special powers.

PAGE 41 **Somes Island:** Jewish refugees from Germany were interned during the Second World War on Somes Island along with their fellow Germans who were known Nazi party members and sympathizers.

PAGE 42 **Sincere Laundry:** A short history of Plum Blossom's family

In 1868, Sam Lee Look, aged twenty-eight, immigrated to the Otago Gold fields in the South Island of

New Zealand. A poor farmer from Kwangtung Province, he was one of twenty Chinese men sponsored by a Dunedin Consortium to rework the Otago claims. The contract was for three years of labor in return for ten New Zealand pounds.

Sam Lee lived with his fellow Chinamen in damp drafty hovels made of sugar sacks and kerosene tins, across from the Central Otago gold town of Lawrence. They worked six days a week, twelve to fourteen hours a day. Their task was to go over the tailings, the rejected mounds of gravel that the Pakeha gold miners had already sifted through. The economics were such that the few ounces of gold they recovered each week made their work very profitable for the Dunedin consortium that owned them. Their social worth was reflected in a local bylaw, where they were banned from entering Lawrence, the nearest and only town they could travel to.

After three years, Sam Lee, ten pounds richer, moved with his surviving male workers to Round Hill near Orepuki in Southland. The Chinese called it Longhilly, the Pakehas, Canton. Here, he lived in a shack actually made of wood and visited the local Fan Tan house and the Chinese temple.

Sam Lee's luck turned in 1878 when gold fetched three pounds fourteen shillings and six pence an ounce. Along with three partners, they made over four thousand pounds. Two years later Sam Lee took his savings and moved to Wellington to open a laundry, the Sincere Laundry on Haining Street.

Haining Street was in the center of a restless Chinese population; many men wanted to sail back to China but were either uncertain as to their fate when they returned or lacked the money for the sea fare. Few Chinese women had immigrated to New Zealand. His two younger sisters, aged twenty-three and twenty-four, finally joined Sam Lee. They had brought over their best friend, an orphan aged eighteen, named Betty Wong. From Long-hilly, Sam had sent letters and small gold nuggets hidden in parcels back as often as he could to his family. In their twelve years of separation, he had dreamed of being re-united with his mother and three sisters. When he met them at the wharf, Sam Look was shocked to hear of his mother's and his older sister's deaths. He also fell in love, on the dock, with the young, serenely pretty and penniless Betty Wong.

Sam Lee, his wife Betty and the two unmarried sisters, soon tired of life in a supposed European city that excluded the Chinese from ordinary life, yet at the same time possessed no European culture. The local police were constantly raiding the laundry, as they were every shop and home in Wellington's Chinatown. Under the 1901 Opium Act, the police needed no search warrant. Chinatown was packed with homesick Chinese men who could neither afford their fare back to their Province nor find work outside Chinatown. They could only gamble, smoke opium and dream of their homeland. Those who could afford it got their shirts cleaned and pressed at the Sincere Laundry.

The rest of the community, the Pakehas, the Europeans, avoided the Chinese and looked down upon them. The Pakehas were afraid of these strange people who had yellow skin, slits for eyes and spoke an indecipherable gibberish. Although there was an active Christian mission in Chinatown, they were still viewed as pagans who did not worship the Lord Jesus Christ. Instead, they let off firecrackers on their New Year's Day, a day that bore no relation to the European New Year.

In fact, these "poker-faced people" had their own calendar, with years for pigs, monkeys, cows and rats. To the Europeans, the Chinese all looked shifty, took drugs and gambled relentlessly. These same Europeans resented the Chinese because there were too many of them concentrated in one city, and therefore, presented a threat to European jobs and European welfare. This same bizarre prejudice would resurface during World War II, when many Chinese, some second or third generation New Zealanders and most of them residents of this country for a longer period of time than their prosecutors, were placed in concentration camps. (Along with German Jews who had escaped the Nazis.) The Pakeha authorities feared the local Chinese would side with the enemy; the dreaded Japanese. This is hard to imagine now, but didn't Japan invade China before World War II broke out? What of the Rape of Nanking? And wasn't China an ally of Great Britain and therefore of New Zealand? Well, the answer was they all looked alike. You could never trust the jaundiced-looking bastards. The Great Prime Minister of New Zealand, the very late Richard Seddon, had said so himself.

Although Sam Lee played Fan-Tan occasionally, he was more concerned with building a nest egg for his family. Betty had three miscarriages before finally giving birth to Sam. Sam was fifty-five and Betty was thirty-five years old. She died in childbirth the next year. Sam, his son and the two elderly sisters moved north to Onehunga, a small settlement on Manukau harbor on the western side of the Auckland Isthmus. Although Sam Lee did not get a good price for the Sincere Laundry, he had enough savings to buy a small house and five acres of fertile land. They became market gardeners.

The Lee family never went hungry, despite two World Wars and a depression. In the early fifties they sold their freehold land in Onehunga for a profit and bought two hundred acres farther away from Auckland in Pukekohe. Following other relatives and kinsmen, they established a thriving market gardening center in Pukekohe, with its rich fertile soil. They supplied the rapidly expanding

City of Auckland with fresh vegetables. If the Pakehas did not accept them socially, they at least bought all the vegetables the Chinese New Zealanders could grow.

PAGE 43 **Tuna:** Maori for eel.

PAGE 45 **Wanganui Computer:** Operational in 1976, the Wanganui Computer Center was a nationwide database of police, justice and traffic files. The database was rumored to include every New Zealander from their birth certificate to their death certificate with any arrests, court cases, traffic cases or other filed reports. There were also rumors that the database included tax records, social security records and other government agency information all linked to an individual's name. The cost was estimated at $21 million, about $7 for every man, woman and child in the database.

PAGE 72 **Marae:** the communal and ceremonial center of Maori life, a traditional building with sacred carvings.

PAGE 73 **Cape Reinga:** the northwestern tip of New Zealand where Maori spirits of the dead fly off into the underworld "Reinga."

PAGE 75 **Tangata Whenua:** literally "people of the land," the original native population, Maori.

PAGE 75 **Maoritanga:** the Maori way of life.

PAGE 146 **Utu:** Standard European interpretations relate utu to the concept of revenge. With a greater understanding of Maoritanga, the Maori way of life and thinking, utu is now being understood to bring balance in life, reciprocity for both good and bad deeds. Trying to define ancient Maori concepts that were communicated orally can lead to much misunderstanding in relation to European culture that is semantically bound by the written word.

PAGE 159 **Tangi:** Tangihana is a Maori funeral, a ceremony performed at the deceased's marae. Because of Hone Wilson's close ties to the Maori protest movement, his funeral was moved from his iwi's home in Hokianga to Mangere.

PAGE 180 **Norfolk pine:** Early missionaries planted Norfolk pine seedlings across Auckland. They believed the cross design of the saplings (when seen from a hill or on top of Auckland's extinct volcanoes) would help Christianize the pagan land.

PAGE 255 **"E Hei Hei, he aha to koha ma ku?!!"** "Hei Hei, what is your gift to me?!!" It was the sentence Potatau called out to Te Rauparaha when Potatau was surrounded by Te Rauparaha's men and was about to be massacred. Hei Hei was well versed in Maori history and immediately understood the meaning of the words, implying an ambush from all sides, while the police had no idea what this exchange meant.

Te Rauparaha was a leading chief of the Ngati Toa tribe who took an influential part in the Musket Wars (initiated by the Ngapuhi) of early 19th century New Zealand. He signed the Treaty of Waitangi twice. He also wrote the haka (war dance) Ka Mate to celebrate his escape from death in one of his many battles. The New Zealand All Blacks perform Ka Mate before they play rugby.

PAGE 256 **"Ena whakamaku ki enei whakamaku!"** "Your popguns against ours!" Hei Hei's reply mimics Te Rauparaha's response.

PAGE 279 **Miles per hour:** In 1975, New Zealand, as part of its metrification, changed the speed limit from 55 miles per hour to 80 kilometers per hour (50 miles per hour.) All the car models in this novel still had miles per hour gauges.

Characters

Police Commissioner Ian Thompson: about to retire, thinks he can handle the Maori gang issue by going after a tribal leader not affiliated with a gang.

Police Inspector Bernie Grimble: a relentless investigator tasked by the police commissioner for an unofficial operation.

Sergeant Cadd: Inspector Grimble's new sidekick.

Donna: Cadd's girlfriend.

Wiremu Wilson: a Ngapuhi leader and Land Rights activist.

Hone Wilson: Wiremu's younger brother, an academic who is researching a Political Science Thesis for his PhD.

Hei Hei: Wiremu's cousin who has his own agenda.

Henry Lotus: a theoretical physicist just returned from New York, having been rescued by his girlfriend.

Dr. Mel Johnson: Henry's girlfriend, a doctor at a new Women's Clinic in Ponsonby. She is skilled in various martial arts.

Clovis Tibet: a large red-haired classical violinist back from New York where he rescued his girlfriend.

Plum Blossom: Clovis's girlfriend, a third generation Chinese New Zealander, who is an actress.

Rodney: a friend of Henry's who is building a yacht.

Terry Turner: "Terry the Turk" Auckland's criminal mastermind, originally from London.

John Eustace: "Big John" Terry Turner's very large and scary looking enforcer.

Moana Wilson: a young relative of Wiremu who has been lured to Auckland.

Lance Beefeater: a gentleman farmer's son from Hamilton.

Alan Crispfeldt: the distinguished attorney who represents Wiremu Wilson and Henry Lotus.

The widow Wadman: lives next door to Terry Turner with her poodle, Ruffles.

Matthew Bounder: Clovis's musician friend, leader of various rock groups, including the recent group Particle Board. Other band members include:

Rua: the large Maori drummer,

Sheila: the brunette bass player with killer legs,

Billy Whitehorn: the lead guitarist and

Rodger: plays keyboards and now looks like a Mormon.

Sam Look: Plum Blossom's guardian and grandfather.

Bruce Look: a third generation Chinese New Zealander who manages a market garden company with his two younger brothers:

Tony Look: the suburban accountant and middle brother.

Chuck Look: Bruce's youngest motorcycle riding brother.

Ricky Wong: owns and operates the Hungry Wok, a takeout shop opposite the Three Lamps and is related to the Looks.

Marty Wong: his brother. They also run a martial arts supply company.

Tony: the four-hundred-pound Rarotongan bouncer at the Gluepot upstairs at the Three Lamps.

Inspector Wallace McShane: head of the Drug Squad. Other members of the Drug Squad include Sergeant Adams, Saunders, Anderson and Karl.

Rangi: the truck driver from Hokianga.

Freddy, Rere and Mokau: close friends of Hei Hei.

Playlist

"Rainy Day Woman # 12 & 35" Bob Dylan

"Have You Heard?" John Mayall and the Bluesbreakers with Eric Clapton

"Ten Guitars" Tom Jones

"Wild Thing" Jimi Hendrix

"Land of a Thousand Dances" Wilson Pickett

"Women of Ireland" Barry Lyndon Soundtrack

"Stranger than Fiction" Split Enz

"House of the Rising Sun" The Animals

"Can't You Hear Me Knocking" The Rolling Stones

"String Sextet No. 2 in G Major Op. 111" Johannes Brahms–Amadeus Quartet with Friends on Deutsche Grammophon

"Bungle in the Jungle" Jethro Tull

"Hungarian Czarda for solo violin" Barry Lyndon Soundtrack

"Sympathy for the Devil" The Rolling Stones

"The Ying Tong Song" from the Goon Show

"Te Po nui, Te Po roa" a Waiata

"Too Much Between Us" Procol Harum

Other books by Nick Spill available as e-books and paperbacks:

Reluctant Q – with George Spill

The Way of the Bodyguard